Platinum Persuasion

Platinum Persuasion

INDIA

www.urbanbooks.net

Urban Books, LLC
300 Farmingdale Road, NY-Route 109
Farmingdale, NY 11735

Platinum Persuasion Copyright © 2021 INDIA

ISBN 13: 978-1-64556-317-4
ISBN 10: 1-64556-317-0

First Mass Market Printing May 2022
First Trade Paperback Printing June 2021
Printed in the United States of America

10 9 8 7 6 5 4 3 2 1

This is a work of fiction. Any references or similarities to actual events, real people, living or dead, or to real locales are intended to give the novel a sense of reality. Any similarity in other names, characters, places, and incidents is entirely coincidental.

Distributed by Kensington Publishing Corp.
Submit Orders to:
Customer Service
400 Hahn Road
Westminster, MD 21157-4627
Phone: 1-800-733-3000
Fax: 1-800-659-2436

This book is dedicated to all the dreamers.

Keep pushing, keep grinding, and you will see the mountaintop.

Acknowledgments

Thank you, thank you, thank you for continuing to support your girl. Words can't explain the gratitude I have for my loyal readers. I've said it many times before and I'll say it again because it's the truth—There is no way I could continue to do what I do without you!

Chapter One

Prologue

From the day Layani Cherise Bell fell from between her mother's legs, the world was betting against her. Born four months premature, the doctors didn't expect her to make it, but she did. At the age of six, Layani was diagnosed with leukemia. Again, the doctors gave her a death sentence, but she survived. As if that weren't enough, at the ripe age of thirteen, she lost her mother and father in a head-on collision with a truck driver who had fallen asleep behind the wheel of his big rig. Although her mother had two sisters and her father's mother was still alive, no one on either side of her family tree wanted to bear the burden of raising someone else's child. Therefore, she became a ward of the state just hours after the accident. Due to being bounced around and lost paperwork, she wasn't even permitted to attend her parents' funeral.

For the first time since birth, Layani was all alone. Every waking moment she spent without her mother and father made her want to lay down and die. However, she knew her mother would be angry if she were to ever give up, so day by day, she pressed forward.

"Don't you know you're a fighter, girl?" her mother, Georgia, would say every time life dealt her precious daughter a low blow.

"Yes, ma'am," the shy child would always reply.

"Then hold your head high, put your dukes up, and yell *bring it on!*"

Just the thought of her mother's voice put a smile on Layani's lips and caused several warm tears to trickle from her large doe eyes down her cocoa-complected face. Usually, she brushed the waterworks away in a hurry, as not to let the other kids know she was crybaby. Today, however, she chose to let them fall freely. Maybe it was the gloomy morning weather peeking through a crack in the blinds, or maybe it was the fact that her birthday was the next day. Whatever it was had her in her feelings.

Soon Layani's soft sniffles turned into loud sobs. She tried to suppress the sound by burying her head into the paper-thin pillow resting atop her twin-size bed, but it was useless. Not wanting to wake her roommate Angel, Layani forced herself from the bed that was too small for her growing five-feet-six-inch frame. Carefully, she took the ladder down from the top bunk and planted her feet firmly onto the carpeted floor.

As soon as Layani put her hand on the doorknob, she could hear a car door close from outside in the driveway. The distraction was enough to stop her tears momentarily as she headed over to the bedroom window to be nosey. Resting in the driveway was a familiar older model gray Buick. Its owner, Mrs. Gail, walked up to the walkway with a briefcase in hand. Layani knew seeing the old, slender social worker on a Sunday was never a good sign.

Tiptoeing over to the bedroom door, she opened it slightly and listened as Mrs. Gail and Mr. and Mrs.

Daniels exchanged pleasantries downstairs. After a few moments of small talk, Mrs. Gail explained that the state audited their records and realized the maximum child occupancy for a home their size was six, which meant they were over by one. Consequently, she would have to remove the additional child and place them at another home. Mrs. Gail also advised that they could at least keep the children of their choice, but the decision had to be made immediately.

Layani eased the door closed as her heart began racing uncontrollably. She'd been with the Daniels for almost the entire two years she'd been in the system. The first home she was placed in caught fire four months after her arrival. Though things weren't bad there, she knew being placed with the Daniels was a blessing. For starters, they treated each of their foster children like family, even the most troubled ones. Mr. Daniels took time out of his busy day as an E.M.T. to spend time with all the kids by taking them to and from after school programs such as karate, cheer, and band. Mrs. Daniels always made sure the children had help with homework, well-balanced meals, and clean clothes to wear daily. The entire family even went to church on Sunday. Being with the Daniels had given Layani's life the structure she'd been missing. She couldn't stand the thought of losing them because it would almost be like losing her parents all over again.

Hearing footsteps and light chatter coming up the stairs, Layani flew back to her bed with lightning speed. She climbed into her bunk and tossed the covers over her face just in time for a knock on the door. Seconds later, the door opened and Mrs. Gail stepped into the room. Layani's eyes fluttered as she tried to play sleep, but it did no good.

"Layani, wake up. I need you to come with me." Mrs. Gail shook Layani lightly.

"Huh? Why?" She yawned, still pretending.

"I'll explain in the car. Grab your things."

"I don't want to leave." Layani sat up and dropped the act. "Why do I have to leave?" She turned her attention to Mr. and Mrs. Daniels, who were standing in the doorway.

"I'm sorry, Layani. The state said we can't keep all of you."

"I've been here for two years!" Layani stated as a matter of fact while jumping down from the top bunk. "Why me?" She wanted to know.

"Layani grab your things now, please," Mrs. Gail instructed. She'd been a case worker for three decades. She knew this was about to go left fast if she didn't get things under control.

"I'm sorry." Mrs. Daniels ran away from the room, bawling her eyes out, yet the tears meant nothing to Layani.

"Maybe you can tell me why?" She walked up to Mr. Daniels, who'd turned red in the face. "What did I do to deserve this?"

"Layani, that's enough," Mrs. Gail hollered.

"I swear to God on my parents' grave, I'll work harder in school. I'll cook and I'll clean," she pleaded.

"Layani, I really wish we could keep you, but we can't." Mr. Daniels put his hand on her shoulder.

"You can't keep me, or you won't keep me?" Layani snapped. "Don't think I didn't realize you're getting rid of the only black kid here!"

"Enough is enough! I'll give you ten minutes to grab your things or we will be leaving without them." Mrs. Gail closed the bedroom door, leaving Layani standing in the middle of the floor with her mouth wide open. She wanted to cuss, scream, and fight everybody in the house, but instead she took a deep breath, remembered what her mother taught her, and walked over to the closet to gather her things, all of which fit into one small, pathetic duffle bag.

Before departing, Layani grabbed a notebook and pen to leave a goodbye note for the friends.

"Layani, are you leaving?" ten-year-old Angel asked from the bottom bunk. She was a hard sleeper; therefore, she'd missed the whole commotion.

"Yes, Angel, I'm leaving. They said I have to," she whispered to her roommate, who was more like the little sister she never had but always wanted.

"But . . . but your birthday is tomorrow." Angel wiped sleep from her eyes. "We were supposed to go out for ice cream, remember?"

Birthdays around the Daniels house were always a big deal. Mrs. Daniels didn't really give the children treats that contained sugar, except for special occasions. Therefore, all the children loved birthdays.

"Yeah, I remember." Layani tried to keep her voice steady. "I guess we'll have to do it another time, okay." She walked over to the bed, bent down, and hugged the girl that had been her roommate for the last two years. Angel was wheelchair bound, so getting up from the bed without assistance wasn't happening.

"I don't want you to go." She began to cry softly.

"I don't want to go either, but I have to." Layani wiped Angel's tears as her own began to fall.

"What am I going to do without you?" Angel was devastated. Layani was her best friend, confidant, and protector. She always pushed her chair and helped her get in and out of the bed. Layani looked after her without making her feel like a cripple.

"Don't worry. We'll be together again." Layani doubted they would ever see each other again, but she wouldn't dare say that.

"Do you promise?" Angel held out her pinky, and Layani wrapped hers around it.

"I promise!" She gave the girl one last hug, flung her bag over her shoulder, and headed out of the room with her head held high.

Standing in the hallway conversing were Mrs. Gail and Mr. and Mrs. Daniels. They stopped talking abruptly and looked at her with apologetic glances.

"I'm ready." Layani rolled her eyes at the Daniels while addressing Mrs. Gail.

"Aren't you going to say goodbye?" Mrs. Daniels asked with her arms opened wide for a hug. Layani descended the stairs without so much as even looking in the Daniels' direction.

"Goodbye!" Layani hollered with much attitude upon reaching the front door. Before she stepped outside, she turned and flipped Mr. and Mrs. Daniels the bird.

Though disappointed, Mrs. Gail smirked inwardly. She, too, had to admit it was a little sketchy of the white couple to rid themselves of their only black foster child. Yet and still, she apologized for Layani's behavior and thanked the Daniels for their hospitality.

Chapter Two

Once inside of the smoke-scented car masked by air freshener, Mrs. Gail tossed her briefcase onto the back seat that was filled with everything from stuffed animals to extra clothing and a first aid kit. In her line of work, you had to be prepared to console a child, clothe a child, and make a boo-boo feel better in a moment's notice. With condemning eyes, she turned to face Layani.

"Mrs. Gail, please don't start with the lectures. This ain't fair and you know it." Layani fastened her seatbelt and crossed her arms, refusing to look at her social worker.

"Baby, life ain't fair." With a sigh, Mrs. Gail placed her wrinkled hand over Layani's. "The sooner you understand that, the better off you'll be. The world doesn't owe you nothing."

Gail Henry had seen her fair share of things over the years. She felt bad for each and every child she came in contact with on the job, especially the ones like Layani, who'd ended up in the system by default, but she knew this too would pass. "Bad times are like storms in our life. We've just got to remember they don't last forever, and there is always a rainbow after the rain."

"It's been raining in my world for two years, though." Layani gazed out of the window with disdain. She was tired of the shuffle and tired of the uncertainty. She desperately wished she could go back to the fateful day that had taken her parents out of this world; if not to change the outcome, then to at least put herself in the car with them.

"Death has to be better than this," she whispered.

"Don't say things like that." Mrs. Gail put her key in the ignition and started the car. "This right here is temporary, but baby, death is forever. I'm pretty sure there are some children in the graveyard wishing they could trade places with you right now!" She paused and tried to regain composure. The job, case files, and innocent faces of those she had encountered over the years were beginning to take a toll on her. Being the first point of contact in these heartbreaking and gut-wrenching situations had become too much.

Just last week, she'd attended funerals for three children who had been beaten and dismembered by their own mother after a psychotic episode. After receiving a call from a concerned teacher, she'd been assigned the case. Although she couldn't put a finger on the problem right away, she knew things were amiss. For four months, Gail pleaded with her boss remove the children from their home. However, due to lack of evidence, the state could do nothing more than random wellness checks. Gail felt guilty for not doing more, but she didn't mean to take her frustrations out on Layani.

"You will age out of the system in three years. Use this short amount of time to do something productive." She reversed from her parking spot, put the car in drive, and pulled off. "What are you good at?"

"I'm good at drawing, but I really like to sing." Layani replied after giving the question some thought.

"Sing me your best song."

"I can't sing in front of people. I'm shy." Just the thought of singing aloud caused butterflies to form in her belly.

"You can't say you're a good singer if no one has ever heard you sing besides you." Mrs. Gail laughed, and Layani joined in.

"My mother used to say I sounded like Whitney Houston." Once again, Layani's unhappy eyes peered out the window. That's when she spotted the ice cream parlor where the Daniels had promised to take her the next day.

Mrs. Gail followed her gaze and decided to pull the car over. "I'm not supposed to do this, and if you tell anyone, I will deny it." She put the car in park. "Since it's almost your birthday though, I'll make an exception this one time." With a wink she grabbed her purse. "What's your favorite ice cream?"

"I love cookies and cream. What about you?" Layani was so happy to get the small treat that it temporarily took her mind off her troubles.

"I'm more of a strawberry girl."

"So was my mom." Layani smiled as they got out of the car and walked up to the window of the small parlor to give the teenage boy dressed in a red-and-white-striped uniform their orders.

"Let's sit over here." Mrs. Gail pointed to a seat on one of the picnic benches resting beneath the awning of the parlor. "I haven't had ice cream in years," Mrs. Gail admitted. Her hectic schedule didn't allow for much social time, which was part of the reason her husband had left her eight years ago.

"Really? What about your grandchildren? Have they gone years without ice cream too?" Layani inquired.

"Here you are, ladies. Enjoy," the young man who'd taken their orders said after placing the tray of ice cream on the table.

"Thank you," they replied in unison.

"Sadly, I don't have any grandchildren." Gail usually kept her personal life private, but today she felt like sharing. "My daughter Naomi died shortly after her second birthday."

"I'm sorry to hear that. How did she die, if you don't mind me asking?"

"She drowned in the bathtub." Mrs. Gail looked away into the distance. "Back then, I worked seventy hours a week, and my husband was no help. I'd just picked Naomi up from the babysitter and decided to kill two birds with one stone by giving us both a bath. With the water still running, I dozed off, and she did too while laying on my chest. The water rose too high and filled her nose and mouth. By the time I woke up, the bathroom floor was flooded, and my precious baby was floating face down."

For the first time since meeting Mrs. Gail in the lobby of her school two years ago, Layani realized that the social worker was human. Instinctively, she placed her hand over the old woman's and comforted her the same way she had been comforted in the car.

"Your ice cream is melting." Layani tried to lighten the mood.

"Apparently, so is my makeup." Using the back of her hand, Gail wiped her face, which caused it to smear. "I'll be right back. Finish your ice cream." Gail tossed her melted mess into the trashcan, then headed into the ladies' room.

As Layani sat on the picnic bench alone, she began to imagine herself running away. She wondered where she would go and how far she'd get before they found her.

"Slow down, Button!" a short lady with blonde braids called after her small son as he darted across the parking lot toward the ice cream parlor. Layani blinked rapidly before standing to address the woman coming toward her.

"Aunt Nova?"

"Layani?" Embarrassed, Nova Stansfield greeted her niece with a half-hearted smile. "What are you doing out this way, baby?" She picked up the little boy, who kicked and screamed. He wanted ice cream. He didn't care about their conversation.

"I'm with my worker, having ice cream for my birthday. We're on our way to my new foster home."

"Oh." Nova shifted uncomfortably.

"Mrs. Gail, this is Nova, my mother's younger sister." Layani introduced the women after the social worker reemerged.

"Well, hello." Mrs. Gail nodded. "Who is this little guy?"

"This is Harvard, my son." Nova fumbled with her large Coach purse. "Layani you're about to be fifteen, right?"

"Tomorrow I'll be fifteen."

"Well then, I got fifteen dollars just for you." Nova produced the crumbled money proudly, like she was doing something. When Layani didn't move, she pushed it into her hand. "Please take this gift, baby."

"Nah, I'm good. Keep your money, Aunt Nova."

"Baby, don't be too proud to take the gift. What's wrong with this child?" Nova asked Mrs. Gail as if she had the answer.

"Aunt Nova, a gift would've been giving me a place to stay. A gift would've been at least taking me to my parents' funeral or coming to see me from time to time." Layani dropped the money. "This ain't no damn gift!"

"Layani, I wish I could've—" She was cut short.

"Yeah, me too!" Without another word, Layani threw her ice cream into the trash and headed to the car. Her actions indicated to Mrs. Gail that it was time for them to go.

After riding across town from the west side to the east side for thirty minutes in silence, Layani finally spoke out. "Can you adopt me?"

Though Gail was startled by the question, she had a ready-made answer. "Unfortunately, I can't do that, Layani. The law forbids a caseworker to become the legal guardian of a client," she lied. Truthfully, she could've gone through the massive red tape to adopt Layani if she really wanted to, but she didn't. After losing her daughter, Gail desperately tried again and again to get pregnant, but it was no use. After years of trying, she accepted the fact that being a mother wasn't for her. Instead of crying about it, she poured herself into work and decided to be there for all the children in her case log, the way she wished she'd been there for Naomi. "I'm sorry honey."

"Yeah, I know. Everybody is always sorry." Layani rolled her eyes to keep the tears from falling down her face.

Gail wanted to stop the car and embrace the little girl who'd been dealt a raw hand, but instead, she kept driving. She didn't want to lead her on in any way or give her false hope.

Moments later, Gail pulled her Buick up to a two-story colonial home in need of a few renovations. "This is it. Are you ready?"

"I guess." With a shrug, Layani got out of the passenger seat and peered down the sketchy city block. There were five vacant homes surrounding the foster home. Across the street was a park that was no longer visible due to overgrown grass and wild weeds. Layani already knew this place would be hell compared to the home she'd just left in the suburbs.

"Well, come on. We don't have all day." Mrs. Gail grabbed her briefcase and walked toward the house. Layani followed her across the dirt-filled lawn with old basketballs and broken toys that had been thrown about. Aside from the hanging gutter and four broken windows, the words "pimps up, hoes down" were spray-painted on the yellow siding. Layani didn't like the looks of this place, but what could she do?

After three knocks on the door, it opened, and Mrs. Gail and Layani were let inside by a tall, dark-skinned boy wearing oversized clothes and a pair of taped-up headphones. "What up, Ms. G." He smiled, a tarnished smile.

"Hello, Roderick. How are you?"

"I'm good. What up with you?" Though he was talking to Gail, he couldn't stop looking at Layani. He could smell fresh meat from a mile away.

"Boy, you're too old to be talking to me like a ten-year-old. How are those grades? Have you been filling out applications? You do know that you age out of our system in four months, don't you?" Gail lit into his ass.

"Dang, Ms. G, chill." Roderick raised his hands in defeat. "Ms. H is in the kitchen. Come on, let me take you to her." He nodded for the social worker to follow him while purposely avoiding her questions.

"Layani, take a seat right there. I'll be back shortly." Gail pointed to a folding chair up against the wall.

Quietly, she took a seat and peeped the scene. The house was clean according to most people's standards; however, it was overcrowded with stuff. There was a bookshelf under the stairs filled with dusty old books. There was a corner with a child's play kitchen, baby dolls, and toy cars lined neatly in a row. The blue couch was worn down and stained various colors. The coffee table and two end tables were covered with board games. The fireplace was adorned with cards, drawings, and old flowers that had turned into potpourri. There were five chairs along the wall and two recliners on the side of the sofa. The recliners and the sofa were being occupied by two girls and one boy. From her position behind them, Layani couldn't see their faces, but she wasn't pressed. Therefore, she didn't even bother to make her presence known by introducing herself.

Instead, she sat on the folding chair quietly. Seconds turned into minutes, and before she knew it, the glass clock on the wall indicated that a whole forty minutes had gone by.

"Who would've known that you'd have to go? But so suddenly, so fast." Layani sang to continue passing the time. "How could this be, that a sweet memory could be—"

"Bitch, didn't you hear me? I said shut the fuck up. I'm trying to watch TV! Are you deaf or something, bitch?" asked the heavyset girl on one of the recliners. Her hair was half braided with a comb in the middle. When Layani looked at her and didn't respond, she got up, walked across the room, and stood over Layani, holding the remote control. "Did your dumb ass hear me, bitch?"

"Bitch? Oh, I got your bitch!" Layani dropped her bag and stood to her feet. If being in foster care had taught her nothing else, it taught her to never argue sitting down. She'd seen way too many fights over the past few years where the person in the chair always got snuck or just beat the fuck up because they were at a disadvantage.

"Yo, y'all better chill that shit out before Ms. H come in here and handle all of us." A tall, lanky boy leaned over the sofa. His hair was bleached an orangish color, both his eyebrows were pierced, and his face had a cross tattooed on the left side. Layani was a bit taken back by his appearance, but she knew not to stare.

"Don't holler at me, Dre. Blame the new girl. She started it." The big girl pointed.

"I don't give a fuck who started it. I'm finishing it." Dre walked over, stood in between the girls, and put his foot down. "Sydney, you know better." He reached down and snatched the remote control from her hand. "You ain't even supposed to be watching TV this week anyway. I wasn't gon' say shit, but since you don't know how to act, go do whatever it is you're supposed to be doing before I get Ms. H."

"Damn, it's like that, Dre?" Sydney smacked her dry lips.

"What did I say, girl?" He looked at her with eyes that said *try me.* Instantly, she backed off. Layani recognized then that his position in the house must've been pretty high. With that kind of authority, she needed to be in his good graces in order to survive in this house.

"Thank you, Dre. I appreciate what you did." She reached her hand out to shake his. "My name is Layani."

Flashing him her best smile, she waited for Dre to shake her hand.

"Layani, or whatever the fuck your name is, save the *thank-yous* for somebody else. I did that shit for me, not you." Dre rolled his eyes. "The Bull don't play no games around here. If one of us pisses her off, then we all have to pay," he warned before returning to his seat on the sofa.

"The Bull?" Layani frowned and flopped back down in her chair.

"Sorry about that, new girl. Sydney be on one sometimes." A little girl with two afro puffs took the seat beside Layani and began leaning backward in the chair. "My name is Daisy." She held out her hand.

"Hey, Daisy, I'm Layani." She was impressed by the little girl's ability to hold grown-up conversation. However, she shouldn't have been surprised. Most children in foster care had the tendency to grow fast. "Daisy, who is the Bull?"

Daisy didn't speak. Instead, she pointed as Mrs. Gail and a tall, large lady with a fuzzy red wig and bull nose ring walked toward them. The sides of her shoes rubbed the floor, and her thighs fought with each other every time she took a step.

"What did I tell you about leaning back in my chair like that? Don't think I won't get you because the social worker is here!" The woman's voice was as heavy as her body mass as she struggled to breathe.

"Layani, this is Ms. Anita Hardy. She will be your foster mom until further notice."

"Hello." With a deep gulp, Layani walked up to the Bull and held her hand out.

"Aww ain't she cute." Ms. H looked at Gail. "Yeah, she'll fit in just fine around here."

"Anita, thanks again for helping us out on such short notice. We really appreciate all you do for the agency and these children." Mrs. Gail waked toward the door, purposely not stopping to say goodbye to Layani. The human side of her wanted badly to hug the young girl and let her know that everything was going to be ok; however, the social worker side of her knew leaving in a professional manner was always the way to go.

"Hey, it's no problem at all. Just remember to ad-just my check and SNAP benefits by end of day!" Ms. H closed the door without making sure Gail had made it to the car.

Chapter Three

Turning to look at the children remaining in the living, who all seemed to be avoiding eye contact with her, she finally looked down at Daisy. "Go show her the room and give her the rules." Without another word, she walked back into the kitchen.

"Come on, Lay. Can I call you that?" Daisy asked as she headed toward the stairs.

"Um, yeah, that's cool."

"All right, bet," Daisy continued. "Well, the rules are simple. Don't get on the Bull's nerves. No loud talking, no coming in late, no asking for seconds at breakfast or dinner, no showers longer than ten minutes. You wash once a week according to the calendar, keep your room clean, and do the chores listed for you on the calendar without being told. If you need personal items like pads or soap, you see Roderick. If you need things like cold medicine or Tylenol, then you see the Bull."

By the end of the speech, Daisy and Layani had made it up the stairs, down the hallway to the third bedroom on the left. There were a total of four bedrooms on that floor.

"How many kids stay here?"

"Ten, if we count you." Daisy began pointing to each room. "The little kids are in the first room. That's me. I'm ten. Then it's Regan and Kennedy, the twins. They are seven. In the middle room it's Micah. He's fifteen, I think. Dre, who you met downstairs, he's seventeen, and

Roderick, he's almost eighteen, so he'll be gone soon. In that room, near the bathroom is where the Bull sleeps. Sometimes her boyfriend Kevin sleeps over too, but we don't suppose to know that. In this room, it'll be Sydney. She's fourteen. Charlotte, she's sixteen, and you. How old are you?"

"I'll be fifteen tomorrow." Layani hated to even think about spending her birthday there.

"My birthday is in seven months. Do you want to know what my wish is?" Daisy opened the door to the bedroom.

"Well, if you tell me, then it won't come true." Layani looked around the small room. There wasn't much to it besides two sets of bunkbeds. Both bottoms were already made, which indicated they were taken.

"It probably won't come true anyway, so I'll just tell you." Daisy went into the closet, stood on a stool, and grabbed a big bag from the top shelf. It was a blanket, pillow, and sheets. "They are clean. We washed them after the last girl left." Daisy unzipped the bag and handed the stuff to Layani. "Anyway, my dream is to be adopted by my next birthday. Do you think it's going to happen?"

"I hope so." Layani didn't want to burst the girl's bubble by telling her that most children over the age of eight never got adopted.

After helping to make up the bed, Daisy left her new friend to go watch TV before television time was up. Layani put her suitcase into the closet and took a seat on the window seat. After being in foster care for the past two years, she'd learned to never unpack until she had been somewhere for a while. After what had happened that day at the Daniels', she would probably never unpack until she was moving into her own house.

For nearly an hour, she sat in silence, pondering her new life. She missed her old life tremendously. She missed her old friends, her old school, and her old neighborhood. How had she gone from that to this? How had the same God that her mama always told her loved her take everything she ever loved?

Layani was beyond irritated and emotional. Things only escalated from bad to worse when she saw Sydney enter the bedroom and close the door.

"What's up now, bitch? Dre ain't in here to save you." She made a show of cracking her knuckles. On instinct, Layani jumped up from the window seat and grabbed the first thing she saw, which was a baseball bat from the corner of the room.

Sydney hadn't anticipated the weapon, but that didn't stop her from coming full force. She lunged at Layani, who dodged the attack and fired back with a blow to the chubby mid-section of her attacker. Next, she swung the bat and cracked Sydney right in the head. It stung like hell but pissed her off even more. Sydney charged at Layani so hard they hit the wall and left a huge hole. Quickly, she hit her with a one-two combo and finished with a blow of her own across Layani's face.

On impact, Layani's top lip split and swelled immediately. Spitting blood to the floor, Layani took the bat and began swinging like a madwoman. She whooped Sydney's ass with the bat all around the room.

The brawl only came to an end when the door flew open. Standing in the frame was the Bull, steaming mad. "I know you little bitches ain't up here tearing up my shit!" She walked into the room and assessed the damage. That was when she spotted the hole in the wall. "Oh, hell no! Hell no!" Snatching the bat from Layani, she began hitting both girls across the ass, legs, and arms with it. "What's the fuck is wrong with y'all, tearing up my shit like y'all pay bills around this muthafucka!"

"Please stop. That hurts!" Layani screamed.

Sydney knew better, so she took the blows without a word.

"Stop what? This?" She began to hit Layani even harder. The skin on her brown body eventually began to turn black and green from all the bruising.

Only after the Bull got tired did she stop the abuse. Dropping the bat onto the floor, she looked down at her victims, who curled up in fear. "You bitches better not even think about coming out of this room until this same time tomorrow. Don't eat my shit, don't drink my shit, and don't use my shit until the lockdown is over." Without saying another word, the Bull left the room just fast as she'd come.

The rest of the day went by at lightning speed. Since both girls were so badly beaten, the only thing they could do was climb into their beds and go to sleep. Layani woke up periodically throughout the day into the night from hunger pains and bladder issues, but she dared not leave the bed. The same could've been said for Sydney, because from time to time, Layani felt the bed shake beneath her, yet Sydney never got up. Layani thought it was ironic that she'd picked the same bunkbed as her enemy. However, she didn't have the strength to move.

Morning came, and Layani was about to pass out from holding her pee. There was no clock in the room, so she didn't know if the 24-hour lockdown was still in effect. It wasn't until Daisy came into the room about an hour later and told them that the Bull said they could come out that they moved.

Both Layani and Sydney had to use the bathroom, but because they didn't want to start another fight, they played a game of rock, paper, scissors. Layani won.

With both legs clenched together, she scurried down the hallway to the bathroom. It was covered in pink and black from the floor tile to ceiling, and it smelled stale and dank.

Layani pulled her pants down and pissed over the toilet seat without even checking to make sure it was clean. Instantly, she felt better. After flushing the toilet and washing her hands, she glanced at herself in the mirror. She was fucked up so bad that anybody who saw her would think she went toe to toe in the ring with Mayweather.

"Damn." She rubbed her lips, gave herself one more look, and then left the bathroom quickly so that Sydney could go. They weren't friends and would probably never be, but that fresh ass-whooping had them acting cordial for the time being.

"It's breakfast in the kitchen. Better hurry up. If you don't get down there in the next five minutes, the kitchen is going to be closed until dinner tonight at seven." Daisy was leaning up against the wall, waiting on her new friend.

"What time is it?"

"Eleven fifty-five a.m, so come on." Daisy pulled Layani down the hallway toward the stairs. She didn't think Layani really understood that if she didn't eat now, then she wouldn't eat until later. "All we got it Cap'n Crunch."

After arriving in the kitchen, Daisy flew around, grabbing the cereal, milk, bowl, and a spoon. "Whew! We just made it with a minute to spare."

"Can we make a bowl for Sydney?" Layani asked before putting the spoon to her mouth. Again, she wasn't trying to become best friends with the girl who caused the ass-whooping last night, but she knew firsthand the hunger pangs Sydney was likely having.

"I guess." Daisy made another made dash around the kitchen, just in time for the clock to hit noon.

"All right, if you don't have it, you won't have it! The kitchen is closed." With her head covered in a floral bonnet and a cigarette hanging from her lips, the Bull entered the kitchen wearing a long nightgown, stretch pants, and dingy Christmas socks. Grabbing the cereal box from the table, she put it into the cabinet. Next, she grabbed the milk and placed it into the refrigerator. Layani looked from the Bull to Daisy, who was as stiff as a board until the Bull addressed her.

"Girl, hand me them locks and shit."

"Here you go." After fumbling in the drawer, Daisy produced several chains and locks.

Layani watched in silence as she walked around the kitchen and literally locked all the cabinets, the pantry, and the refrigerator and freezer. Layani couldn't believe the lady was actually locking up the food.

"New girl, today is your day to clean my kitchen. Daisy will show you where the supplies are, unless you got a problem with that." After staring at Layani for a few uncomfortable seconds, she finally walked into the living room.

Sydney arrived in the kitchen a few seconds later. She saw the locks and cursed under her breath because she knew what time it was.

"Here. Daisy made you a bowl." Layani handed the bowl of cereal to Sydney, who took it but didn't say thank you. Instead, she nodded her head in appreciation and began wolfing the sugary breakfast down like it was going out of style.

Chapter Four

After being shown where the supplies were and being told how the Bull liked to keep her large, dated kitchen with mismatched appliances, Layani got to work. She washed, dried, and put up all of the dishes. She wiped off the counters and the worn kitchen table, then cleaned the stove and the microwave. After taking out the overflowing trash, she began to sweep the kitchen floor.

Her body was racked with pain from the beating and physical labor, so she started singing to take her mind off it. Singing was something she usually did in private, or at least when she thought no one was listening, because she was shy.

"I will cross the ocean for you. I will go and bring you the moon." She crooned the old jam her mother often sang while using the broom as a microphone.

"Damn, girl. You sound good!" Micah walked into the kitchen, careful not to step on the pile of trash resting in the middle of the floor.

"Oh, thanks." Layani was startled and embarrassed that he had caught her little impromptu performance.

"Keep going," Micah urged.

"Nah. I'm good." Layani timidly turned away.

"Please, gorgeous, continue for me," he begged. Even with bruises, he thought she was a beautiful girl, with almond-shaped eyes, a small button nose, and pouty lips. Her skin was the color of mocha, and her smile was warm. She reminded him so much of his mother.

"Handsome, I said I'm good." With a smirk, Layani returned his compliment with one of her own. It wasn't hard to do, because Micah wasn't bad-looking at all. With catlike hazel eyes, deep dimples, and skin the color of rich cocoa, he could've easily won the hearts of many.

"Girl, God put something special on your vocal cords. You need to be singing every chance you get." Micah hopped onto the counter and watched her finish sweeping. He was done with his chores for the day. Usually, he would have offered to help, but the Bull had worked him and Roderick like dogs that morning, and he was tired.

"God don't mean shit to me," Layani stated as a matter of fact.

Taken aback by her choice of words, Micah frowned. "God is the reason you woke up this morning. Don't you know that, girl?" His mother had raised him in the church. If there was one thing he knew for sure, it was how to praise the Lord and give thanks for all his blessings.

"Well, if God is supposed to be looking out for me, why didn't he let me die with my parents?" Layani was angry. She resented God and everything about Him for leaving her an orphan.

Micah knew her pain because his parents were also deceased. They had died in an apartment fire three years earlier, while he was at school.

"Trust me, I know where you're coming from, shorty, but God does everything for a reason." Micah hopped off the counter and wrapped his arms around the new girl. It was a forbidden gesture at the foster home. The Bull didn't play physical contact of any kind, unless it was an ass-whooping, but Micah knew she needed a hug. The embrace lasted for almost five minutes, until they heard heavy walking upstairs.

"Maybe God kept you around to bless people with your voice."

"Thank you. I never thought about it like that." Layani sniffed before pulling away. It was the first genuine embrace she'd received since her parents died.

"No need to thank me, shorty. I'll always be here if you need me. We foster kids got to stick together." Micah smiled. He liked the girl standing before him as much as any teenaged boy could like anybody. She was very pretty, with super fine hair, and she was curvy, too. "Now, can I hear you sing again?"

"Nope." Layani shook her head with a smirk.

"Why not?" Micah leaned back on the counter with his arms folded and licked his lips. Even as a kid, his swag was apparent. Most girls flocked to the six-foot boy with the football player build. His hair was naturally curly, and his teeth were perfectly straight.

"I'm shy." Layani looked down at the white laminate floor she was sweeping.

"You shouldn't be." Micah lifted her chin.

Both felt the chemistry between them, but neither knew exactly what it was.

"Check it. Let me drop you a beat, and you just chime in when you're ready." He began to tap on the counter while making beat-box noises with his mouth.

"Dang, you sound fresh!" Layani was impressed. If she wasn't watching the music come from his body with her own eyes, she would've sworn the radio was on.

"Thanks." He smiled while still keeping the rhythm. "I'm going to be a famous music producer when I grow up," Micah declared. "I love making music."

"A producer?" Layani frowned. As far she was concerned, the real money was in singing and rapping. "I ain't ever heard of a rich producer."

"Who do you think make all the beats for the rappers and singers?" Micah informed her. "Shit, they get paid first even before the artist do."

"Oh, I didn't know that." Layani felt enlightened.

"You should join my team and get this money." Micah didn't actually have a team, nor was he making any money, but he wanted to make Layani think he was doing something.

"What does your team do exactly?" she asked before going back to getting the trash on the floor.

"We make the dopest music this side of Detroit. Mark my words, we will be famous one day."

"Oh, yeah? What's the name of your crew?" She paused and waited for an answer.

"We go by the Dream Team!" He had come off the cuff with that one, but it sounded good.

"Who's on your team?" Layani needed to know all of the specifics before she got on board.

"Me and you, if you want to be down." Micah smiled, and Layani did too.

"You have a way with words. I hope you know that." Layani shook her head. She couldn't believe this boy had her going this whole time.

"So, are you in or what?" Micah extended his hand.

"I'm in!" Layani reached out and placed her palm into his.

"Bet!" Micah exclaimed while pulling his hand back. "I only got one rule, though."

"What's that?" Layani peered into his eyes.

"They say that money change people, so we have to promise to stay down with each other no matter what." He spit into his hand and held it back out.

"All right, bet. As long as you got me, then I got you too," Layani added before spitting into her hand and shaking his.

Chapter Five

Present Day

"Can I have your autograph, please, with your fine ass?"

Layani looked up from the song sheet she was holding and smiled. "Hey, baby, are these flowers for me?"

"Of course they are, superstar." Micah presented Layani with a large bouquet of red roses.

Inwardly, she gushed, feeling ever so lucky to have Micah in her life. Ten years had passed since they'd made the childish pact that day in the Bull's kitchen; however, the pact was still good. During their time in Ms. H's foster home, they'd endured some bad days and some good together. They'd also gained some new friends and lost some old ones, but thankfully, they were never separated. Once they aged out of the system, the couple decided to make it official and move in together. They couldn't wait to begin a new life together, get married, and possibly have children; however, right now the sole focus for both parties was to make their dreams a reality.

Micah worked relentlessly to make Layani's presence felt on the music scene, while getting her booked back-to-back for singing gigs. Layani also worked odd jobs to help keep the bills paid. No matter what, they knew they were destined for greatness and would stop at nothing until they both were finally famous.

"I think this is it, girl. You have to go out there and kill it." Micah began pacing back and forth in the back room of the Cocoa Club. It was an intimate spot for local artists to perform new music, comedy skits, and poetry. Truthfully, the club wasn't a club at all. It was more a lounge with a large stage, two bars, and leather seating for 300 people. It was something like Detroit's own little Apollo on Woodward Street. Micah had started working part time at the lounge five years earlier, helping acts bring in equipment, changing stage lights, and plunging dirty toilets. He had just wanted to get his foot in the door for Layani to one day grace the stage, and now here they were. Tonight was the big night.

Micah was dressed to the nines in a black suit, white shirt, and black tie. He'd borrowed the clothes from his boy Lavelle, who was the personal driver for some corporate attorney that worked downtown.

"Do you need some water? How about some tea?"

"Micah, calm down, boy. You're making me nervous." Layani was standing at the mirror, looking at the red gown practically safety-pinned to her body. It was borrowed from her friend Sonshine, a drag queen from the west side of the city. In fact, Sonshine had put her whole look together—red lace gown, matching gloves, and silver high heels. Her hair was pin-curled to her scalp, and there was a red rose behind her ear. Sonshine said she was giving off the *Sparkle* vibe, but Layani felt like a drag queen herself. Her makeup was over-done and the outfit was dated, but she didn't want to piss off her free stylist, so she obliged.

"Two minutes, guys." Terry, the stage manager at the small venue, tapped on the door.

"Okay, Lay baby, go out there and do your thang. Don't worry about who's in the audience except my pretty ass," Sonshine coached. She was wearing an orange fishnet pantsuit with gold accessories.

"Fuck all of that!" Micah chimed in. "I need you to perform like Henry Wells in the audience, because he is, and this is our one shot to knock his socks off." Mr. Wells was the CEO of Platinum Records. His career went as far back as the seventies. He was known in the music industry as the black Clive Davis. He may have been old, but his ear was always in tune with the next big thing.

"I've got you." Micah held up his knuckles.

"And I've got you back." Layani pressed her gloved fist against his.

"Aww, ain't y'all cute." Sonshine sashayed out of the makeshift dressing room, and Layani followed suit.

Things went in slow motion as Layani waited on the side of the stage. She could hear her heartbeat through her ears. Sonshine squeezed her hand, then went out onto the mainstage. "Ladies, how y'all doing? Fellas, y'all good?" As the head MC every night at the Cocoa Club, addressing the crowd was a cakewalk for Sonshine. "I've had the pleasure of introducing some very talented people during my young twenty-five years on this earth." Immediately, the crowd burst into laughter. Sonshine pretended to be offended; however, some of these same people were just partying with her last month for her sixtieth birthday. Her age was no secret.

"Damn, y'all just won't let a bitch live, I guess." She smacked her lips, and again the audience chuckled. "Okay, let's start over. I've had the pleasure of introducing some very talented people during my young forty years on this earth." This time, the crowd laughed so hard it even made Layani giggle. "Fuck it, then. I'm sixty years young, and I'm okay with that." Sonshine did a slow spin and showed off every inch of her silicone body to the audience, who in turn gave her a standing ovation. "Anyway, as I was saying, this young lady coming to sing for you tonight is simply amazing! Her voice is straight from Heaven. When she sings, I swear I see God, so I call her my angel. But the world knows her as Layani!"

Layani took her cue and nervously stepped on stage from the right. Sonshine exited the other side and quickly left from backstage so that she could see her girl sing.

"If I . . . should stay . . . I would only be in your way." Before the first phrase was out of Layani's mouth, the crowd erupted into clapping and cheering. She carefully hit every note and carried every tune. By the end of the song, there was not a dry eye in the house, nor a single ass in their seat.

"Thank you." She smiled graciously and did a small bow.

As soon as she got off stage, Micah wrapped his arms around her. "You did it, baby. You did it."

Micah wasn't a soft man at all, but just thinking about the possibility of Mr. Wells signing them tonight had him in tears. They'd come so far for this moment. After growing up in foster care, having no family support, and working around the clock to make ends meet, it was hard to believe the moment they'd been praying for was finally here.

"No, we did it, Micah. You know I am nothing without you." Layani loved her man, and she owed everything she had become to him. If it weren't for Micah believing in her, coaching her, writing for her, and keeping her booked, she'd be just another girl with a little talent and a dream.

"Excuse me, y'all, but someone wants to see you." Mr. Hearns, the owner of the Cocoa Club interrupted the couple's embrace.

Micah and Layani turned around to see none other than Mr. Henry Wells. He was dressed down in a pair of blue jeans, leather jacket, and leather riding gloves. There were two women standing at his side, one white, and the other black.

"Excuse my attire. I was on my way to the airport when my man DeAngelo told me to come down to his club to check out this pretty little thang with the angelic voice." Mr. Wells leaned in and kissed Layani's hand and then shook Micah's.

"We appreciate you stopping what you were doing to come and check Layani out. I'm Micah, by the way. I'm her manager. I hope you were beyond thrilled with the show."

"Thrilled?" Mr. Wells shook his head. "That, my boy, is an understatement. Layani has it, and by *it*, I mean the whole package. I've already called my attorney to draw up a contract. It should be ready for you to review first thing tomorrow morning." Mr. Wells looked down at his Rolex. "Let's say around ten. I can come to you, or you can come to me. I've extended my stay in the city for another night."

"We'd be happy to come to you tomorrow at ten." Micah nearly choked on the words that he couldn't believe he was saying.

"Awesome." Reaching into his pocket, Mr. Wells produced a business card. "Micah, this number goes directly to Chandi, my personal secretary. Call her in the morning, and she will give you the address. If the contracts come any sooner than ten, can I have Chandi call you?"

"Hell yeah." Micah practically snatched the card. "They could come tonight at midnight and we would be on our way."

"Good, good. Keep that same energy. We've got a lot of work to do." Mr. Wells bid Micah farewell with another handshake. "Layani, my dear, welcome to Platinum." He kissed both her cheeks and walked off with his women.

Chapter Six

Sleep didn't come easy to Micah or Layani that night as they lay in their compact studio apartment atop the mattress on the floor in the corner. Beside it was a box being used as a nightstand. The home was modest and unique. Over the years, Layani and Micah had furnished their place with random finds from multiple second-chance stores and garage sales through the city. There was a yellow two-seater sofa with a red coffee table in front, and two mismatched end tables, one black, and the other gray. Layani tried to tie the colors in with a multicolored throw rug, but all it did was add more unnecessary color to the room. In the center of the kitchen and dining space, there was a wooden folding table and two folding chairs. The couple never ate at the table. It was used as Micah's office and covered with tons of paper.

The night before, dozing off into the best dreams they'd had in a very long time, the pair went through a ball of emotions that neither of them could control. First was excitement, then there was nervousness, and that was followed by anxiety. Once those feeling ran their course, sadness crept in as they both thought of their parents and how proud they might've been. The big moment was definitely bittersweet.

As soon as the clock struck six a.m. the next day, Micah was back in grind mode. "Come on, Lay. Get up and get yourself together, baby." He nudged his sleepy-headed girlfriend.

"Baby, why do we have to get up so early?" Layani asked with one eye open. "The man said ten."

"The early bird gets the worm, so come on now." Undressing, Micah tossed his T-shirt to the ground. Then he went around the room looking for something clean and presentable to wear to the meeting. "Babe, have you seen my khakis?"

"No, but I do see that big-ass dick swinging between your legs." Layani was now sitting up on the full-sized bed. It was tight for them to sleep on together, but they'd slept on worse, so neither of them complained. "Mr. producer, can you bless me with a little sample before it's time to go?" Layani playfully removed her nightshirt, exposing her round, 40D breasts.

"Bae, we don't have time for this right now, but as soon as that contract is signed, I promise I will fuck you every which way but loose." When Micah was in grind mode, nothing could take him out, not even Layani or her perfect pussy.

Layani and Micah showered and dressed hastily before making their way out of their studio apartment toward the elevator. Micah took in the sight of food stains, broken toys, and a bag of trash left behind, and he smiled. The first thing he planned to do once they signed the contract was find a nicer place to live.

"Remind me again why we are leaving so early?" Layani's watch read 8:03 a.m.

"I figured we could grab a coffee and a doughnut from the shop downstairs to celebrate, and then I'll call Chandi." Micah pressed the down button on the elevator.

"Nigga, we had coffee and Pop Tarts back at the crib. What's really going on?" Layani wasn't stupid. She knew when Micah was hiding something.

"I didn't want to say anything, but Boost turned our phones off this morning. I need to call Chandi from the phone at the doughnut shop downstairs so we can get the address." He looked at her apologetically. He'd spent the last of their savings on the rent last week. There was nothing left to pay the cell phone bills. He figured he'd at least have until next payday, but that wasn't the case.

"All you had to do was say that in the first place." Layani kissed her man just as the elevator arrived.

Mrs. Carol got off and smiled at the lovebirds. "I heard you did good last night. All the neighbors are talking about it. I hate that I missed it, but Earl has been down with the flu."

"That's okay, Mrs. Carol. Please give him our love." Layani stepped into the elevator.

"Tell him we're going to sign a contract right now!" Micah added as the door closed.

Layani slapped him playfully on the chest. She didn't want him spilling the beans until they had signed the contract and everything was official.

Once outside, Micah spotted trouble coming their way. "Hey, bae, go on ahead inside and order for us. I'll be inside shortly."

"What's up?" Layani saw two men crossing the street. One of them was Dre, a boy from their time at Ms. H's foster home. He'd aged out two years before them, which meant he was now about 27.

"Go ahead inside, Lay. I'll be in there shortly." Micah hated when she didn't listen. "Now!"

"Fine. You ain't got to holler." She rolled her eyes.

"What's up, Layani." Dre nodded. He was now sporting a beard and long braids. His facial tattoos had multiplied, but at least the orange hair was gone.

"Dre." With an attitude, Layani left the men to talk while she retreated inside of the doughnut shop.

"Man, why the fuck is you snooping around my crib?" Micah was instantly on defense. He knew Dre and his goon came with nothing but trouble.

"Man, why the fuck haven't you returned my calls and texts?" Dre folded his arms.

"My bad about that. My shit is disconnected."

"Which brings me to my next question. How the fuck is you going to pay me my shit back when you can't even pay your got damn cell phone bill?" From time to time, Dre fronted Micah pounds of weed and sometimes cocaine to get on his feet when money was tight. Micah always paid him back on time, with interest. However, after this last deal two months ago, Micah got ghost.

"I will have your money soon. You know I'm good for it, so don't come and try to front on me like that." Micah did have Dre's money as scheduled, but then Layani went on and on about a necklace she'd seen in the mall that reminded her of the cross her mother used to wear. She said the minute she had enough money saved, she would go back and get it. Never wanting his woman to go without, he bought Layani the necklace and decided to rob Peter to pay Paul in other ways to get Dre his money.

"Nigga, I want my shit, and I want my shit now." Raising his shirt, Dre exposed the gun in his pants.

"Nigga, I don't have your shit now, but on my mama, I'll have it for you by the end of the day." Micah stared at his so-called foster brother.

"You should just pop this nigga, man," Dre's friend chimed in.

Before he knew what was happening Micah caught him with a left hook and right jab. Dre watched for a minute before pulling the men apart.

"Micah, you know I don't like looking like a clown out here. You're only getting this extension because we're something like family." Dre reached for a dap and then pulled Micah in close. "But if I don't get my muthafuckin' money by tonight, I will come back and shoot you and then fuck your bitch!"

Micah wanted to fuck Dre up, but he knew to leave well enough alone. Not that he was scared of Dre or anything like that, but he knew that business was business. If Micah was in the same position, he would've played it the same way.

"What the fuck was that?" Layani asked when Micah took a seat across from her at their favorite booth in the back of the establishment.

"Don't worry about it." Casually, Micah grabbed the menu, though he already knew he was ordering the same shit he always ordered.

"Micah, you better tell me something right now before I make a scene in here." When he didn't say anything Layani leaned over the table and whispered, "Are you still selling drugs for him?" She'd warned Micah about fooling with the likes of Dre. She knew he was a knuckle-headed nigga with nothing to lose. "Micah, you don't need to be dealing with him, period."

"After we meet with Mr. Wells, I'll pay him back and that will be a done deal. I swear."

"How much do you owe him?"

"A band," he said, referring to the sum of one thousand dollars. Micah shifted his gaze from Layani back to the menu.

"What the fuck did you need that kind of money for?" While waiting for him to speak, she looked down at her necklace. It was the only thing that could've cost that amount, so she took it off. "Here. I don't want it. Take it back."

"Put the necklace back on."

"Not if it means you'll still owe Dre." She slid the necklace forward. "Take it."

"Lay, don't make me mad. Put the got damn necklace back on." He stood from the booth and walked toward the back near the bathroom. It was one of the few establishments that still had a public phone for use.

Micah dialed and redialed the telephone number fifteen times before deciding to give it a rest. He'd left a message the first and the sixth time. By the time he got back to the table, Layani was eating her beloved doughnut holes and drinking hot chocolate. Micah loved apple fritters, and there was one waiting on him with a hot cup of black coffee.

"What did Chandi say? Did we get the address?" Her mood was noticeably lighter.

"Nobody answered. I called fifteen times." Though he didn't speak on it, there was an uneasy feeling in the pit of his stomach. Micah hoped like hell Mr. Wells hadn't changed his mind and was dodging his calls.

Layani could see the panic in her boyfriend's eyes, so she decided to take his mind off things with a game they used to play back when they lived with the Bull. "What is the first thing you're going to buy with our check?" Her eyes danced at the possibilities.

"I don't know." Truthfully, Micah wasn't in the mood to count dollars he didn't have today. He needed Chandi to answer the phone.

"Well, the first thing I would buy is a six-bedroom house."

"Why six bedrooms?" Micah looked at the wall clock behind Layani. It was 8:56 a.m.

"One for us, one for our office, and four for all of the babies I can't wait to have with you." She smiled.

"Girl, ain't nobody thinking about babies right now. You have music to make. The world is about to sing your praises. You are about to blow up!" He stood from the booth and headed back to the phone. "Beyoncé better move out the way for Layani Bell," he hollered while walking down the hall.

While waiting on Micah to come back, Layani grinned from ear to ear as the thought of being rich invaded her mental space. For the first time in life, she wouldn't have to worry about paying bills or having money. She couldn't wait to tour the world and learn new things. Her luck was finally turning around, or so she thought.

"Hey, turn that up!" Someone sitting at the counter hollered for the owner to adjust the volume on the television mounted to the wall.

Layani looked at the television screen to see what the story was about.

"Frank, unfortunately, we've got some sad news coming to us this morning from Bloomfield Hills. We've just been told that music mogul and adored hitmaker Henry Wells has been found dead in his residence at approximately two a.m. At this time, police do not speculate any foul play but will not have an official cause of death until the coroner completes his report. Henry Wells was eighty-three years old. He leaves to mourn eight children, thirty grandchildren, nineteen great-grandchildren, and millions of fans. Mr. Wells was one of kind and will truly be missed. We will update you as soon as we know more. Back to you at the studio."

Almost as soon as the story went off, everyone in the building went into an uproar. Some got on their cell phones, while others began chatting with other patrons about the death of the music legend.

The bubble Layani had been living in since meeting Mr. Wells last night had just burst all over the got damn place!

Chapter Seven

For almost twenty-four hours straight, neither Layani nor Micah said a word to one another. In fact, they hadn't watched television, eaten, or done anything. She stayed in the bedroom part of the apartment, and he stayed in the living area. They weren't angry with each other. They just needed time to process what had just happened. Both felt bad for the other one even more than themselves. The loss of this opportunity felt like the loss of a loved one. Therefore, they each needed time to grieve.

"Hey." Micah stepped into the bathroom where Layani sat in the bathtub, soaking and sulking. She'd been in there for hours. The water was probably ice cold.

"Hey." Looking up at her man, she noticed how he'd seemingly aged overnight. There were new bags under his eyes and even a few gray hairs that hadn't been there yesterday. He was beyond stressed, and she knew it.

"I just wanted to tell you that I love you." He avoided her gaze. "I got to step out for a minute, but I should be back in a little while."

"You should be back, or you will be back?" She looked him up and down and noticed he was dressed in all black.

"Should be back," he repeated for clarification before leaning down to give her a kiss.

She reached around his body and felt the presence of a gun. On cue, he stepped away, but she was right on his heels, butt naked and all.

"Micah, please don't do this."

"Everything will be all right. I promise." Grabbing his black hoodie off the bed, he tossed it over his head. During his twenty-four-hour downtime, he decided that the only way out of his financial turmoil was to do what he knew best, beside producing music.

"You promised the last time was the last time!" Layani used the back of her hand to wipe away her tears. Back in the day when she and Micah first aged out of foster care, he stole high-end cars and sold them to his boy who owned a chop shop. It was a dangerous profession with huge consequences if he ever got caught. During that time, though, it didn't matter. They needed the money, so Micah did what he had to do for them to survive. After they were able to stash enough money away to live comfortably for a few months, they both got honest jobs, and he had been on the straight and narrow ever since.

"Lay, I know what I said, but, baby, I'm drowning." Micah peered down at her with hazel eyes that begged for her to see his side of things. "I owe Dre, we need our cell phones turned on, and any day now the bills will start coming for next month."

Without a word, Layani removed her necklace and placed it into his hand. "I love this necklace, but I love you even more. If you go out there tonight and get killed or locked up, this piece of jewelry can't do shit for me," she cried. "Take it back to the store, take it to a pawn shop, or sell it. I don't care what you do with it. Just take the money and pay Dre. We will figure out the rest later. I can't lose you, Micah." Wrapping her wet arms around her man, she held on for dear life.

With tears in his eyes, Micah accepted what she said and nodded his understanding. Silently, he vowed to buy her another necklace that was bigger and better once he was able. Layani had just saved him from doing something stupid, and quite possibly had saved his life, too. He knew she deserved the world, and he would do anything to give it to her.

Three weeks after Mr. Wells passed, everything was back to business as usual. Micah had sold the necklace to one of his rapper friends and paid $750 to Dre, with the promise to pay the rest by the end of the month. Layani had picked up extra shifts at the hospital where she worked in housekeeping. Micah worked around the clock in a plant that made parts for Chrysler, and at the studio putting tracks together for other artists.

One day while on a lunch break at the plant, Micah received a courtesy call from Chandi, Mr. Wells' personal secretary. The call was to inform him of what he already knew. Without a signed contract, the record label executives wouldn't honor Layani's deal. Chandi apologized profusely for the unfortunate situation and gave Micah the number to Wolf Wells, one of Mr. Wells' grandsons. She said he was the new CEO of Platinum Records and thought that if Micah could talk to him and convince him of Layani's talent the way he had convinced his grandfather, then maybe they still stood a chance. Micah wasn't optimistic this go-round, but he didn't want to blow it for Layani, so he gave it a shot.

After calling Wolf and leaving messages practically 24/7 for almost a week, Micah was granted a meeting downtown. The meeting was scheduled for the next day at 2 p.m. His shift was from 8 a.m. to 4:30 p.m., so he asked his boss, Raymond, if he could work until noon, then leave for his appointment and come back when it was over to finish his shift. Micah even offered to work overtime if they needed him to. The plant rarely granted days off that weren't scheduled months in advance, but he lied and said he had a doctor's appointment. Still, Raymond said no and told Micah if he left before 4:30 the next day that he might as well not come back ever because he'd be fired.

With much thought and careful consideration, Micah threw caution to the wind and clocked out of work at exactly noon the next day. Raymond watched from his position in his office as the young man defied everything he'd said yesterday. In his opinion, he didn't think Micah knew how good he had it. There were thousands of people waiting for the company to hire them, and here Micah was just throwing his job in the trash.

"Another one bites the dust," he mumbled before calling up to the security and telling them not to let Micah Green back into the building if he tried to come back. Next, he called up to the Human Resources Department to start the termination process.

Micah knew that he couldn't afford to lose his job, but then again, he couldn't afford to lose this second opportunity either. Layani's career was on the line, and so was their future. Micah knew you missed one hundred percent of the shots you never take, so he had walked out of the plant and didn't plan on looking back.

"Micah, come on in." Wolf welcomed the young man in sweatpants and a T-shirt into his oversized office.

"Thank you for agreeing to meet me." He extended his oil-stained hand and saw Wolf hesitate to shake it. "Sorry about that. I left work and caught the bus straight over here. I didn't have time to change or clean up."

"No problem. I understand." Wolf walked over to the bar in the corner and poured a shot of Cîroc vodka. "Care for a drink?" He removed the jacket of his suit and undid his tie.

"No, I'm good. Thanks."

"Well, I'll cut to the chase. Chandi told me about your deal with my grandfather to sign your client, Layani Bell. I listened to some of her covers on YouTube, and she sounds amazing. Her range is out of this world, and her sound is unique." As Wolf downed his vodka, Micah couldn't stop from grinning like a Cheshire cat. "I wish Platinum had a place for her, but at this time, we don't. I'm sorry."

"Wait! What?" Micah was utterly confused. "If she sounds a great as you say she sounds, why wouldn't you have a place for her under your label?"

"My grandfather was a sucker for R&B. He loved doo wop music because that's the sound of his generation. I am the generation of hip hop and rap, as I'm sure you can understand. R&B is cool, but it's dated. Nobody wants to hear about another love song or a broken heart. People want to hear club music and gangster rap. Starting next quarter, I will be pushing the label into more of a hard-core rap direction." Wolf poured another shot of vodka. "Layani might be great for a hook or two, but other than that, we have no use for her at Platinum."

"Why the fuck didn't you just say that shit over the got damn phone?" Micah was pissed and seeing red.

"Excuse me?" Wolf was taken aback by his bluntness.

"I basically got fired from my fucking job to come here and take this meeting thinking that you wanted to sign Layani." Micah ran his hands over his face. He couldn't believe his luck. Not only did he not have a job, but he also didn't have a deal—again!

Chapter Eight

Micah was beyond pissed and sick to his stomach after leaving Wolf's office. He wanted to break the CEO's face and smash everything in his office, but what good would that do? Micah would be in jail pronto, turning a bad situation into a worse one.

He didn't know how to tell Layani he'd lost his job. He didn't want her to see him as a failure. Instead of heading home, he headed to the only place that gave him peace, his studio. It was a small building on West Seven Mile that Micah named M'Powered House of Music. He rented the building from an Arab guy name Aman for $650 a month. Every other month, Micah couldn't afford the rent for this reason or that one, but Aman didn't care. His family was pretty wealthy. He took it easy on the gifted producer because he liked to be able to get free tracks from Micah here and there. Aman had been trying his hand at rapping for the past few years. He thought he was the next Tupac. With beats from Micah, he knew superstardom wasn't too far from his grasps.

After getting off the bus, Micah walked three blocks down the cold city streets to his studio, which sat on the corner, next to a dry cleaner. His mind was all over the place. Therefore, he didn't see the stretch limo idling in the parking lot. Reaching into his pocket, he placed the key into the door and felt a soft tap on the shoulder.

"Excuse me. Do you know where I can find Micah?"

"Depends on what you need." Without even turning to face the woman, Micah unlocked the door and stepped inside of his fortress. The inside of the building was nicely decorated in red and black. There was a small waiting area, one bathroom, and two studios. Micah only worked in one studio. The other one was being used as storage by Aman. He turned on the lights and removed his jacket.

"My name is L-Rae Rose. My friend Z Muney sent me here to listen and quite possibly buy some of your beats. He said you're the best in Detroit."

"Did you say L-Rae?" With a smile as big as Texas, Micah turned around to face the newly signed rapper to Universal Records. She was taking over the charts single after single. "I'm sorry for being rude. Would you like some water or something?"

Leading her into the studio, Micah glanced around to make sure everything was neat and in place. He'd never had an artist as big as L-Rae in his building; therefore, things had to be right. She was a beautiful Black woman from Atlanta. Her smile was almost as big as her ass, yet her voice was as small as her waist. In fact, it was the tiny voice that intrigued most of her fans.

"No thanks. I'm good." Taking a seat on one of the leather chairs, L-Rae removed her black fur coat to expose a tiny pink tube top, black biker shorts, and hot pink thigh-high boots. Her wig was neon green to match her nails. She smelled like candy.

"So, what exactly can I do for you for, Ms. Rae? Z didn't tell me you were stopping by or I would have been more prepared." Micah took a seat and tried to calm his nerves. He didn't want to say the wrong thing, and he didn't want to blow this opportunity.

"We tried to call you a few weeks ago to tell you that I would be in town and wanted you to produce a song or two on my next mixtape, but it said the phone was disconnected." L-Rae sat back in her seat. "We probably dialed the wrong number or something. My bad."

Micah knew that she hadn't dialed the wrong number and that his shit was cut off at that time, but he didn't tell her that. "No worries. You're here now, and I would be honored to produce a song or two for you. How long are you in the D?" He stared at her and purposely kept his eyes off the breasts that threatened to escape from her small shirt at any second.

"I'll only be here until tomorrow morning, unfortunately." L-Rae looked at the fine producer and tried to remain cool. There was something about him that turned her on. Maybe it was his good looks and swag, or maybe it was his ordinariness. She loved that he wasn't all suited and booted with flashy jewelry and expensive clothes like the other producers she was used to. The industry hadn't taken him over yet, and she appreciated that.

"Well, let's get to work." Micah turned on his equipment and began asking L-Rae questions about what she liked in music sounds, who her inspirations were, and what her vision for the new mixtape was. By the time he finished interviewing her, he was able to come off the cuff with two very unique beats.

L-Rae stepped into the booth and put down her lyrics effortlessly like a professional. She hadn't written a thing, but the way her voice rode Micah's beat was simply magic.

"Oh my God! I can't believe we just got two songs in less than three hours." She was so excited that she called her manager and played the songs. Instantly, Sheryl, her manager, was in love and said she would wrap up her meeting and head to the studio shortly. "Micah, you are a musical genius." L-Rae rubbed his thigh.

"Thank you." He rolled his chair away from hers and began adjusting the knobs on his sound board.

"I know your mama is so proud." L-Rae reached into her Fendi bag and applied a fresh coat of lip paint. "Does she ever come down to the studio to watch you work?"

"No." Micah shook his head, not wanting to go into details.

"My mama doesn't support me neither, so don't feel bad. She ain't never came to school performances or a club showcase. Real talk. The only time I see that bitch is when she looking for some money."

"Don't call your mama a bitch." Micah shot the superstar a look that meant business, but she didn't care.

"That bitch is a bitch!"

"Girl, you better watch your mouth and love on your mama while you can. She won't be here forever." As he looked at L-Rae, he noticed she was crying, causing her makeup to melt a little.

"I'm sorry for being emotional. It's just that every time I think about her never being there for me no matter how much I need her or how proud I try to make her, I get upset."

"Look, I don't know your mom's story or your situation. That's none of my business. But take it from a friend—your mother won't be here forever. Let that resentment go and try to move forward. Maybe seek counseling or something, but try to salvage whatever relationship y'all got left. You don't want to wake up one day with any regrets on what you wish you should've said or could've done."

"Thank you, friend." L-Rae wiped her eyes.

Approximately thirty minutes later, Sheryl barged into the studio with her cell phone glued to her ear. "Hey, Fish, I'm here now with Rae. I'll call you shortly." Sheryl ended her call and held out a hand for Micah to shake. "Sheryl Martin. Pleasure to meet you," she said in a British accent.

"I'm Micah, and the pleasure is all mines."

"So, Micah, I was just on the phone with Kenny Fisher, the A & R over Rae's album. I filled him in on the amazing songs you guys just did in record speed, and he has offered to fly you out to Atlanta, all expenses paid, to produce Rae's entire mixtape." Sheryl could hardly contain herself.

"What! Really?" Micah's luck had been so bad lately that he was reluctant to get excited prematurely.

"Yes, darling! Fish wants you to exclusively produce her mixtape. If all goes well, this would be the start of your career in the big league." Reaching into her purse, Sheryl produced a stack of rubber-banded money. "That's four thousand dollars. Two thousand each for both of the songs you did today."

Micah only charged three hundred dollars for his beats, but he didn't tell her that.

After pushing the money into Micah's hand, Sheryl went back into her bag. "And as a sign of good faith, here is a check for twenty thousand. The label wants the mixtape to have at least twelve to fifteen songs. This is half of the money, and you will get the remainder at the completion of the album."

"Damn, so this is how ATL get down, huh?" Micah thumbed through the bills before staring down at the check. He couldn't believe that afternoon he was unemployed, and just a few hours later, he was a thousandaire. He couldn't wait to tell Layani.

"Do this right and there is more where that came from." Sheryl winked at her future client. Though she'd never managed any other producers, she knew she'd be able to make Micah just as wealthy as she'd made the other clients under her management.

"Thank you, Ms. Martin." Micah couldn't stop himself from wrapping his arms around the older woman.

"Don't thank me yet, baby boy. The cash is all yours to keep, but the check won't be signed until after you come to Atlanta and sign the contract."

"No offense, but can I—"

Sensing that Micah was reluctant, she cut him off by pulling out her cell phone, dialing Fish, and placing the call on speaker. "Hey, darling, it's me again. I think we've got that new genius producer Micah from Detroit on board, but he needs a little more encouraging. Can we add anything to sweeten the pot for him?" She winked at Micah, who remained silent. He was already good with the deal, but a little extra cheese on his sandwich wouldn't hurt.

"Did you tell him that there are thousands of producers ready and willing to work on L-Rae's album?" Fish sounded irritated. Nothing pissed him off more than when nobodies tried to negotiate.

"I did, darling, but then he asked me if any of them were able to finish two songs in three hours the way he has." Sheryl used this opportunity to flex her muscles and show Micah what he'd be getting if he signed on with her as his manager.

"Jesus Christ!" Fish paused for a second. "Send me the got damn tracks and I'll call you back. I need to see if this little punk is really worth my time and my money."

Without another word, Fish hung up the phone. Sheryl sent the tracks to him, and then the trio shot the breeze in the studio for only ten minutes before her phone rang back. "Talk to me, Fish."

"Tell Micah and Rae I loved the tracks. They were edgy yet classy. Simple yet over the top. That boy had the golden touch! With Rae on his tracks, we are destined for platinum status. Of course, we will pay for his travel and living expenses while he's here, but if he agrees to do the entire mixtape of fifteen songs in sixty days, the label will pay him an additional twenty thousand and sign him on as the exclusive producer for all of our top artists."

"He's listening. I've got you on speaker phone." Sheryl smiled at Micah, who was leaned against the wall with his eyes closed. "So, what do you say, baby boy? Do we have a deal?" She extended her hand.

"Hell yeah! Shit! When do we leave?" Micah shook her hand so hard that a bone popped.

"We fly out tomorrow. However, I'll set up your flight for Monday morning. That way, you can settle your affairs here and be ready to hit the ground running as soon as you touch down."

This was the deal of a lifetime. Micah knew a blessing when he saw one. Things were finally about to change for him and Layani. Silently, he praised the Lord in his head and thanked God for His angels providing a path to success. He thanked L-Rae and Sheryl for choosing to do business with him, and then he locked down the studio. It was time to go home and break the news to Layani that they would be moving to Atlanta for a few months.

Before he caught the bus home, he made a stop at the jewelry store and once again purchased Layani another diamond cross necklace. This one was bigger and better. He couldn't wait to give it to her.

Chapter Nine

As soon as Micah made it down his street, flashing lights and sirens captured his attention. The commotion was coming from in front of his apartment building, but he didn't think much of it. Every other day, the ambulance was there responding to an elderly resident who had fallen or burned themselves, or a domestic dispute. He thought today was no different until Mr. Lang, his next-door neighbor, met him on the walkway.

"Micah, that's you girlfriend. You need to see about her. Lots and lots of blood." His English wasn't the best, but Micah got the picture.

"Excuse me, sir. What happened to my girlfriend? My neighbor said he saw a lot of blood." Micah tried to remain calm as he ran up to a man standing at the back of the ambulance, although his heart was about to leap through his chest.

"Calm down, sir. What apartment is yours?" the paramedic asked before releasing any information.

"Four oh nine." As Micah waited on the paramedic to say something, Layani arrived on a gurney being pushed by another paramedic. She was covered in sweat and blood. Her eyes were closed, and she wasn't moving. "Layani, baby, get up. Please baby, get up. What happened?" He was frantic.

"I will tell you that we did respond to a 911 call from your apartment. However, due to HIPAA regulations, I cannot tell you the reason for the call. We're going to Sinai Grace. Can you meet us there?" the paramedic asked.

"I don't have a car." He shook his head. "Can't I just ride in the back, please?"

The paramedic wanted to advise that ride-alongs were typically prohibited for any patient besides minors. However, he could see the desperation in the man's face, so he obliged.

During the ride, Micah watched as the paramedic attached monitors to Layani, who was still unconscious. "Man, please tell me what happened," he asked while grabbing a hold of her hand It was cold. "Is she dead?"

"She's just sedated right now. Don't worry. She'll be okay." The paramedic didn't offer any other information, and Micah didn't ask. Instead, he went into prayer mode, asking God to bring Layani back to him and make everything okay.

Immediately after arriving at the hospital, Layani was taken into surgery. It wasn't until nearly three hours later that he was finally permitted to see her. She was in the recovery area.

"Bae, what happened?" He rushed behind the curtain where her bed was. She was laying on her side, looking at the wall. "They wouldn't tell me shit, but I saw all of that blood and thought you were dead." He bent down and kissed her forehead.

"I had a miscarriage." She sniffed while doing her best to blink back tears. "The pregnancy was two months."

"A miscarriage?" Micah asked for clarification, and she nodded then went on to tell him that she didn't even know she was pregnant. In fact, Layani hadn't even missed a period the last two months.

"The doctor said other than my cholesterol numbers being a little off, I'm healthy. So, the most likely possibilities of the cause of the miscarriage would stem from the pharmaceutical therapies I had as a child with Leukemia, or stress." She looked at Micah, who was still trying to process the whole miscarriage. "Either way, our child is gone because of me." At this point, she began to cry uncontrollably.

"No, bae, this is not your fault. God knows we aren't ready for a baby just yet. That's all."

"Micah, I don't care what you say. I wanted that baby." She sobbed. "I just want something in this world to call my own."

Micah felt helpless. There was nothing he could do or say to comfort her in this moment. She was entitled to her feelings, and he knew it was a hard pill for her to swallow having to grieve yet another loss. Though he was fucked up about losing their child, he saw this as a blessing in disguise. Layani was destined for greatness, and he knew she would never be able to reach her fullest potential with a baby on her hip.

"I was going to wait to give this to you, but I think right now is as good a time as any." Reaching into his pocket, he pulled out the new necklace and placed it around her neck. She looked at him and was about to demand he take it off when he told her exactly how he'd gotten the money to pay for it. "Bae, they got sixty thousand with my name on it if I can produce L-Rae's mixtape in sixty days. We fly out on Monday."

"When do you come back?" she asked nonchalantly. Her mind was already preoccupied with more pressing matters.

"We come back in sixty days when the mixtape is done, but truthfully, we ain't never got to come back if things take off for us in the A. This right here is our moment. Once I get my feet wet at Universal, I could slide you right into the mix. By this time next year, you'd be a signed artist with your own music out."

"Micah, I don't want to go." She couldn't look at him as she spoke. "You go and do the mixtape. I'll be here when you get back. Besides, I need a break from music anyway." Truthfully, she was tired of all the shows, recording sessions, vocal lessons, and industry talk. Today, when she lost her baby, reality hit her hard. She was sacrificing her health to chase a dream that was probably never going to come true.

"Bae, this opportunity to do what we love is all we ever wanted in life."

"Micah, this opportunity *was* all I ever wanted, but after realizing that I was this close to being someone's mother, I now see there are other things I want in life." After struggling to sit up, Layani reached over and grabbed Micah's hand. "I'm still in this with you. I just need a break. You go to Atlanta and make that money. I'll be here waiting on you to come back."

"Baby, I don't want this if you ain't going on the ride with me." Micah shook his head.

"I promise I'll be here ready to work the minute you step off that plane in sixty days." She puckered her lips for a kiss; however, when Micah when to kiss her back, she fell backward and started to foam at the mouth. Her body jerked uncontrollably as the machines she was connected too sang like a choir.

Before Micah could holler for help, a team of medical staff rushed into the area. Once again, he was asked to wait in the waiting area, completely unsure of what was going on.

For the better part of an hour, Micah waited on edge. Every fifteen minutes, he checked for an update with the front desk, but there was none. Finally, just as he approached the desk for the fourth time, Layani's doctor was coming out to see him.

"What's up, doc? Is she okay?"

"She's fine, just resting now. Micah, it appears Layani had a seizure. The seizure could have been caused by anything, including the stress we attributed to the miscarriage. Seizures can be a one-time thing, and sometimes they can be a lifelong thing. We have given Layani a little medicine to help her really rest. Tomorrow, we will perform an electroencephalogram, in other words an EEG. It's a test used to detect any brain abnormalities. With the medicine, she's probably going to sleep for most of the night, so I would probably go home for the night if I were you. We'll take her down for the test about eight o'clock. So, come back about nine o'clock and she should be alert and ready to see you." The doctor patted Micah's shoulder before walking away.

Usually, Micah would have stayed at the hospital and been by Layani's side, but it had been an extremely rough day. He was overwhelmed and needed to close his eyes and lay down in a comfortable bed. There was also so much to think about. On one hand, he wanted to stay and be with his girl because she needed him, and he needed to know that she was okay. On the other hand, he knew this deal was the opportunity of a lifetime. If Micah could secure this bag, then all their dreams would be at his fingertips.

All night, Micah tossed and turned. He didn't know what to do at that point besides get down on his knees and pray. He prayed for God to point him in the right direction. He also prayed for God to make Layani better. He couldn't imagine living life without her.

By morning, Micah was even more tired than he had been the night before, yet and still, he got dressed and headed downstairs to the donut shop. He ordered an apple fritter and a coffee, then took a seat at the counter. Without Layani, he didn't want to sit at their favorite booth.

"Hey, Micah. Where is Layani?" In the past three years, the owner, John, never recalled seeing one without the other.

"She got sick yesterday. She's at the hospital. As soon as I leave here, I'll be headed back up there." Micah played with apple fritter, breaking a small piece here and there.

"I'm sorry to hear that. Please give her my love." John walked away and went to help another customer. Things were always busy in the morning, but he couldn't help but notice the young man's body language. Just by looking at Micah, John could tell the weight of the world was on his shoulder.

"Hey, what's going on with you?" He leaned over the counter when he came back.

"I'm good. Just got a lot on my mind."

"Come take a break with me in the back." John removed his apron and headed to the back of the building where his small office was located. The room was nothing special, just a desk, two chairs, a computer, and a phone. "Micah, you look like you're minutes from losing it. I'm concerned, but I'm not nosey. I didn't bring you back here to dig into your personal life. I just really wanted to say that whatever is going on, this too shall pass. I know things seems rough right now, but God has the final say. When I look at you, I see a man destined for great things."

John didn't know much about Micah other than he was known around the west side of the city as a very talented music producer. Being in business at the donut shop for over thirty years, he'd seen many young punks come and go, but Micah was different. He didn't try to be street. He didn't try to be a thug. He worked hard and made an honest living.

"Your time may not be right now, but your turn is coming. Just stay faithful to God, and God will remain faithful to you." John didn't know if Micah was religious, but the Bible was all he knew, so he said what was on his heart.

"Thanks, man. I appreciate everything you just said more than you know." Micah believed God sent John to deliver the message that his time wasn't now, but his turn was coming. Micah believed wholeheartedly that he needed to be there for Layani; therefore, after wrapping up the conversation with John, Micah called Sheryl. He told her there was an unforeseen emergency with his girlfriend that required him to stay in Detroit. He thanked her for the opportunity and told her if they ever needed more music not to hesitate to hit his line. Of course, she was displeased but told him that family came first, so she understood. Micah ended the phone call, took a deep breath, and tore up the $20,000 check.

Chapter Ten

Thankfully, Layani's test came back normal. The seizure appeared to be something random and related to stress and the lack of rest. She was released from the hospital after a two-day stay. Micah committed to spoiling her rotten, and she didn't have to lift a finger. In fact, he had her quit her job while he took on three jobs. He'd somehow gotten his job back at the plant, which he worked Monday through Friday. He also worked security at night at a bar on the weekends and worked for John in the mornings. Initially, Layani was happy to hear that Micah wasn't going to Atlanta, but after a while, she felt guilty. She knew how important music was to her man, and with him working so hard to provide for her, he had no time to spend at the studio.

Six months after getting nothing but rest, Layani finally went back to work. She'd started at another hospital in the housekeeping department. She wanted to alleviate the stress on Micah so he could quit at least one of his jobs and return to what he loved.

It was just after noon when Layani crawled into their full-sized bed and closed her eyes. She'd just pulled a double shift, and the girl was tired. Layani hated pulling trash, washing soiled bed linen, and cleaning up after other people—especially the sick ones—but it was what it was. The job only paid $10.65 an hour, but it was enough to help keep the lights on and put food on the table. Layani knew housekeeping wasn't the most glamorous job, but it sure beat the fuck out of the unemployment line.

"Hey, bae, get up. We got to go!" Micah barged into their studio apartment sounding like he was speaking over a bullhorn. He was wearing work clothes covered in dirt and oil.

"Unh-uh." Layani groaned. Her pillow was perfectly folded beneath her head, and the sheets were crisp and cold, just the way she liked them.

"Come on, Lay. Get up!" Micah barked. This time, he clapped his hands together loudly. "We got shit to do." He hadn't been this excited in a long time.

"Why are you home anyway?" Layani knew Micah should've had his ass at work this time of the day.

"Well, at work we listen to the radio, right," he eagerly tried to explain the moral of his story, but Layani wasn't interested in the long version.

"Bae, get to the point. What the hell does the radio have to do with the reason you're home?"

Micah was too excited to let her kill his vibe, so he blew her off and continued. "I heard that Dernard Perry will be at WJLB until two o'clock today, so I clocked out and came here to get you." Though Micah had already learned the consequences of leaving work early, he knew today would be different. The third time was the charm. He felt in his spirit that things for him and Layani were about to take off for real this time.

"Who is that?" Layani half heard him as she dozed off.

"D-Money!" Micah exclaimed. "Come on, bae, D-Money! How can you not know who I'm talking about?"

"Oh, shit! Are you referring to the CEO of the Black Millionaires label?" Layani was now up and fully alert.

"Hell yeah!" Micah exclaimed as he saw Layani's eyes dance in anticipation. Dernard Perry was a major player in the music industry. Word around the way was that he started his company with ill-gotten gains, such as drug money, but Layani couldn't care less. The Black Millionaires label was solely responsible for the success of the best of the best. Mariah Mariah, Lil Caine, and Jake had gotten their starts from the label. If Layani could get down with the hitmakers at Black Millionaires, she knew superstardom was really within her grasp.

"Come on, girl. Let's go!" Micah was more excited than his girlfriend; however, to be clear, he wasn't on no groupie shit. He knew this was the break he and Layani needed to change their lives forever. Sure, signing with Mr. Wells would have been great until his grandson took over the business, and doing L-Rae's mixtape would have been amazing, but D-Money was currently the head nigga in charge on the music scene. He was young, rich, and talented. D-Money had owned and dominated the charts for the past fifteen years.

"Give me ten minutes." Layani sprang from the bed as if it were on fire. Maybe it was the long break Micah had given her from music, or maybe it was knowing exactly who she was going to meet that had her excited.

True to her word, it didn't take long for Layani to shower, apply a touch of makeup, brush her teeth, and curl her hair. Micah wanted her to go as is, just to ensure they made it to the radio station on time, but Layani knew beauty was what really signed contracts. A girl could be the most gifted soul on the planet, but if she wasn't easy on the eyes, then no one would be checking for her.

"What do you think?" After doing a slow spin, revealing the red Spandex dress and black patent leather heels, Layani posed in the bathroom door with a Kool-Aid smile.

"Got damn!" Micah was in awe and truly taken aback at the sight before him. Naturally, he knew his queen was gorgeous, but she hadn't dressed up in so long that it surprised him.

"Do you like it for real?" She played with her hair.

"Baby, you are so fine that I can't even let you catch the bus looking this good." Pulling out his phone, Micah secured and Uber ride to the radio station.

Fumbling with a loose string hanging from the tight dress, Layani shifted nervously from one leg to the other. They had just stepped through the doors of the radio station, and the pressure was on.

"You got this," Micah whispered into her ear before strolling up to the reception desk like he owned the place. A young chick who barely appeared to be twenty sat there glued to her iPhone.

"May I help you?" she asked after noticing the man in dingy overalls, dirty fingernails, and work boots.

"Is Dernard Perry still here?" Micah asked casually.

"That depends on who wants to know." She eyed him suspiciously. More times than she could count, people came up to the station looking to nag the superstars with sob stories and demo tapes. Every morning at the team meetings, she was reminded to ask the fan to leave and call security any time they refused.

"Thanks." Micah walked away with a smirk. He knew by the way the lady responded to his question that D-Money was still in the building.

"What did she say?" Layani shifted nervously again from side to side. It looked like she had to pee.

"We have to wait, but he'll be out here shortly." Micah took a seat on one of the leather chairs in the lobby and grabbed a magazine. He was probably more nervous than Layani, but he wouldn't dare show it. Their entire future was riding on her shoulders, which was why he didn't want to induce more stress on her, so he played it cool.

An hour later, the main door behind the receptionist opened. Layani looked up to see an entourage of black men in suits emerge. Nevertheless, only one of them meant something to her. Standing there in a custom gray Tom Ford suit with canary yellow diamond cufflinks was Dernard Perry. He was dressed to the nines and looked even better than he did on television. Layani couldn't believe she was a mere ten feet away from the music mogul.

Micah looked up and followed her gaze, then stood to his feet. He grabbed Layani's wrist and pulled her toward the crowd. Most men would've been intimidated to approach a man of Dernard's stature, especially in dirty work clothes, but Micah was confident about his shit. Although he wasn't rich, he was fine according to most women, and he knew it. The boy was built rock solid, too. Micah also knew Dernard was the missing piece between the life he lived today and the one he prayed for tomorrow. He would never let pride get in the way of his dreams.

"What's up, Dernard? My name is Micah Washington." Micah reached his hand out. A dude wearing a red tee with the word *security* on it tried to block the exchange.

"No need for that, Rallo. The man is just saying hello." Like a gentleman, Dernard extended his freshly manicured hand and shook Micah's while looking him in the eye. "What's up, Micah? What can I do for you, man? Would you like an autograph or a picture?" Dernard stared at the brother with rough hands and wondered what he was about to say.

"Nah, none of that, fam. Actually, my girl Layani is a beast with her vocals. We've been working on a few songs that I planned to package up and send out to all the labels, but when I heard you would be down here at the radio station, we decided to come through so we could show you in person." Micah pointed to where Layani stood.

Right off the bat, Dernard liked what he saw in the curvy young woman, but he didn't have time for an impromptu audition. They usually were a waste of time anyway.

"Yo, Micah, I'm sorry, man, but I got a plane to catch," he lied. Dernard always traveled by private jet, and he told the pilot when it was time to leave.

"Please, man, just hear her out." Micah felt the opportunity of a lifetime slipping through his fingertips. "Before Mr. Wells died, he wanted to sign Layani, and Universal was interested too." Micah embellished the truth.

"My man, what the fuck did he say?" The security guard tried to boss up.

Micah was about to get buck with that nigga, but he didn't get the chance. On cue, Layani started singing "I Will Always Love You," the same song she won Mr. Wells over with. Instantly, everyone stopped what they were doing. All eyes were on her, and all ears were pleasantly surprised as she did Whitney's vocal tricks with her throat. Layani was so loud that people started coming from the back of the radio station just to see where the angelic sound was coming from. One of the men in Dernard's entourage even pulled out his cell phone and started recording the a capella singer. Layani stared at her man while giving it all she had. If nothing else, she owed him that much, and Micah couldn't have been any prouder.

By the end of the song, the entire lobby erupted into praise and thunderous applause. Micah didn't say a word as he turned back to look at Dernard, whose mouth hung in awe.

"This girl is unsigned?" he asked Micah, still trying to grasp how talented this woman was.

"Unsigned, unless you have a place for her at Black Millionaires," Micah replied.

"Danielle, come over here." Dernard snapped his fingers and yelled for his assistant. She practically fell over herself to see what her boss wanted.

"Yes, sir?" Danielle asked with a pen and a yellow notepad in hand. Ever since she began working at the label, they'd become permanent fixtures in her hand.

"Get Mr. Washington's information," he instructed. "Micah, I'll be in touch." With a smile as large a Texas, he asked, "What's your name again, sweetheart?"

"Layani. Layani Bell."

"Ms. Bell, you are truly a sight for sore eyes, and your talent is raw and unmatched. I'll be getting with your manager by the end of the day, okay?"

"Thank you, sir." She was so nervous, she bowed like he was king or something.

"Talk to you later Ms. Bell." D-Money put on his Gucci hat and walked off with his entourage behind him.

Chapter Eleven

An entire week had gone by, and not a word from Dernard, who'd initially said they would hear something by the end of the day. Micah wanted to be angry, but he had been let down so many times in life that the shit was beginning to feel like nothing more than business as usual. Layani was irritated at yet another disappointment; however, she followed Micah's lead and got back in the studio. He told her to stay ready just in case and reminded her that God would come through for them as long as they didn't lose faith like John had said.

Sitting shirtless at keyboard in the living room, Micah played around with some tunes. He'd been there for the better part of an hour, trying to find the right sound for the new song on Layani's demo. Other than the television on near the bed and the sound of the keyboard, the studio apartment was quiet. Layani was out grocery shopping.

"And the winner of the BET Music Takeover award goes to none other than L-Rae!" At the mention of L-Rae's name, Micah got up from the keyboard and headed to the bed, where he took a seat. He watched as the superstar, who'd been in his studio months ago practically begging to work with him, graced the stage. She was wearing a beautiful off-the-shoulder gown, sporting pink hair. Micah listened as she thanked God and then her fans for their loyal support. Next, she thanked her record label, her manager, Sheryl, and then she called Yazonthebeat up onto the stage with her. He was a new producer from North Carolina. Micah noted that the record label must've hired Yaz to work on L-Rae's mixtape after he declined.

"I just want to especially thank my boy Yazonthebeat! Without your raw ear for hits, I know this mixtape would not have gone platinum."

At the mention of the album's platinum status, Micah's stomach did a back flip. That could have been him on that stage, receiving those accolades in the prestigious room filled with his peers. Yet here he sat, on the edge of the bed, feeling like a failure.

"Your turn is coming." Micah looked at himself in the dresser mirror. "Your turn is coming," he repeated once more before standing and walking back over to the keyboard. There was no sense in sitting around moping when there was work to be done.

Thirty more minutes passed before there was movement at the front door.

"Hey, baby." Layani walked into the studio apartment, kicking off her shoes and placing her bags down onto the counter.

"What's up, boo." Micah didn't bother to look up from his keyboard as she walked over and kissed his cheek.

"What are you working on?" Layani went about the kitchen, putting up the canned goods, milk, lunch meat, and potatoes that she'd just brought in from the store.

"Huh?" Micah erased something on his paper and rewrote something new.

Layani knew that when her man was working in a zone, he barely talked, ate, or slept, much less heard anything she said; however, that didn't stop her from continuing the conversation. "I heard that girl from *Detroit's Own* got a record deal with Uptown."

"What's that, bae?"

"*Detroit's Own* is that new show I told you about. People from Detroit go on there to sing, dance, and do all kind of stuff. The show is mostly just for entertainment, but every now and then, those contestants catch the eye of someone big." Leaning up against the counter, Layani hopped up on it for a seat. "I know the management part is usually your thing, but I filled out an application to be on the show today online."

"That's good, bae." Micah still had no idea what she was saying, but she sounded excited, so he followed her lead.

"Anyway, I feel confident about them calling us to come down there and be on the show." She giggled. "Oh yeah, I forgot to tell you that I saw a limo downstairs. I wonder who was in it," she said more to herself than to him as she rolled up her store bags and placed them under the kitchen sink. Due to the area they lived in, she knew the limo was way out of place.

"Hey, Lay, come here for a sec." Micah jotted something down on a piece of paper and handed it to her. "Sing this in your second range. Wait eight counts after I drop the beat to come in."

Layani looked at the paper for a second. The words read: *If love was all I had, I'd give it all to you. They think they know about us, but they don't have a clue. Many say on dreams alone, we won't make it far. But in my eyes, you're already a star.*

Layani always loved Micah's lyrics. He was an excellent songwriter who could write about anything. She couldn't wait to see his name in lights. She couldn't wait until they accepted their first award together. She couldn't wait for the day they traded in their studio for a mansion and their bus passes for the foreign whips all the rappers talked about. Together, they had overcome many hurdles. In all honesty, Layani couldn't imagine her life without her man. Micah was the Yin to her Yang. Without him, she would've never realized that her voice was a gift, and she most definitely wouldn't have overcome her fear of singing in public.

"Come on, baby. You ready?" Just as Micah struck a chord on the keyboard, there was a light knock on the door. He was so in the zone that he didn't hear it.

Layani held up her finger and went to see who was knocking. The peephole was about two inches higher than her five-foot frame, so she stood on her toes to look through it.

"Who is it?" she asked the female on her doorstep. She had never seen the lady before and was instantly suspicious. The black fitted suit and glasses the woman was wearing made her look like an official representative of some kind of corporation, but Layani was still wary. Silently, she began wondering if they had paid the rent. After remembering that she had paid the rent, Layani looked around the apartment to see if they had anything someone would come to repossess. There was nothing in the apartment worth reclaiming, so Layani instantly put her hand around her necklace. Micah had told her he'd paid it in full, but maybe he lied. Not wanting to part with her jewelry, she slowly backed away from the door as if the lady on the other side could see her.

"My name is Veronica Joseph. Is Micah Washington or Layani Bell home?" Veronica adjusted the ivory Jimmy

Choo glasses on her nose and shifted her weight from one leg to another.

"Micah, do you know why this lady named Veronica is looking for us?" Layani did her best to whisper. However, through the paper-thin walls, Veronica could hear every word. Micah didn't know anybody with that name, so he shook his head.

"Um, can I take a message?" Layani couldn't think of anything else to say, so she came off the top of her head with that one.

"I would rather talk in person. Do you know when they are available?" Veronica tried hard not to show her irritation, but she had better things to do with her time than stand here playing guessing games.

"Do you have a card or something? I'll have one of them call you."

"Listen, I'll be in town until tomorrow. Please have them call as soon as possible." Veronica reached into her brown Hermes bag and slid a card under the door.

Layani reached down and picked it up. Her stomach hit her toes when she saw the Young Millionaires logo on the card.

"Oh, shit! Veronica, wait!" Layani hollered while unlocking the door. Their apartment was in the hood, so Micah had installed three deadbolt locks to ensure Layani's safety when she was home alone. "I'm sorry. I am Layani," she said, out of breath once the door was finally open.

"May I come in?" Veronica was halfway down the dingy hallway, but she still turned around with a smile.

"Yes, ma'am." Layani's heart raced as she stepped aside to let Ms. Joseph enter.

Micah was still sitting at the keyboard, puzzled, but he remained silent.

"Thank you, dear." As Veronica made her way into the bare apartment, she was reminded of her days in college, when ramen noodles were dinner every night. Now, at the age of 32, she was accustomed to the finer things in life. Her bed linen was Louis Vuitton, and her bathroom towels were made by Gucci. She was very uncomfortable in this roach motel, but she played it cool. Silently, she counted the minutes until she could be back in her limo, headed to her executive hotel suite to indulge in a lobster dinner and the best red wine the Motor City had to offer.

"Baby, we have company. Go put your shirt on." Layani took a seat at the folding table and gestured for her guest to do the same.

"No need. I won't be here long. You must be Micah. I'm Veronica Joseph, the VP of talent scouting and operations for Black Millionaires." She extended her hand to the shirtless, handsome young man.

Immediately, Micah stood to his feet, trying hard not to let his heart leap through his chest. "Ms. Joseph, please have a seat. Would you like some water?' Micah asked nervously. He couldn't believe this was really happening.

"No, thank you. I'll be brief." Veronica smiled. Truth is, she wouldn't have taken a seat nor drank from a cup in this apartment, even if someone had paid her good money to do so. The apartment was clean, but the building and its surrounding looked atrocious. "Dernard likes Layani's look, and he was very impressed with her sound when she performed at the radio station. He flew me here personally to sign her right away."

"Oh my God!" Layani screamed while jumping up and down. "Are you serious? I knew Dernard was going to come through."

"I've got the paperwork right here." Veronica tapped the snakeskin purse resting across her shoulder. "All I need is your signature on the dotted line, and you will be the next official face of Young Millionaires."

"Just like that?" Layani beamed with joy.

"Just like that." Veronica snapped her freshly manicured fingers.

"Wait." Micah paused. "Don't we need a lawyer?" He was elated that his prayers had seemingly been answered, but he still erred on the side of caution.

"Well, Micah, having a lawyer look at your documents never hurts, but I can assure you that this contract is most gracious." Veronica knew getting lawyers involved could be messy, so she tried to make the contract sound like the cat's meow.

"What's your definition of gracious?" Micah folded his arms across his chest and put on his best poker face. Layani, on the other hand, didn't care what was gracious or not. She was ready to sign, right then and there.

"Here. You can take a look for yourself." Pulling a manila folder from her bag, she presented it to the couple. Veronica watched closely as they read the document line for line, until they got to the part about a five hundred thousand dollar signing bonus. Micah and Layani stopped and eyed each other.

Veronica was sure these two had never seen that many zeros on a check before, so she pressed on. "Dernard is ready to get to work pronto. He even has studio sessions booked."

"Everything looks legit, Ms. Veronica, but let me consult my lawyer first." Micah was nobody's fool. He was not about to let nobody "Cadillac Records" him.

"Micah!" Layani groaned. "We need that money." Her eyes pleaded with him to forgo the legal shit so that they could secure the bag.

"Lay, I ain't gonna let you sign this until we make sure it's right." Micah folded the contract and proceeded to thank Veronica for taking the time to stop by.

Forcing a smile, Veronica placed her hand on Micah's shoulder to calm him. "Look, I have a little pull with the boss. If you sign the contract tonight, I'll have him throw in another hundred grand and a brand-new car for you. Within reason, of course." Veronica had been given strict instructions to snag Layani, even if it meant pulling out all the stops.

"Oh my Lord! More money and a car? Where is the fucking pen?" Layani squealed, but Micah remained calm, still with the contract folded in his hand.

"I have one right here." Veronica reached into her purse and pulled out a custom pen with the record label's logo on it.

"That additional money and brand-new car is all fine and good, but I still want to have these documents checked." Micah knew if Veronica was willing to toss in more money and a car like it was nothing just to get the documents signed tonight, then they definitely needed to be reviewed.

"Suit yourself, but Dernard doesn't wait long." Veronica was irritated. "Layani, you have my card. Just call me when you are ready to change your life. I'll be in town until tomorrow evening."

"I'll be in touch, Ms. Joseph." Micah retrieved the card from Layani and walked their guest to the door.

Pausing in the doorway, Veronica looked as if she wanted to say something, but she didn't.

"Do you mind telling me what the hell was that about Micah?" Layani asked after Veronica was gone. She was beyond pissed. How dare he close the door on their dream like that? Especially after all they'd gone through these past few months.

"Bae, just chill and trust a nigga. Don't I always have your best interest?" Micah walked up and wrapped his arms around Layani's ample ass.

"Yeah, you do." Layani couldn't argue with facts. She laid her head onto his broad shoulder and exhaled to calm her nerves. From the foster home until now, her boyfriend had never steered her in the wrong direction. She'd be foolish to think he'd start now, especially when he wanted her to make it big more than she wanted it for herself.

"All right then, so just relax. I got you." Passionately, Micah leaned in and kissed Layani's plump lips while caressing her ass. For the first time in a while, things were really looking up for them. Tomorrow, their lives would be different, so for now, he took advantage of the moment. "I love you so much. I can't wait to make you my wife and give you the world."

"I can't wait to be your wife." She could feel his manhood rise through his basketball shorts. This immediately caused her womanhood to pulsate and cream. Instinctively, Layani reached down into Micah's boxers to free the giant from its lair. He watched as she stroked his joint up and down before dropping to her knees.

"Oh, shit!" He moaned as Layani took all eight inches of his dick into her mouth. Her tongue felt good, but her tonsils felt even better as she deep-throated that dick for nearly ten minutes.

"Hmmm." She vibrated her throat, which caused every hair on Micah's body to rise. He had to lean back onto the wall to keep his knees from buckling. "You like that, baby?" Layani asked after pulling back and leaving a thick coat of spit behind.

"I love that shit!" Micah reached down and forcefully pulled Layani up.

Before she knew what was going on, she was upside down, with her pants pulled to her ankles. With one hand, Micah pinned Layani up against the wall, and with the other, he parted her pussy lips. It was freshly shaved, just the way he loved it. She was already moist and creamy, so he dove right in with his tongue.

"Damn, baby!" Layani screamed as blood rushed to her head. She wasn't sure if it was from being upside down or because of what Micah was doing, but she didn't care. Layani was a low-key freak, so she liked weird shit like this. Normally Micah was more of a traditional lover, so she enjoyed random moments like this. Straining her upper torso, she pulled her body toward his and took his penis back into her mouth.

For several minutes, they pleasured each other like never before. Micah finally noticed that Layani was turning a reddish-burgundy, so he gently placed her onto the floor.

"Give me that dick." She was ready to feel penetration.

"Beg for it!" Micah stroked himself while Layani rubbed her erect nipples.

"Please, baby, give it to me." Layani played along with the skit. Micah's shit was swollen as he bent her legs back toward her head and plunged deep inside of her.

"Shit, daddy!"

"Is this my pussy?" Micah didn't have to ask. He knew he was Layani's first and only, and she was his. They knew each other's bodies like their own.

"You know it is, baby." She threw her hips back at him so hard that Micah could barely contain himself.

Within ten minutes, they had both climaxed and passed out on the floor, where they panted and gasped for air.

After gathering the strength to turn on her side, Layani faced Micah. "I can't lie. I stop thinking about the contract."

"Me too." Micah kissed her shoulder. "We've been let down so many times that I don't want to be excited, but I can't help it." The possibility of having all of that money at their disposal was borderline overwhelming.

"I know we had a few setbacks along the road, but I feel in my heart that this was how it was supposed to happen. I think of all the offers, Young Millionaires is the best fit." Staring up at the cracked ceiling, Layani wanted to grab the phone and call Veronica back. Just imagining how different life would be for them had her on a cloud and ready to spend money the way she'd watched other celebrities do for years.

"I think you're right. We just have to make sure this shit is accurate, though." Micah had come too far to be getting played with some wooden nickels. He knew Layani's talent was unmatched and valuable. He wanted to make sure she got everything she deserved.

Chapter Twelve

The next day, Micah and Layani headed down to Wayne State University's law department. They didn't have money to hire a real attorney to review Layani's contract, nor were they willing to part with any contract money to hire one. After pondering over it all night, Micah had the bright idea to visit one of the law professors at the local university. Micah knew they worked pro bono and were just as knowledgeable. In fact, most of them had practiced law for decades and been at the top of their game before settling down and becoming professors.

"Hello, Dr. Girard. Again, my name is Micah, and this is my artist, Layani Bell." Earlier, Micah had called down to the university and explained his situation to Dr. Girard, an older black man with completely white hair on both his head and mustache. He was courteous enough to agree to meet with them between classes. "Here's the contract that we discussed."

"Come on in and take a seat while I take a look." Dr. Girard hit the light on the wall of his small office. There was an L-shaped desk with two chairs for guests and one for the professor. There were a few bamboo plants lining his window seat, and a few papers lying over the keyboard of his computer.

Completely engrossed in what he was reading, Dr. Girard searched his pocket for the rimless glasses that were tucked into his pocket protector. With one hand, he put them on. Carefully, Dr. Girard inspected each document, page by page, while using a yellow highlighter to mark places of interest. For nearly thirty minutes, Layani and Micah watched in silence as he highlighted damn near the entire contract.

"Do you think the contract is bogus?" Micah sat up in his chair with his eyes on the verge of popping out of his head. Layani was practically in tears as she looked down at all of the yellow markings.

"Well, I wouldn't call it bogus, Micah, but it's very tricky. For starters, there is a clause in section six of page two that states the entire sum of the artist's advance payment must be repaid in ninety days or the amount to be repaid is doubled. Yet here in section two of page eight states the record company has twenty-four months to release the artist's album." Dr. Girard looked up at the young couple. "I'm no mathematician, but how can you repay something in ninety days when your album won't be released for possibly two years? This is a tactic to keep the artist in debt, in my opinion."

"Wow." Layani looked from Dr. Girard to Micah with admiration. He was right about having the contract reviewed. Had she eagerly signed last night, she would be locked in a dummy deal.

"Micah, on the phone you said the record company offered to buy Ms. Bell a car, right?" Dr. Girard asked.

"Yeah, that's right," Micah replied.

"Well section three point four states that any gifts, jewelry, clothing, housing, vehicles, and makeovers, including plastic surgery, is to be repaid by the artist to the company with royalty money made off album sales and such. Quite frankly, they aren't buying her a car. They're basically loaning her the money, but she has to repay them from the profits of album sales and concert tickets."

"Damn." Layani felt the excitement slowly ooze from her body. Here was yet another disappointment.

"Lastly, in section six point eight, there is a clause which states Ms. Bell will only receive three percent of her sales total."

"Can you give it to me in layman's terms, sir?" Micah knew what he was saying, but he wanted further clarification.

"If she sold ten million dollars' worth of records this year, her take-home profit would be only three hundred thousand." Dr. Girard removed his glasses. "I would suggest you call this company and do some serious negotiation."

Layani looked to Micah again, this time with watery eyes. She didn't want to cry in the presence of a stranger, so she walked out of the office into the hallway.

Micah didn't want to let his lady down, but he knew he was no match for a powerhouse such as Dernard. The minute he got on the phone spewing demands and contract changes, all bets would be off. Talent and pretty faces came a dime a dozen in America. If Dernard didn't sign Layani today, he wouldn't lose any sleep about it, and Micah knew that.

Dr. Girard understood the pickle the young couple was in and offered his assistance, though technically his contract with the university clearly stated he could not act as a practicing attorney under any circumstances without written permission from the university. "Micah, if you'd like, I can make the call on your behalf."

"Thank you, Dr. Girard. I really owe you one, man." With sincere gratitude, he reached into his pocket and produced Veronica's business card.

When Dr. Girard contacted Veronica, she sounded a bit surprised that he was real attorney. She knew most people threw the word *lawyer* around just as a scare tactic for negotiations, but she had to give credit to Micah for really following through.

After hearing Dr. Girard out and discussing the concerns with Dernard, Veronica was told to patch the lawyer through to the record labels' legal team. Dernard saw great potential in Layani, which was the only reason he obliged her contract review.

For the next hour, Dr. Girard and the legal team at Black Millionaires discussed terms of an agreement that would suit both parties. When it was all said and done, Dr. Girard was able to finagle a deal for Layani that increased her royalties by thirty percent. In addition to that, all of her advances were hers, free and clear, including the car. There were a few minor things that the label didn't budge on, like the ownership of her name and her recording masters for the next fifty years. Be that as it may, everything else in the contract swayed in Layani's favor.

Dr. Girard made the record label fax a new contract directly to his office just to make sure they didn't pull a switcheroo later. Layani signed and dated right beneath Dernard's signature and date, and then they faxed it back. Ten minutes later, Veronica called Micah to confirm that everything was received and to personally welcome Layani to Young Millionaires. She also invited them to a special dinner that night in Layani's honor at one of the most expensive restaurants on the Detroit River.

Micah and Layani thanked Dr. Girard profusely and invited him to dinner. Though the older man declined any gift, be it financial or otherwise, Micah promised to return the favor in some way or another.

Micah and Layani left the campus of Wayne State University on cloud nine. Not only was Layani an officially signed artist, but she was also rich!

"Baby, I can't wait until we get that check from Veronica. As soon as we deposit that bad boy, we are on the first thing smoking out of Detroit. We need a getaway." She fantasized as they walked down the street to the bus stop.

"Bae, I hate to break it to you. There won't be any vacations for you or me in the near future. You already know they're going to put you to work as soon as possible."

"Damn, just that fast, I forgot about all of that."

"It's on and popping now. You're in the major leagues." Micah sped up the pace as he saw the large bus approaching the stop. "Come on." Grabbing Layani's hand, he pulled her with him. They made it just in time, paid their fare, and took a seat.

"What are you cheesing so hard for?" Layani nudged her man. He'd been grinning ear to ear ever since they took a seat on the semi-crowded public transportation.

"I just thanking God for blessing us. Do you realize after today our lives will change forever? This is our last bus ride. This is our last day being nobodies."

Layani didn't respond. Instead, she sat back in her seat and pondered what he was saying. She couldn't believe her dreams were finally coming true.

After getting off the bus at the stop two blocks from their apartment, the couple walked gleefully to their home in silence. Nothing and no one could change their moods, and things got even better when they approached their building to see a silver-and-chrome 2020 3.0L V6 Supercharged HSE Range Rover with an oversized large bow on it. Already knowing the car was hers, Layani ran up to it and looked inside.

Micah took note of the Town Car sitting behind the Range Rover. On cue, a gentleman in a suit got out of the car and approached Layani.

"Ms. Bell, my name is Peter. I was told to deliver this envelope to you. Can you sign here?" Peter handed Layani a clipboard, and she signed. "This is for you." After handing Layani the large manila envelope under his arm, he bid them both a good day.

Instantly, Layani ripped into the heavy package and pulled a small envelope and then the key fob to the Range Rover. At the bottom of the envelope were several neat stacks of money. She handed that to Micah and opened the smaller envelope, then read aloud.

Congratulations, Layani, and welcome home! We here at Black Millionaires are excited about your career, and we hope you are too! We anticipate getting to work as soon as possible, so we have arranged for you to join us here in New York City in two weeks for artist development. Enclosed, you'll find the sum of $50,000. The remaining $550,000 will be electronically deposited into your account within in the next ten business days. In the meantime, enjoy the Range Rover and your time with loved ones. Rest up. Once you arrive in New York, sleep will be a thing of the past!

Warmest Regards,
Dernard
CEO of Black Millionaires

Chapter Thirteen

Layani finished reading the letter aloud, then placed it into her purse. "Bae, let's take her for a spin. You drive." She wasn't much of a bragger, but after all they had been through, she felt they'd earned the right to show off their newfound wealth just a little.

Micah didn't need to be told twice. It took him a minute to figure out how to start the keyless car, but eventually he got it, and they were on their way. As Layani rubbed on the shiny black leather seats and opened all of the SUV's compartments, Micah played with his seat's recline button and then the XM/FM radio. He rolled down the tinted windows so everyone on the street could see them. He wanted everybody to know they'd finally made it.

The first stop on their joy ride was to Somerset Mall. It was the most prestigious, expensive mall near Detroit. For hours, Micah and Layani went store to store, buying any and everything their hearts could imagine from socks and underwear to the more expensive things such as Gucci, Hermes, Louis Vuitton, and Fendi. They had so many bags that a rep from Gucci instructed mall security to bring the couple a dolly and escort them outside to their vehicle.

After loading the SUV with all the bags, Micah encouraged Layani to treat herself to getting her hair and nails done, but she had other plans.

This time, she hopped behind the wheel of the Range, plugged an address in the GPS, and pulled off. Micah had no idea where they were going, but he sat back and enjoyed the ride.

After driving for nearly thirty minutes, Layani pulled up to a quiet subdivision in Southfield, Michigan. Micah was confused when they pulled into the driveway of a two-story home.

"What's up, Lay?"

"Come on. You'll see." Without another word, Layani got out of the truck and approached the house. Standing in the doorway was an older lady with keys in her hand.

"Hello there. You must be Micah and Layani. I'm Beth." She extended her hand and they all exchanged pleasantries. "I was so happy to get your call, Layani. My client has been very anxious about this property being put in the right hands. As I told you on the phone this afternoon, she is in Florida caring for her ailing mother, so she can't keep taking the time to fly back and forth to check on this house."

Beth unlocked the front door and let everyone in. "This home was built in 1993. It's four bedrooms, two and a half bathrooms, living room, dining room, large kitchen, fair-sized back yard, and a fully finished basement."

Layani had fallen in love with the space when she saw Beth's ad resting on a table in the women's bathroom at the mall earlier. She didn't care anything about the tray ceilings, sparkling hardwood floors, and brand-new appliances. In her mind, anything was better than their studio apartment.

"Bae, we can't afford to buy a house right now," Micah said in a hushed tone after Beth gave them some time alone to walk around the house. He knew Layani's intentions were good, but he didn't want her to blow all of advance money on a house they wouldn't probably live in long.

"Micah, we're not buying. We're renting. The lease is only for two years. The owner needs someone to occupy the house in her absence, and we need another place to stay. For one thing, I'm tired of being cramped in that tiny studio apartment, and for two, you know good and well we can't park this Range Rover there. Now that people in the building know that we got a little something, they will try us."

Unfortunately, Layani was right. In the area they currently lived, there was a lot of crime and jealousy. A lot of people in her neighborhood had the "crabs in a barrel" mentality. The minute they saw someone on the rise, they did whatever in their power to bring the person down.

Micah knew she was right, but he still wasn't sold. However, things began to change the more he walked through the house. Room by room, he began envisioning their new life there. He could see Layani in the kitchen, preparing some of her famous dishes, and him in the basement, watching sports on a large television.

"What do you guys think?" Beth was waiting on the back deck. She was taking in the scene while sitting on the patio chair.

"It's very nice." Micah rubbed his chin.

We'll take it!" Layani jumped up and down before kissing her man. She couldn't wait to christen the house.

"Awesome! Let's go ahead and sign these papers really quick." She reached into her bag and slid a folder toward them. "This just states that the lease is for two years. At that time, the owner may choose to reoccupy the property, offer to extend your lease, or sell the property. Of course, you would have the first option to buy. The total due today would be the sum of two thousand seven hundred dollars, which is first and last month's rent, plus a refundable deposit. Everything else is standard for damages and such, but please read over it yourself, sign it when you're done, and the home is yours."

After skimming through the paperwork, Layani and Micah signed on the dotted line, and the deal was done. Beth left the couple with two sets of keys and two garage door openers. She told them that they had one week to get the utilities on in their names, because that's when they would be turned off in the homeowner's name.

Once Beth was out the door, Layani was on Micah like a magnet. Something about having such a great day had her on him like a dog in heat.

"Baby, there is nothing I would love more than to take you down right now, but we have to get ready for your big dinner," Micah said in between passionate kisses. Honestly, he wanted to say to hell with the fancy dinner and just stay home and order in, but business was business. Black Millionaires had really come through for them today. The last thing he wanted to do was shit in their face.

Begrudgingly, Layani pulled herself off Micah because she knew he was right. With only a few hours to spare, they made a quick run to Meijer's to grab cleaning supplies, a few towels, a set of sheets, a king-sized blow-up mattress to get through the night, and some personal items. Next, they headed back and unloaded the SUV. Since all their new clothes were with them, they decided to get ready from the house instead of driving all the way back to their apartment building.

Though the house was bare, it was an amazing feeling for them to be able to take showers and get ready in different bathrooms at the same time. Layani was beyond happy that she could flat iron her hair in peace. Micah was elated to brush his teeth and trim his hairline without knocking over all of her makeup and hair products.

"Lay, it's time, baby. We've got to." Micah fumbled with the bow tie around his neck and gave himself the once-over in the mirror. He was fresh to death in a pair of Gucci loafers with the gold buckles. His shoes were complemented by the Gucci tuxedo pants, white button-up shirt, and royal blue Gucci suit jacket. The gold Cartier buffalo frames on his face gave his look some Detroit flavor. After adding a splash of 1 Million cologne to his body, he was ready for whatever the night had in store.

"Come on, baby," he hollered down the hallway.

Seconds later, Layani opened the door, and Micah's heart skipped four beats. She looked like nothing less than an angel in her snow-white lace gown. The body was fitted, and the mermaid bottom had a slight train. Layani rocked a stunning pair of silver Louboutins that complemented her new diamond earrings perfectly. Her makeup was subtle, just the way Micah liked it, with a pair of faux eyelashes, a little foundation, and lipstick.

"Baby, you are absolutely radiant." He licked his lips, and she blushed.

"You are quite the looker yourself, handsome." With a smile, she walked up to her man and held out a box. "This is for you to wear tonight."

"Bae, you really shouldn't have. I already felt bad for even allowing you to spend money on me today." Micah was a real man. He didn't feel comfortable taking anything from his woman. Low key, even though he hadn't said anything, just the thought of Layani now being the breadwinner had him in his feelings. He felt like there was an invisible shift in the dynamic of their relationship.

"Micah, you have been here for me when nobody else was. You have literally put your dreams on hold just to take care of me, and I will never forget that. May our love be as timeless as this watch." Blinking back a few tears, Layani opened the large leather box and presented her man with a gold-and-platinum Rolex President.

Micah stared at the watch in silence while he digested a few feelings. His first emotion was that of irritation. Though he loved the thought behind her gift, Micah was irritated with the fact that he didn't have his own money to buy her something just as nice. The second emotion he tried hard to suppress because he wasn't emotional was that of extreme gratitude. Just the thought alone of being broke last night and being able to receive such an expensive gift like this today was a miracle. Micah lowered his head and silently praised God as a lone tear rolled down his face.

Chapter Fourteen

Micah gathered himself, turned his swag back on, and led Layani toward the vehicle. The ride was silent aside from the faint sound of the radio in the background. The tables had turned for the young couple in such a major way, it was hard to digest.

Twenty minutes passed before Micah pulled up to the valet. Looking and smelling like a million dollars, he and Layani headed into Roma's on the Riverfront, a large, swanky Italian restaurant right off the water on the Detroit River. The establishment had only been around for five years, but in that time, it had served some of Michigan's most elite. Many athletes, rappers, actors, and affluent professional had parties there. Tonight was Layani's night. Her turn had finally come.

"Welcome to Roma." The young man in a black valet vest smiled.

"Thank you." Micah handed over the keys and then hustled around the front of the SUV to open the door for Layani.

"Good evening." A young woman smiled as they approached the oversized wooden door, which was at least fifteen feet tall. "My name is Becca. I'll be your personal concierge for the evening, Ms. Bell. Your party is inside. Can I start you guys off with a few libations?"

"A few what?" Layani asked Becca, but looked to Micah for an answer. He shrugged.

"Spirits?" Becca nodded.

"Nah, we ain't into that shit." Micah shook his head adamantly. He didn't believe in anything but God.

Becca could sense the couple had no idea what she was referring to, so she dropped her restaurant etiquette at the door. "Spirits as in cocktails or drinks." She laughed, and Layani did too.

"Well, in that case, I'll take an amaretto sour. He'll take a Hennessey straight."

"Absolutely. Let me show you to your table, and I will bring the drinks right over to you." Becca pulled another set of doors open, and Layani was amazed by the party going on inside. The place was crowded with a whole lot of unfamiliar faces. They were partying like it was going out of style.

The entire venue was decorated in black and gold. There was even an ice sculpture in the center of the floor made to resemble the Black Millionaires logo. Layani pointed for Micah to see that the DJ booth was suspended over the crowd that was going ape shit on the dance floor. The song at the moment was an old school joint by Juvenile. The man behind the beats was none other Money Mone, the number one DJ on Detroit's favorite radio station, WJLB.

"Shout out to Detroit's very own princess and the newest face of Black Millionaires, Layani Bell! Hey girl, I'm so happy to see you in the building tonight!" Mone gave Layani a shoutout like he'd been friends with her for years.

As the crowd erupted into cheers and applause, Layani noticed the spotlight hit her and Micah. The entire restaurant was staring at her. She wasn't sure what to do, so she took a bow. When she lifted her head up, someone was pushing a microphone into her hand.

Layani hated public speaking. She wanted to hand the mic to Micah, but she knew she had to say something. After all, these people had come out just to celebrate her.

"Detroit, we made it!" she said in a soft voice. Again, the crowd erupted into applause, and she handed the mic back to the person who'd given it to her.

"There is Veronica." Micah pointed, grabbing Layani's hand and led her toward back of the restaurant. On cue, the crowd parted like the Red Sea.

"Congrats!" a few people shouted.

"Can't wait for your album to drop!" another one said.

"Hey, Layani, look right here real quick," the woman said before pushing her face up against Layani's and snapping a few pictures.

"Layani, do you remember me?" the man not far from the woman taking pictures asked. When Layani didn't reply, he continued. "It's me, Darren. We went to high school together."

"Sorry, I don't remember." With a smile, Layani continued through the room of people and praises until she finally made her way toward the table by the picture window, where Veronica stood, waving.

"Layani, darling, you look stunning! Micah, you are such a handsome man. Have you ever thought of modeling?" She smoothed down her red Prada pantsuit and greeted them with hugs. "Did Becca get you started with drinks?" Veronica had personally hired the concierge to cater to all of Layani's needs that night. She wanted Becca to wipe Layani's ass if she asked her to. This was the way Black Millionaires wooed their clients.

"Yes, she did. Veronica, this is such a big turn-out. How do all of these people know me?"

"Darling, this room is filled with radio station employees, local club DJs, music executives, and a few randoms, just for good measure. We like to invite the people out to get to know you and put a face with the name. That way, you're easier to sell when your music is ready to be released and we need to get you on the radio, in clubs, and on award shows."

"Hello, I'm Asia. Nice to meet you, Layani." She was a beautiful woman with caramel skin and long blond hair, which was parted in the middle and braided in two braids. There was a heart tattooed on her face, and both her nose and left brow were pierced. Asia was dressed in a crisp white jean set. Her shirt was a wife beater, and she wore a chain that hung almost down to her vagina. Asia grabbed Layani's hand and kissed it.

"Hello, I'm Layani, and this is my boyfriend, Micah." Layani smiled. Asia and Micah exchanged a handshake.

"Asia is a very talented rapper. She has a few deals on the table and is currently trying to decide which label is the best fit for her. We've been trying to show her that Black Millionaires is her home, but maybe you can convince her." Veronica saw someone she needed to chat with, so she excused herself.

"If you don't mind my asking, what made you sign with Black Millionaires?" Asia stared at Layani intensively.

"Honestly, I just wanted to be signed. I'm not like you. I don't have deals on the table. I had a few things come up here and there, but everything fell through. This company came at a time when I needed it the most." Just as Layani ended her sentence, Becca walked up and handed her and Micah their drinks.

"What do you think about all of this? Your girl is now a member of a traitorous industry. Relationships don't usually last in the music business," Asia said.

"Layani and I are different. Many music business relationships start after one or both parties are already famous. Me and my boo got out the mud together. Our love is strong, and our loyalty is solid. She's a big girl. She'll be all right." Micah pulled his girl in and gave her a passionate kiss.

"I feel ya." Asia raised her hands in surrender. "I didn't mean to come off rude. I just know shit can go left quick." She leaned in. "You just be careful, Layani. I heard Black Millionaires have a lot of staff members that can't keep their hands to themselves. Remember what happened to Isys."

Isys was a white singer out of Canada. Just five months after being signed to Black Millionaires, she filed a lawsuit about being raped during a studio session by three of the record label's producers. The story was in the headlines for nearly two months before everything went silent, which everyone chalked up to a large payoff.

"Micah, she's right. Maybe you should come to New York with me." Suddenly, Layani was nervous. She was afraid to be alone.

"Baby, I can't go. You know I got to work, but I promise anytime I can take a few days off work, I'll be there. Furthermore, if some shit happens that makes you uncomfortable, I will be on the first thing smoking."

Micah did his best to ease Layani's reservations. She had already signed the contract, and they had spent way more than they would ever be able to pay back right now. This was their dream, and he wasn't about to let Asia fuck this up. Besides, they had come too far to turn back.

Raising his glass, he toasted his woman, and everyone within ear shot did the same. "Baby, you are meant for this! Cheers to seeing you on the main stages all over the world. I love you!"

Chapter Fifteen

For two weeks, the lovebirds played house at their new rental home until it was time for Layani to leave Michigan for New York. Instead of taking the small vacation she wanted to take before leaving, they decided to furnish the house and spend as much time together as they could. That in itself felt like a vacation because they had money to buy and do just about whatever they wanted. In all the time they'd been together, they had never enjoyed a luxury like that.

"Come on, Lay, baby, the plane leaves in three hours. You need to be there at least in the next forty minutes." Micah had already loaded her bags into the car and had been waiting downstairs in the living room for her to come down.

"Baby, I don't want to go." Layani flopped down the stairs solemnly. Emotionally, she was a wreck. Not only was she afraid of leaving Micah, but she was also afraid of the unknown. Would the people at the label like her? Would she be able to prove her worth? What if no one liked her music? Would she fail? Several discouraging thoughts raced around her mind, and it was making her physically sick.

"Bae, come on." Micah grabbed her hand and pulled her out of the house. "Staying is not an option, and you know that. To whom much is given, much is required.

Remember that." He opened the SUV and damn near had to pick her up to force her inside.

"What if I can't sing like they want me to?"

"Baby, the man has been in the music industry for years. If he didn't see something in you, he would not have signed you, gave you the contract you negotiated for, nor had his people throw you a party." Micah tried to share his logic on her, but Layani had tuned him out with her sobs.

For nearly the entire ride to the airport, Layani cried like a baby. She had done her makeup that morning, but by the time they pulled up, she had to wipe her face down with a few baby wipes and start over.

"Micah, please come with me," she begged one final time.

"Bae, you can't have any visits the first thirty days of artist development. I'll be down there on day thirty-one. I promise."

When Veronica had sent the email confirmation with all of the important information Layani needed for the artist development procedures, the very first rule was no visitors.

"Until then, I will talk to you on the phone every morning, every night, and anytime during the day when you have a break. You are smart, beautiful, and courageous. This here is temporary. We will be back together in no time. In the meantime, I need you to go to the Big Apple and show them niggas how Detroit does things, okay?" He pulled Layani's face up and dried her eyes.

From the moment Layani stepped onto the Delta aircraft, she felt like royalty.

"Welcome, Ms. Bell." The stewardess took the ticket and showed Layani to an oversized leather recliner. Her seat was in first class, which allowed her to board ahead of all the regular passengers. "Would you like something to drink or eat?"

"No, thank you." Layani smiled politely. Whenever she was nervous, she became attached to the bathroom. Today, she didn't need any food or beverages contributing to her toilet visits.

"Is this your first time flying, dear?" an elderly white woman asked while taking the seat beside her.

"Yes, ma'am, it is."

"You'll do fine." She patted Layani's hand with a wrinkled one of her own. "Planes are less likely to crash than motor vehicles, you know."

The woman thought she was helping; however, the last thing Layani wanted to do was think about was the plane crashing. She pulled out her cell phone and dialed Micah. She really hated that he wasn't there with her, but she knew it was what it was.

"What's up, superstar?" he answered with a smile. Although he had practically just pulled away from the airport, he had to admit he already missed his girl tremendously. In fact, the moment she had walked into the airport and the doors closed behind her, he felt like his heart was breaking into a million pieces.

"I'm scared," Layani admitted.

"Scared of flying?" Micah rolled up the window to hear better. "You'll be fine. Just close your eyes, and you'll be there in no time." The flight was only two hours.

"Micah, I'm scared of everything." She sighed. "I wish you were right here next to me. This is our dream, so why am I here alone?" For the first time since meeting each other, the couple was apart. Micah was Layani's security blanket. Without him, she felt lost.

"Lay, like I told you already, I'm right there with you. Baby, I'm always in your heart and on your mind, or at least I should be, superstar," he joked, which lightened the mood.

"You are always on my mind."

"All right now, don't go acting brand new on me after you get around them shot callers." This time, Micah was only half-joking. He was secure about his shit, but he knew sometimes just being around men with money and power made some girls go crazy. Although he trusted Layani, he knew she was human.

"Boy, stop!" She giggled.

"Have a safe trip, baby. Hit me up when you get there." Micah pressed his lips together and made a kissing noise before hanging up. Layani smiled, turned the cell phone off, and prepared to take flight.

Just as Micah suggested, Layani used the travel time to catch a quick nap. The flight from Detroit to New York was short, but just enough to give her what she needed to reboot. When she opened her eyes, the captain was announcing their arrival. Layani held her stomach as the plane descended toward the landing strip. The plane shook wildly and made a loud screeching sound. If Layani wasn't looking out the window and saw that they were already on the ground, she would've have pissed herself.

"It wasn't that bad, was it, dear?" Her neighbor smiled with stained teeth.

Layani shook her head. "Yes it was!"

As Layani was wiping sleep from her eyes, the plane was pulling up to the gate. Layani stood, grabbed her carry-on, and told the old woman goodbye. Since she hadn't checked any luggage, she was able to head straight to the pick-up door. Micah had encouraged her to send her clothes to the address where she'd be staying because it was cheaper than paying for all the luggage.

The airport was huge! It took Layani nearly fifteen minutes just to make it to the pick-up area. When she got there, she noticed an older man wearing an African caftan holding a sign with two names. Layani recognized her name and walked over to him.

"Are you Layani Bell or Mackena Moore?" he asked.

"I'm Layani." she replied while looking around the airport as if she were going to spot a familiar face.

"Ms. Bell, it's a pleasure to meet you. My name is Akebo. I'll be your chauffer while you're in New York."

"Nice to meet you as well, Akebo. Do you know when the other girl will be here?" Layani probably sounded impatient, but she was only making small talk.

"Her flight from Baltimore should've arrived fifteen minutes before yours. I didn't see any delays on the board." Akebo shrugged. "We'll give her a few minutes if that's okay."

"It's cool with me." Layani took a seat near the window and leaned up against the glass. After pulling out her cell phone, she shot a quick message to Micah to let him know she was in New York. He quickly shot back a text saying that he loved her and that he was proud. Next, she took the time to post on her social media accounts and snap a few pics.

While Layani and Akebo waited, she took the opportunity to people watch. The Big Apple was home to a

variety of folks from all walks of life. Being a quiet girl
from Detroit, the new setting was almost a culture shock.

Akebo glanced at his Fossil watch for the second time
in five minutes. He was about to put an APB out on the
missing chick, but then she rounded the corner.

"My bad! These dumb fucks lost my luggage!" a thick
girl with red hair and a fat ass yelled from several feet
away. She was dressed in a pair of Spandex leggings, a
tight tank top, and wedge sneakers. The nose ring in her
nostril was connected by chain to her ear. Her fingernails
were long and represented every color in the rainbow.

"You must be Mackena Moore." Akebo smiled. "I'm
Akebo. I'll be your driver."

"Call me Mack!" She looked past him to the plain
chick behind him. "What's up?" Mack nodded while
looking her over with a microscope. In her opinion,
Layani was beautiful, but her style needed work. There
was nothing about her that screamed statement.

"What up, doe. I'm Layani." Layani nodded her head
back. She wasn't sure of this girl's angle, so she played it
safe, not wanting to be too friendly.

"So, what you do, rap or sing?" Mack raised a brow.
She wanted to know if Layani was competition.

"I sing." Layani smirked. "Let me guess, you rap?"

"Yeah, I rap. What gave me away?" Mack handed her
bag over to Akebo, and the ladies followed him outside
toward the waiting Lincoln Navigator.

"You come off rough, like a rapper." Layani didn't
want to offend her new label mate, but it was the truth.
This girl looked like she could use a dab of classy
femininity.

"Baby girl, in a male-dominated industry, that's how
you got to be." Mack reached behind her ear and pulled

out a Newport cigarette. "Where you from?" she asked after lighting it.

"Detroit." Layani fanned away the smoke. She'd come too far to let this smoke ruin her vocals.

"D-Town. Y'all niggas be live."

"You're from B-more, right?" Layani stepped inside the SUV and placed her carry-on on her lap.

"Born and raised." Mack flicked her cigarette and hopped into the whip. "How you get your deal? Did you fuck anybody at the label?" she asked casually while rolling her window down.

"Bitch, no I didn't. Did you?" Layani was done being polite. This girl had her fucked up.

"I ain't trying to offend you, baby girl. I just need to know."

"Like I said, no! Did you?" Layani repeated.

"Hell no, but if the opportunity would have presented itself, I sure in the fuck would have." There was no shame in Mack's game. "Girl, I done fucked some bum-ass niggas for free just because I liked them or thought I loved them. So, got damn right I would have fucked for a record deal." She busted out laughing, and Layani did the same.

During the ride, the two women got the chance to get to know one another a little better. Lay told Mack a little bit about how she grew up and about Micah. In turn, Mack told Lay about her life in Baltimore and the son she'd left at home. In fact, she'd just given birth four months ago. Layani thought it was crazy to leave a newborn baby behind. On the other hand, she understood that Mack only had one shot at her dreams, and she did what she thought she had to do to make his life better. Mack rationalized that she'd have an album out and have tons of money in the bank by the time her son turned two, so the risk of missing his baby days would be worth the reward in the long run.

"Sorry to interrupt the conversation, but we're here, ladies." Akebo put the SUV in park.

Both ladies peered out of the windows to see a large studio before them. The lighter neon letters indicated that the place was called the Track House. Layani had heard mention of the infamous studio on various songs and hip hop shows. She felt blessed to be there and wanted to capture the moment. Quickly, she took out her phone and snapped two pictures for the Gram.

"What the fuck is you doing?" Mack smacked her heavily glossed lips.

"I'm capturing the moment," Layani replied with a smile showing all of her teeth.

"Girl, you are about to be star! You can't be doing no amateur shit like this." Mack thought she knew everything about being famous and wanted to share her game with Layani. "These niggas can smell fresh meat from a mile away. You have to act like you ain't new to this, but you're true to this." Mack winked at her new friend before stepping out of the Navigator like the celebrity she thought she was.

Layani shook her head and got out to follow her inside.

The Track House studio was unlike anything Layani had ever seen before. Yet and still, she played it cool. Following Mack's advice, she pretended not to notice the gold and platinum albums, flat screen televisions, or celebrity pictures adorning the wall.

"There are my girls." Veronica Joseph met them in the hallway with a smile. She was dressed in a white blouse and tightly fitted black pencil skirt. "How were your flights?" she asked while pressing the button on the solid gold elevator.

"It was cool," Mack replied.

Layani was too nervous to speak. She remained silent as they stepped inside the elevator. Internally, she was still screaming with excitement for even being inside of the iconic building.

"Well, Dernard wanted to get you girls in the booth ASAP. He has a team of songwriters and producers upstairs waiting for you." Veronica pressed the fourth-floor button.

"Oh, I write my own stuff." Mack spoke up without a second thought.

"You'll get to do that soon, but Dernard wants you working with a seasoned writer for now." Veronica politely shut her down without so much as batting an eyelash.

Mack wanted to check her but decided to let it go. She knew she had the tendency to be abrasive and outspoken, and she didn't want to burn any bridges this early, so she took a page out of Layani's book and just got silent.

The moment the women stepped off the elevator, weed smoke filled their nostrils. It was so foggy that Layani started to pull the smoke alarm.

"Damn." She coughed.

"Wayne is down the hall. I'm sorry about that." Veronica fanned the smoke as she led the ladies down the hall.

"As in *the* Wayne?" Mack asked, completely forgetting to act like she wasn't an amateur as she'd just told Layani to do.

"Yup, that's the one," Veronica replied without a second thought. Behind her back, both girls squealed like schoolgirls. Right then in that moment, they both knew they were in the big league.

Chapter Sixteen

Veronica escorted the girls into the room that was labeled STUDIO B. Inside were two men collaborating at the keyboard. The beat they were engineering was already dope as hell. Instantly, Mack and Layani started bobbing their heads.

"Hey, guys, meet Mackena Moore and Layani Bell, the newest additions to Black Millionaires. Ladies, meet So-Low and Naïve, two of our best producers." Veronica waited for the group to exchange pleasantries before pointing to the back of the room. That's where an overweight lady sat with a notebook and pen. "That's Jayko, your writer. She is fire with her pen."

Mack wasn't feeling the chick off jump, so she didn't speak at all. Layani didn't mind having a writer because she was used to Micah writing for her, so she smiled and waved. "Hello, nice to meet you."

"What's up." The chick nodded back. She could tell Mack was acting funny, but it didn't faze her. Jayko was from the Marcy housing project. She didn't give one fuck about this new bitch. These hoes came a dime a dozen. All she was concerned about was writing this song and getting her check.

"What's the name of this song?" Layani leaned against the wall.

"The last time," Jayko replied. "I just finished the last verse. Do you want to look it over and then go in the booth and add your flavor?" She handed the notebook to Layani.

After a quick glance at the words, Layani knew the song was about leaving a nigga after he cheated on her for the last time. She thought that there was so much more in life to write about, but she didn't complain. Instead, she carried the notebook into the studio and took a stab at singing Jayko's lyrics. Layani wanted to prove that she was a team player who knew her position. One day, she would be a playmaker, but for now, she was content just being off the bench.

Within an hour, her vocals had been laid down and the song was starting to come together. Everyone loved the new girl's voice, but no one wanted to blow her head up, so they didn't say anything. Layani had the sultriness of Whitney, the pitch of Mariah, the range of Beyoncé, and the sexiness of Janet. She was a deadly combination, and everyone who ever crossed her path knew it.

"You did amazing!" Mack clapped for her new friend when she noticed that no one else in the room intended to.

"Thanks, Mack. Your turn." Lay grabbed a bottle of water from the mini fridge and gulped it down.

Mackena took Jayko's lyrics into the booth and tried to ride the beat with her own flow, but it wasn't working. Because the words weren't hers, it really messed up her process; therefore, she was in the booth for nearly forty minutes and still hadn't put down her verse.

"I'll be right back," Layani told Veronica before leaving the room, pretending like she had to use the restroom. Truthfully, she was going to see if she could spot Wayne, or any other celebrity for that matter, and introduce herself.

Imagine meeting a big celebrity on my first day? she thought.

Nervously, she adjusted the hair resting on her shoulders and straightened her back. The music coming from down the hall rattled the walls, and that damn smoke cloud was still present.

Knock. Knock. Layani tapped on the door and then realized that no one could hear her over the music. She pushed lightly on the door, and it opened. Peeking her head inside, she was surprised by what she saw. There was a middle-aged man on the sofa, getting head from two Hispanic-looking women, while another black woman squatted over his face and held on to the wall for dear life. Inside of the booth was another dude rapping and smoking a blunt at the same time. The Asian engineer in the chair was oblivious to it all, or at least he pretended to be while he played with the buttons on the keyboard.

"That shit is crazy, right?" A male's voice came out of nowhere from behind, startling Layani.

"Shit!" She jumped before closing the door and turning around to see none other than Dernard Perry himself, grinning from ear to ear.

"Those Red Bottom niggas get down with some crazy shit, don't they?" The Red Bottom Crew was a group of young men out of Memphis. They were some ghetto country boys with dread-locs and gold grills. They had released a song and video on YouTube and it instantly went viral with over four million views. Dernard had flown to Tennessee personally and signed them the very next day. Though they had some crazy studio tendencies, Dernard let them do whatever they wanted because they had been very valuable and worth their weight in gold so far. "Were you looking for someone, Layani? I thought I booked you in Studio B."

"Um . . ." Layani stalled nervously. "You did. I just finished my part of the song and went to the bathroom. On my way, I guess I got a little lost."

"Is that right?" Dernard raised a thick brow. He knew she was lying and was just being nosey, but he went with it. "Would you like me to take you back to studio B, or would like to come with me? I'll give you the official tour of the building." He unloosened the Armani tie around his neck. It had been a long day of meetings discussing video budget and concert dates for various artists. He welcomed the down time.

"Are you sure?" Layani couldn't believe her luck. "I don't want to overstep my boundaries."

"I don't think the boss will mind." He chuckled and extended his arm for her to grab.

Layani hesitated briefly before wrapping her arm around his. She tried to pretend that she didn't feel the muscles beneath his fancy suit jacket or smell the expensive cologne dripping from his body. Dernard was eye candy for sure, but Layani played it cool and forced herself to think of Micah the whole time.

Chapter Seventeen

The tour of the Track House studio building lasted
for just about thirty minutes. In that time frame, Dernard
showed Layani each of the twelve studios units, his personal office, the executive board room, all six apartments
for artists needing overnight accommodations, and the
game room. The latter was her favorite because she was
a huge gamer whenever time permitted. The extra-large
room housed every game system or arcade game you
could imagine. Dernard wanted his employees to be
comfortable and to be able to relax after a long day of
studio sessions. Also, if they ever got stuck on a song and
needed to unwind, they could use the game room, clear
their minds, and come back to the drawing board with
fresh ideas.

The small one-bedroom apartments were nice too.
Originally Dernard had added the basic apartments to
the building in case there was ever inclement weather
and he or one of his artists got snowed in; however,
after noticing most of his artists spent days in the studio
and ended up sleeping over, he had all six redone and
completely upgraded. Dernard wanted to provide a place
with all the comforts of the finest hotels for his artists to
shit, shower, and shave if need be. The apartments even
came with maid services.

"This place is amazing," Layani said after stepping off the elevator back onto her floor. Though she was already happy to be in the iconic building, having the private tour made her appreciate her time there that much more.

"Thank you for saying that. I worked hard as hell for this place to be what it is today." Dernard rubbed the wall as they headed back to her studio session with admiration. "It all started with a dollar and dream," he said while recalling building his vision brick by brick with blood, sweat, and real tears some days.

"Layani, may I ask, what's your dream?"

"Well, I don't know honestly." She shrugged.

"What is the one thing you want to accomplish before you leave this earth? Is it being rich? Is it seeing the world?" Dernard peered at the doe-eyed girl inquisitively.

"I don't need a billion dollars. I don't want one hundred houses, and I don't have to see the whole world. I guess all I want is to just leave my mark on the world, ya know?" She smiled; it was contagious.

"That was beautiful." Before Dernard knew it, he was smiling too. He liked this new girl—maybe a little too much. He knew he was a dog who wouldn't do her any good, but he was also a man who always went after what he wanted. His mind told him to leave her the fuck alone, but his dick was throbbing at the thought of what her guts felt like. "You've already made a mark on me. The rest of the world should be easy." Dernard licked his full lips. "You're beautiful, and your voice is pure."

"Thanks, sir." She blushed nervously. Though she had received thousands of compliments throughout the years, receiving one from someone of Dernard's caliber was one for the books.

"Please, call me D."

"Is that what all your artists call you?" Layani asked in a flirtatious tone. She wasn't even trying to sound that way. It just happened. Maybe it was the heat she sensed between them, or maybe it was the fact that he was Dernard Perry. Whatever it was, it had her feeling a little too school-girlish with him.

"Nah, but my friends do." He winked before opening the door to the studio and watching her round ass sashay back into the room.

"Damn," he mumbled under his breath. Normally Dernard was attracted to the tall, skinny model type, but Layani definitely had a natural sex appeal that he was drawn to. She was superstar potential. Once his team made her over, she would be a thoroughbred no doubt.

"D-Money, baby, what's up." So-Low stood and gave his boss a dap.

"What's up, y'all? How are the newbies working out?" Leaning up against the wall, he crossed his arms.

"We're still working, but it's coming together." Naïve nodded before being cut off by Jayko.

"Look, your singer was fine. She took my words and killed it! But your rapper ain't really cutting the mustard."

"Cutting the mustard as in she can't rap, or she just can't rap your shit?" Dernard leaned off the wall and waved Mack back inside.

"D, we've been in here for more than an hour and we don't have shit to work with." Jayko smacked her lips as Mack entered the conversation. Veronica didn't want to be in the drama, so she pretended to take a phone call out in the hallway.

"Mack, how do you feel about the song?"

"I like the song. I just don't like my verse." She handed the paper with her lyrics to him.

"What don't you like about it? Be specific." Dernard looked over the paper.

"The shit is corny as hell! I mean, do I look like the type of bitch that sit and home crying because some nigga is cheating?" She made it a point to make eye contact with everyone in the room.

"What kind of bitch are you then?" Dernard asked like he really wanted to know.

"I'm the bitch that will bust out windows, slash tires, and cut up clothes if I have to, after first going out and getting me a new nigga," Mack stated as a matter of fact. "Look, the lyrics might be cool for somebody else, but not me. My fan base would be utterly disappointed if I released some shit like that. It goes against everything I stand for."

"Okay, I hear you, and I do understand." Dernard placed the paper down onto the table. "I give you permission to go in the booth and freestyle on this one with your own words. If the shit turns out dope, you can write all of your shit going forward. If the shit is trash, then you will go back to having a writer, and it will remain that way until I say otherwise. Understand?" he first asked Mack, and then asked Jayko. They both nodded in agreement. "All right then, I'll leave y'all two. I look forward to listening to this in the morning. Eight o'clock sharp, So-Low!" he hollered on his way out of the door.

Layani thought there would be some tension after Mack and Jayko's disagreement, but surprisingly, things went exceptionally well. Mack went in the booth and murdered her verse, just like she said she would. Everyone in the room sang her praises when it was over, especially Jayko. They even hashed things out with a hug. Jayko told Mack that she was glad as women they were able to iron out their differences, because it was already too many industry beefs amongst women.

Shortly after wrapping up the song with ad libs and fillers, the girls left the studio to allow the producers to put their magic touch on it. Veronica offered to treat them to dinner at Sylvia's, a famous soul food restaurant not too far from the studio. Both Mack and Lay were tired and wanted to get some rest, but Veronica warned both women that it would be their last good meal before they had to start eating like birds. She told Layani that she was expected to lose at least twenty of the one hundred thirty-five pounds she currently carried. Mack, on the other hand, was only expected to maintain her current 150 pounds.

"Why I gotta lose weight and she don't? I'm already smaller than she is." Layani rolled her eyes as they got into Akebo's truck.

"Ever since Nicki came on the scene with that big ass, female rappers are expected to be a little on the thicker side," Veronica explained nonchalantly.

Mack wanted to tell her a thing or two about basically calling her fat, but she let it go, not wanting to get into it with another person today.

"Singers, on the other hand, should be slim."

"Why should my weight matter?" Layani asked, puzzled. As a singer, the only thing that should matter was her vocals.

"Layani, your weight matters because in this industry, image is everything," Veronica replied.

Layani wanted to dispute the claim; however, her dream was at stake. If losing a few extra pounds would help her achieve success, then so be it.

Fifteen minutes later, the trio pulled up to the small but quaint restaurant and were immediately shown to a table. The restaurant was filled with patrons, but the staff knew Veronica was with the Young Millionaires label, so they treated her order with urgency. Within twenty minutes, the waiter was coming out with their food. Veronica had ordered her usual, fried chicken, collard greens, corn bread, and yams. Layani ordered the same, and Mack ordered pork chops, greens, hot water bread, corn, and a peach cobbler dessert. Layani wanted some dessert but didn't want to add to her pounds, so she passed.

Once dinner was over, the ladies did a little sightseeing around New York. Akebo took them to see Madison Square Garden, Chinatown, the 911 Memorial, and the Statue of Liberty from a distance before dropping them off at their new residence. The building was a sixty-seven-floor high-rise building smack dab in the middle of Manhattan.

"We're here, ladies. These are your keys." Veronica handed each girl one key hooked to a keychain with a microphone on it.

"This is our crib?" Mack couldn't believe it. In Baltimore, they didn't have buildings this big.

"Yup, it's all yours." Veronica exited the truck and glanced down at her gold watch. She was due for a conference call in twenty minutes, so she didn't have time to show the ladies around. "Girls, I'll catch up with you tomorrow. Don't hesitate to call my cell, should you need me. The place is fully furnished and stocked with food. Get some rest! Tonight is the last chill day you will have for a while, so enjoy it." Veronica waited for the doorman to come out and assist the women with their luggage before hopping back into the truck with Akebo and pulling away.

The inside of the building looked as good as any five-star hotel either girl had ever seen. There was marble flooring throughout the lobby, with wood grain and silver accessories.

"Hello, ladies, my name is Braxton. It'll be my pleasure to show you to your dwelling. Ms. Layani, the items that you shipped have already been delivered to your suite," the middle-aged black man in a burgundy jacket and gray slacks, said while rolling the luggage cart toward the waiting elevator.

Once it arrived, the trio got on, and Braxton pressed floor number 50. After serving the last ten record label tenants who lived there, he knew the apartment by heart.

"What would you like me to call you?" he asked.

"You can call me Mack, and call her Lay. Don't ever forget those names. We will blow up!" Mack slapped fives with Lay.

"May I have an autograph, Ms. Mack and Ms. Lay?" Braxton pulled a notebook and pen from his pants pocket. In his line of work, he always stayed ready to get John Hancocks from any and everybody that stayed in the Young Millionaires apartment. Though some of those people never turned into the superstars they thought they would be, most of them did. Braxton planned to one day retire off his collection of famous signatures.

Ding! The elevator buzzed, and the girls followed Braxton to their new home. Just by the way the hallway looked, Layani knew the apartment had to be grand. Holding her breath, she used her key and turned the lock.

"Oh my God!" she exclaimed. The place was off the chain, with high ceilings, hardwood floors, and a panoramic view of the city. The living room consisted of tan leather furniture with gold pillows and three stone coffee tables. The kitchen was an open concept, with granite countertops and stainless-steel appliances. Gold records of artists from the label lined the walls leading to the bedroom. This made Layani hopeful that hers would be there soon.

When she and Mack opened the two bedroom doors, they fell in love instantly. Both rooms were the exact same in terms of size and décor. The cherry on top would've been to have an en suite bathroom, but instead, they were sharing the bathroom off the hallway. Still, neither woman complained. This apartment was a big step up from what they both were used to.

"Moving on up." Mack danced like George Jefferson from room to room while snapping pictures on her cell phone. She and Layani both completely ignored Braxton, who stood in the living room, unloading the luggage. He was used to being invisible once the new artists got into the apartment.

"I thought you said we shouldn't take pictures." Lay smacked her lips playfully.

"Is that what I said?" Mack laughed while snapping another one.

"Whatever, girl." Layani dialed Micah, totally oblivious that Braxton had let himself out already.

"What's up, boo?" Micah answered after looking at the screen. He hadn't heard from her all day, but he expected that, so it was no big deal.

"Baby, this place is amazing!" Layani went on to describe the apartment. "I wish you were here to see this. It's some real boss type of shit!"

"Don't worry. I'll be there soon enough." Micah missed Layani something terrible, but he knew the separation was necessary. "How is the Big Apple? Did you take a tour yet, or was today all about work?"

"So far, I'm loving it," she squealed like a kid in a candy store. "Today was a little bit of both. We saw a few things, but the main thing was the tour Dernard personally gave me of the Track House. Bae, it is super dope. I even got to lay down a track."

"Good. Good." Micah nodded as if he could be seen.

"My roommate is a rapper from Baltimore. Her name is Mack. She's on the song too." Layani looked across the hallway at Mack, who was still dancing.

"I know it'll be fly. I can't wait to hear it, baby. I'm so proud of you."

"This is just the beginning. We're on our way!" Layani was smiling so hard.

"I told you God answered prayers, bae." Micah never doubted the call on his life, but he knew Layani was different. So many times, she had threatened to throw in the towel, but Micah urged her to keep the faith. "Treat this time in New York like a school assignment. Learn as much as you can, make as many connections as you can, and you'll blow up in no time."

"You're right, Micah. I'm on it. I'm going to set the path for you too, baby. Me and you together in this industry is a goldmine."

"Yeah, you do that, bae."

The couple talked for two hours as Layani unpacked her bag. She was so excited to be talking with him about her career. Though they'd had this conversation thousands of times over the years, Layani was revitalized and talked as if all of this were new to her. Micah listened intently until his eyelids were too heavy to hold open. Finally, Layani ended the call because she knew he had to work in the morning.

After placing the cell phone on the charger, she headed over to see Mack.

"Damn, I didn't think you were ever going to get off the phone, girl." She was sitting on her bed, drinking from the neck of an almost empty champagne bottle. "I tried to wait for you, but—" She paused before belching.

"I'm sorry. That was my boo, Micah." Layani took a seat on the bed beside her roommate.

"I used to have one of those," Mack slurred. "Then that nigga cheated, and I dumped his monkey ass! Niggas ain't loyal."

"Micah is." Layani defended her man. "He loves me."

"Okay, if you say so. Niggas need pussy. You're in New York, and he's in Detroit. Lay, you do the math." Mack smacked her lips. "Anyway, you can have love. I'll take the money."

"Why can't a person have them both?" Layani knew there was no point in arguing with a drunk, but she still waited for the answer.

"Girl, there ain't no love in hip hop. Don't you know that?" Mack frowned. "How many relationships have you seen survive the music industry? Don't worry, I'll wait."

"Well—" Layani was about to mention Bey and Jay, but after recent headlines surrounding the couple, she remained silent.

"That's what I thought." Mack smirked.

Silently, Layani processed the point her roommate had made and prayed like hell she and Micah would be the exception to the rule.

Chapter Eighteen

After spending most of night drinking and talking, Layani and Mack fell asleep in their clothes sometime after two a.m. Layani was sleeping well, until she arose to the sound of a ringing telephone at four o'clock in the morning.

"Hello?" she answered, half awake.

The female caller on the other end demanded that Layani come down to lobby dressed and ready to sweat. Layani really didn't know what that meant.

"Huh? Who is this?"

"If you want to be something that the music industry will remember, then I suggest you have your narrow behind downstairs in fifteen minutes," the woman barked.

Layani didn't even know who she was talking to; nonetheless, she did as she was told. Forcing herself out of bed, she flew into the bathroom and brushed her teeth, then washed her face and got dressed. She checked in on Mack, who was still asleep, to see if she had gotten the call too.

"Mack, wake up, girl." Layani nudged her roommate for several minutes, but it was no use, so she closed the door and let her sleep.

Within ten minutes, she was on the elevator headed downstairs. When the elevator door opened and Layani could see who was waiting, she smiled from ear to ear.

Standing before her was Kandy K, vocal trainer to the stars. She was known for pushing people to their limits, but everyone loved her for it.

"Good morning, sunshine." Kandy was dressed in blue Spandex tights, a purple leotard, yellow leg warmers, and hot pink running shoes.

"Good morning, Ms. K." Layani tried to contain her nervousness. She couldn't believe she was in the presence of music royalty. During Kandy's fifteen years in the industry, she had propelled many newbies into superstars within their first year. Layani felt privileged to be under her wing.

"Call me Kandy, superstar." She rested a gentle hand on Layani's shoulder.

Layani knew this was only the calm before the storm. After following Kandy's career and seeing her on several music-related reality shows, she knew Kandy could turn into a monster without so much as batting an eyelash.

"How was your first day in the Big Apple?" Kandy asked while stretching her legs. Layani followed suit.

"It was exciting! Honestly, I'm still in shock that I'm even here."

"Good. Good." Kandy smiled. "So many people in your position take their blessing for granted. Always remember that there is someone at home right now, praying for an opportunity like yours." Kandy let her words sink in with the young girl.

However, Layani didn't have to be reminded. Hell, just two weeks ago, she was that person at home, praying. Now that her moment had come, she wouldn't dare let her dreams fall by the wayside. She owed herself, she owed her parents, and most of all, she owed Micah to give it her all.

"With that in mind, there is only one question left to ask." Kandy smirked before asking, "Are you ready to work, beloved?"

"Yes, ma'am." Layani nodded.

"Did you come to work?" This time, Kandy yelled to the top of her lungs.

It was very early in the morning. Layani didn't want to wake her neighbors in the building, but she didn't want to disappoint her vocal coach either.

"Yes, ma'am!" Layani screamed.

Kandy smiled. "So, let's work then!" Kandy turned on the balls of her feet and started sprinting toward the door. Layani did the same.

Kandy and Layani began jogging around her neighborhood. Twenty minutes in, Layani wanted to stop. Her legs felt like limp noodles, but she dared not complain. To make matters worse, Kandy made Layani sing the national anthem over and over again. Her lungs burned a little, and her throat was dry from the alcohol the night before, so she stopped singing but kept running.

"Don't stop until I tell you to," Kandy snapped.

"I can't do this," Layani admitted on the verge of passing out.

"It may seem hard now, but you'll get the hang of it. When you vocalize while running, you increase your stamina to sing and dance on stage at the same time without getting winded," Kandy explained.

"Okay, but why do I have to sing the national anthem of all songs?" Layani asked in a breathy tone.

"You'd be surprised how many times you'll be asked to sing that song. Most singers don't know it, but I bet you'll never forget it after today." Kandy turned around to face Layani while running backward. "Trust me." Kandy chuckled.

Layani was too tired to return the gesture. Her feet hurt, and her body ached. "Superstar, sing the national anthem like your career depends on it."

"Kandy, I can't."

"You can't, or you won't?" Kandy stopped running and jogged in place. "Because if you won't, then we might as well stop here. I don't have time to play with someone who isn't serious!"

"I can. I just don't feel good."

"Superstar, that right there sound like an excuse. Excuses are monuments of nothing that build bridges to nowhere. Now, you can't, or you won't?"

"Oh, say can you see . . ." Layani belted the song out like it was the last time she'd ever sing it.

"That's my girl." Kandy K clapped as they continued to run.

For two hours, the women jogged and Layani sang until she was on the brink of tears. Kandy new she had done a number on Layani, but she didn't care one bit. Everybody wanted to be star overnight, and nobody wanted to work for it. She could tell the girl had skills, but there was still a ton of work needed to get her to the next level. She vowed to not give up on Layani, as long as Layani didn't give up on herself. Too many times Kandy saw talent come and go. She learned long ago not to become attached to artists, but she really liked Layani. In fact, after getting to know her, Kandy silently prayed that she would be one of the ones who made it.

"All right, superstar, this is the last lap."

"Yes!" Layani pushed through her pain and sprinted all the way. Kandy was on her heels, clapping and cheering until they reached the end.

"You did it!" Kandy said after they reached the awning of Layani's building.

"I did, didn't I?" Layani was drenched in sweat. She felt great now that the torture was over.

"It won't be so bad tomorrow." Kandy wiped her face with the back of her hand.

"Tomorrow?" Layani frowned.

"Tomorrow, superstar!" Kandy replied while walking off down the street.

"Ain't this a bitch!" Layani mumbled as she walked into the building.

Just as Layani slid her key into her door, she felt as if she would collapse. Her limbs felt like noodles, and all she wanted was some water and a shower. She hadn't worked out so hard in God knows how long.

Buzz. Buzz. The sound startled Layani as she stepped inside. It was coming from the wall by her ear. She looked over to see an intercom.

"Hello," she said after pressing talk.

"It's Akebo here for Ms. Bell."

"It's me, Akebo. What can I do for you?" Layani was confused. From where she was standing, the wall clock told her it was six o'clock. The sun was really just coming up.

"Ms. Bell, you have a studio appointment in thirty minutes."

"Give me a second and I'll be right down." Layani wanted to grumble and complain, but she was too blessed. She also wanted badly to shower but decided against making a bad impression by showing up late. Funk in tow, she headed back downstairs to meet her driver.

"Good morning." She smiled as Akebo held the door open for her.

"Morning, Ms. Bell. Did you sleep well last night?"

"Yeah, I did for all of two hours."

"Wow! Was the Big Apple too noisy for you?" Akebo peered at her through the rearview mirror.

"No, it wasn't that. Me and Mack stayed up drinking, and now I'm paying for it."

"Oh, I see." Akebo smiled.

The rest of the ride to the studio was silent. Layani used the travel time to get some sleep, but just as it was getting good to her, Akebo stopped the car.

Grabbing her purse and cell phone, she exited with a yawn. Upon entrance into the Track House, the receptionist greeted her with a warm smile before telling her which studio she was in. It was the same studio as yesterday, so Layani knew exactly where she was going. From the elevator, she could smell that damn weed smoke again and wondered if Wayne was back. Curiosity almost made her walk down to his studio and see, but she knew it was time to do what she came for, and that was to work.

"Welcome back." So-Low smiled from his seat.

"Hey." Layani yawned.

"Dana, this is Layani Bell. Lay, this is Dana. She is the writer for today's session."

Layani set her bag on the couch and shook Dana's hand. She was a white woman with sandy brown hair, blue eyes, and full lips. "What's this song about?" Layani leaned against the wall.

"We actually have two very important demos to do today." Dana handed Layani a tablet with the words.

"Demos?" Layani frowned, knowing that meant the music she was singing today wouldn't actually be hers to keep.

"Yeah. These demos are going to be in an upcoming movie under Lionsgate. The finished tracks are going to be done by none other than Beyoncé," So-Low informed the newbie.

"Oh my God! Are you serious?" Layani was now super nervous yet excited to do the demo.

"Cross my heart and hope to die." Dana did the motion with her hand.

"Come on. Let's get it cracking." Naïve walked into the room and took a seat next to So-Low.

Layani grabbed a water from the mini fridge and took it into the booth along with Dana's tablet. She was excited, but unfortunately the first crack at the song didn't go as planned. Her pitch was off because the producers insisted that she sing the song in a key she wasn't used to. It was a hard thing to do, but in the end, after nearly eight hours of singing and re-singing the song, Layani pulled from everything she had in her soul and placed it on the track. When it was finished, everyone in the studio was cheering and applauding. Quietly, they all thought Layani should've been given the song to record for the movie, but everyone knew it wasn't happening. Queen B was, well, Queen B! She'd earned her clout, and Layani still had a way to go.

Akebo was standing at the receptionist's desk making small talk when Layani got off the elevator. "Here you are, Ms. Bell." He handed her a green drink and a straw. "This is just what the doctor ordered for you to sober up and put a little pep in your step."

"No, thank you. All I need now is to go home and get in the bed." Layani tried to hand him back the smoothie.

"Ms. Bell, you still have a long day. It'll at least be another two, maybe three hours before I'm scheduled to

take you back home. Do yourself a favor and drink the
smoothie. It's apple, spinach, kale, pear, ginseng and
B12." Akebo told the receptionist goodbye and held the
door open for Layani.

"Where could we possibly be going now?" She was
irritated but tried hard not to let it show.

"You are due at the Magic House in thirty minutes."
Akebo held open the door to his truck.

Layani didn't bother asking the what the Magic House
was. Instead, she sipped her juice and closed her
eyes. When she reopened them, Akebo was pulling into
the parking lot of a small, black building. He parked the
truck near the front entrance, and Layani got out before
he could get to her door.

"I appreciate you, but you don't have to open the door
for me every time."

"It's my pleasure to do so, Ms. Bell." Akebo smiled
before going to open the door of the building. "If you
need me, I'll be outside waiting until you're done."

Layani walked into the office building's all white in-
terior, white furniture, and silver accent pieces hesitantly
and was greeted by a six-foot tall person dressed in drag.

"Hey, sugar, you must be Layani. I'm Christina." She
extended her long hands with a perfect French manicure
and smiled. Christina was dressed in a long, red bodycon
dress. Her makeup was flawless, and her lace-front wig
looked like it had grown directly from her scalp.

"Nice to meet you, Christina."

"Do you know why you're here?" Christina led Layani
toward the back of the building, which appeared to be a
big dressing room. There were mannequins, wigs, clothes,
and jewelry placed very neatly throughout the space.

"No, ma'am." Nervously, Lay sipped on her drink.

"This place is called the Magic House because this is where all the magic happens. Here is where you will learn how to walk, talk, dress, and act like the star you are. Now, let me see you walk." Christina took a seat on a chair in front of the mirror.

Layani felt silly, but she put her cup down on the table and walked around the room.

With one brow raised, Christina shouted, "I said walk, bitch!" She snapped her fingers.

After all the running she had done, Layani didn't have it in her to strut the way the lady wanted, but she tried.

"Booooo." Christina held both her thumbs down. "With a walk like that, you will never be a standout star. Sit down and let me show you something, little girl." She got up and let her student take a seat.

Once she had Layani's full attention, Christina walked around that room like it was the runway at Fashion Week in Paris. Her shoulders were still, yet her arms shifted effortlessly. Her feet were pointed and straight, yet her hips slung from the east to the west.

"Baby girl, when you become a big name, the paparazzi will be paid good money to catch any photos of you slipping. From here on out, everything you do must be on purpose. Ain't no more leaving the house in your rollers and shit! Ain't no more sweatpants. No, no, Ms. Thang, you got to be on point." Christina folded her arms. "Do you know Tyra, Naomi, Cynthia, Kimora, Giselle? I taught all of those beautiful ladies and a few more."

"Wow!" Layani was impressed. "What do I need to do to be as beautiful as them and you?"

"First off, ain't nobody said you were ugly! You are very beautiful. Embrace that and build on it. With just a touch of makeup, a new hairstyle, and a few new articles of clothing, you'll be all set."

After the pep talk, Christina went to work. First, she placed a number of wigs on Layani to see what her new signature style and color should be. After settling on a long black wig with a part down the middle and soft curls, Christina braided Layani's hair and then sewed the wig down. Next, she jotted down the exact style number for the wig and color on the custom card she'd created for everyone she ever worked with. This card held the preferred hair color, skin texture, makeup preference, body measurements, dress style, and shoe size. That way, if ever the artist needed Christina's team to send anything for them, she already knew what inventory to pull from.

As Christina applied the makeup onto the right side of Layani's face, she told her exactly what to do to make the left side match. "Sometimes, child, you won't have a makeup artist at your disposal, so you have to know how to do this stuff yourself in case of an emergency."

Christina then pulled three looks for Layani to try on. The first one was a strapless black one-piece, a silver necklace, strappy black Louboutins, and a small black clutch. "This is something you would wear throughout the day to business meetings, lunch dates with friends, or just out shopping by yourself. The second outfit was a long-sleeved white bodycon dress with white wedge shoe-boots. "This is your weekend look, simple yet classy. This could be worn to a grand opening of something, a charity event, or even an informal red carpet."

As Layani slipped into the third outfit, she stared at herself in the mirror. With the hair and makeup, she could barely recognize herself. In the red satin gown, she felt like she was already famous. Her confidence was through the roof as she walked back into the room with

Christina. Taking in everything she'd learned, Layani strutted into the room like she owned it.

"Yes, bitch! You better walk!" Christina cheered. Layani looked stunning. "Hell, you make me want to take you somewhere right damn now."

"Thank you so much."

"Baby, don't thank me. That's just what fairy glam mothers do." She smoothed down the dress and then stood back and admired her work.

"Other than hair, makeup, and wardrobe, is there any other advice you have for me?" Layani wanted to soak in all she could, not knowing when she would get another opportunity to be in her presence again.

"I know this is all new and exciting, but when you're out in public or in the company of people you don't know, be mindful of your surroundings. Unfortunately, a pretty girl like you has more to worry about than looking good for a picture. It's some rough people out there, especially in this industry. They will charm you with their million-dollar smiles and fancy titles just to lower your guard long enough to sink their hooks in. Once those hooks are in you, these vultures will drain the dreams out of your young soul. I know your mama taught you all of this, but at these parties, don't leave your drinks with nobody, and don't accept no party favors either!"

"My mama died before I got that speech, so I appreciate you sharing." Layani looked down at the ground. "Sorry to sound dumb, but what is a party favor?" In her world, she was used to party favors being gifts for party guests, but she could tell by the way Christina said it that she was talking about something different.

"Baby, I'm sorry to hear about your mother, and you're not dumb. The only way to be dumb is to not ask questions. In the entertainment industry, party favors are usually little cute packs of sniffable cocaine and laced marijuana joints. Nowadays, they also give out heroin."

"Oh my God, are you serious?"

"Yes, child. Over sixty-nine percent of the people in this industry are getting high. Some of them are probably some of your favorite celebrities, too." Christina smirked.

"Oh, please tell me one. At least one," Layani begged.

"Nah, now I don't give up the goods that easy." Christina laughed. "At least invite a bitch to a proper lunch before expecting me to spill this tea."

"Yes, ma'am, I will definitely do that. Thank you again for getting me together." Layani hugged Christina. "What do I owe you?"

"Everything is yours, the makeup, the wig, the shoes, and the clothes. Dernard paid for it this morning. He sees something in you, girl. He usually doesn't fork over big money like that until after an artist has proved her worth."

"Well, thank you again. I will be calling you for lunch." Layani waived and headed outside, where Akebo was waiting.

Chapter Nineteen

It was just after six o'clock when Layani made it back to her apartment with all her bags in tow. She was exhausted, and all she wanted to do was shower and sleep. After placing her key into the door and turning the lock, Layani called out for her roommate, but there was no answer. She hit the light and saw a note on the table. It said Mack was out grabbing something to eat and she would bring Layani back a salad. There was a smiling face at the end to indicate that the salad was only a joke.

Layani headed to her room, dropped off her things, and took out her phone. She video dialed Micah and smiled when he answered.

"Hey, baby."

"Bae, you look amazing! What's the special occasion?" Micah stared at his girl with so much infatuation.

"Apparently, I needed to enhance my look." She smiled. "I met with a fairy glam mother who basically told me how to walk, talk, dress, eat, and sleep going forward."

"I love you for you, but I ain't going to lie, I love this look. You really look beautiful, Lay." Micah took another long look before changing the subject. "So, tell me how day two went." He'd called Lay that morning. When she didn't answer, he figured she was working, so he didn't call back.

"Bae, do you know I went to bed at two o'clock, got up at four o'clock, and had to run for two hours while singing the national anthem. I was tired, ready to cry, and about to throw up."

"Damn, running for two hours and singing sounds like some Kandy K type of shit." Micah shook his head.

"Oh my God, that's exactly who it was!"

"Are you for real?"

"Yes, bae, and she is just as intense in person as she is on TV. As soon as I was done with her, I had to go straight to the studio to do two demos for a movie. Guess who will be singing the final version of the songs I demoed?"

"Who?" Micah eagerly asked.

"The fucking Queen Bey herself!"

"Shut the fuck up. Damn, Lay, that's major, bae."

"I know, right! It took me a minute to get the first song right, but eventually I nailed it. Then Akebo, our driver, took me to Magic House for the makeover. I'm hungry and tired. If things stay busy like this, I won't have a problem losing that twenty pounds they want me to lose."

"Baby, you sound like you had a pretty eventful day. Take a shower, grab something to eat, and get some rest. I love you."

"I love you more, Micah." After blowing a kiss, Layani ended the call and went to take a bath.

After soaking her joints in the spa tub, Layani put on a pair of pajamas and walked through the apartment to see if Mack had returned, but she hadn't. There was a note on the counter from Mack. It read:

Hey, bitch, I thought we could go sightseeing today, but when I woke up, you were gone, so I went by myself. I can't wait to tell you all about it.
Mack

Turning over the note, Layani wrote one of her own.

> *Mack,*
> *Sorry I missed you! I hope your day was as great*
> *as mine. I'm exhausted. When you come in, no need*
> *to wake me up. See you tomorrow.*
> *Xoxo*
> *Lay*

The next morning, things switched up slightly. Layani had a studio session at six a.m. scheduled before her morning run with Kandy K. Therefore, she woke up early to curl her weave and apply makeup the way her fairy glam mother had taught her. Though she was nowhere near as good as Christina, no one would ever think she just learned how to apply makeup the day before.

After sifting through her clothes to find what Christina would deem appropriate, she settled on a black romper with ruffled sleeves and a pair of black Gucci ballerina shoes.

Akebo was waiting outside the truck when she got downstairs with another green smoothie. "Thank you." Feeling refreshed from a good night's rest, Layani gleefully got into the truck and took a sip of the healthy drink. Instantly, she thought of what Christina said about leaving her drinks with strangers. For a split second, she wondered if Akebo would try some funny shit with her, but she quickly decided he wasn't cut like that.

Once at the studio, Layani was yet again assigned to B. As she came off the elevator, she was nearly knocked over by an Asian lady who appeared to have been crying.

"Are you okay?" Layani was concerned.

"Yes." The woman frantically pressed the button, but Layani was holding the door open.

"What's wrong?"

"Nothing. I'm fine. Please let me go."

Layani couldn't force the woman to tell her what happened, so she moved her hand from holding the door open. As it closed, Layani could see blood coming from between the woman's legs. She knew something wasn't right, but what could she do?

Doing her best to clear what she saw out of her head, she went into the studio session and put down another track. This time, it was only Jayko and Naïve in the room. The new song was another love song about a couple who had an argument and too many days had passed before they spoke again. Layani wished Micah were there with her. She knew his songs would kill Jayko's. Nonetheless, she didn't complain.

After finishing her studio session, Layani told the gang goodbye and headed out. On her way to the elevator, she was met by a tall, light-skinned, tattooed man with dreads.

"Jackson Mills, is that you?" She immediately recognized the Atlanta-based, two-time Grammy award–winning singer.

"Hello, love." Jackson looked up from his cell phone and was caught off guard by the beautiful new face. "What's your name, sweetheart?"

"Layani Bell."

The elevator arrived, and they both got on.

"That is a very beautiful name for a beautiful woman." Jackson winked. "What are you doing in these parts? I've never seen you before."

"I just got signed." Layani smiled. "I came in from Detroit a few days ago."

"Congratulations, sweetheart. Maybe we can exchange numbers. I would love to show you around the city. I've been living in New York for about four years now. It's not the A, but it'll do."

"Oh, I have a boyfriend. I don't think exchanging numbers is a good idea." Layani knew he was also expecting a baby with his on-again, off=again girlfriend from Curacao. She was a beautiful black model with a mean walk.

"I'm not trying to wife you, sweetheart. I was just trying to be friendly." Jackson laughed.

"I didn't mean to offend you." Layani instantly felt terrible for making the assumption that he was flirting. Though Jackson was a bonafide playboy with a bad temper, she knew she would probably never be his type.

"No offense taken." He grabbed her phone and dialed his cell phone. "Lock me in and call me whenever you need a friend in the city. I promise to be a perfect gentleman." After handing the phone back to her, Jackson went his way, and she went hers.

Akebo took Layani back to the apartment, where Kandy K was waiting in the lobby.

"Good morning, superstar."

"Good morning. Would you like to come up while I change?"

"No, you go ahead. I'll be right here waiting for you." Kandy started stretching.

Within ten minutes, Layani was dressed and back downstairs. It was before noon, and Mack was still asleep. Layani was jealous, but she didn't complain. Instead, she made the morning workout her bitch! She wanted to make up for how she had acted the day before, and she wanted to prove to herself that she could do it.

When it was over, she willed herself into the building, then onto the elevator and finally, into the apartment. The smell of bacon greeted her at the door.

"Shit!" Mack grabbed a butcher knife and pointed it at Layani, who damn near jumped out of her skin as she walked through the door.

"What the hell are you doing?" she hollered.

"My bad, bitch. I thought you were a robber or some shit." Mack dropped the knife.

"A robber with a fucking key?" Layani dangled her key mid-air. A few seconds passed before both women broke out into laughter.

"My bad. I'm from the hood. Old habits die hard. Do you want a breakfast sandwich?" Mack went over to the stove to check on her bacon.

"No, I'm good. After all that running my ass just did, all I want is a shower." At this point, Layani smelled horrible, and she knew it. The only reason Mack might've not smelled her was the bacon.

"I was knocked out. I didn't even know you were gone until I checked your room and saw your dress on the bed." Mack grabbed some grape jelly from the fridge for her sandwich.

"Yeah, my vocal trainer came through shortly after I got back from the studio. I came up here to change for the run," Layani replied.

"Y'all singers be spoiled. I ain't get no fucking vocal trainer." Mack pretended to be jealous.

"You can have her, as long as you do my two-hour sprint every day."

"I'm cool on that." Mack shook her head.

"I'll be back. I need to get in some water." Layani headed toward her room while removing her clothes. She felt dirty and couldn't wait for the water to hit her body.

Being nude in the presence of Mack didn't bother her one bit. Growing up in foster care had taught her to share her space well. She tossed her clothes into the hamper and crossed the hallway to the bathroom.

The minute she turned the light on, she yelled, "Mack, what are you doing in here?" All of her roommate's clothes were hanging across the shower door and atop the sink. The girl had only worn two damn outfits between the first day and yesterday, but there had to be at least five on display.

"My bad, Lay." Mack flew into the bathroom while eating her breakfast. "I'll get them out of your way."

"Why are they in here all wet and shit?" Layani looked bewildered. Mack looked down at the ground before replying.

"Truth moment." She sighed.

"What's a truth moment?" Layani asked.

"We are girls, right?" Mack looked into Layani's face as she nodded. "Well, a truth moment is where we can tell each other the truth no matter what and not be judged afterward," Mack explained. "In Baltimore, I come from the hood where shit gets real. My family ain't got no money, and we fell on hard times. My mama used her last check to buy my plane ticket. It was either that or pay the water bill, so I came here with a suitcase full of dirty clothes."

Mack looked embarrassed, but the truth was the truth. Life hadn't always been easy for her family. However, the minute she got signed to the label, she knew God was about to change things.

"Damn, Mack." Layani felt bad for making a fuss. "As soon as I take a shower, we can go find a Laundromat and wash your shit the right way." As plush as their apartment was, Layani found it silly that there was no washer and dryer.

"I ain't got the money for all that. This way is just as good." Mack tried to laugh it off, but she was ashamed.

"Mack, do you have any money?" Layani didn't really want to ask the intrusive question but felt the need to do so.

"Nah, I'm as broke as a joke, but my ends are coming, believe that."

"Didn't you get an advance or something from your contract?" Layani frowned.

"No." Mack shook her head. "My contract stated that the label would only cover my room, board, and anything to do with my career until my album dropped. I won't see my first dime until after I sell some records." Mack felt that her contract was sheisty, but it was the closest thing she had to a meal ticket at the moment, so she took it.

"Well, my man gave me a little something before I left, so I got you." Layani omitted the fact that she actually had received a nice lump sum of money from the record label. She didn't want to make her new friend feel slighted. "As soon as I shower, we can go to the Laundromat."

"You don't have to do that." Mack shook her head. She wasn't one for handouts, never had been and never would be, as long as she could help it.

"Girl, bye!" Layani waved her hand dismissively. "Give me fifteen minutes."

"With the way you smell, I'll give you thirty minutes." Mack started collecting her things from the bathroom while pinching her nose. Both women laughed at the joke and silently thanked God for the camaraderie amongst them.

Chapter Twenty

An hour later, Layani and Mack set out on a mission to find the nearest Laundromat. They stopped downstairs to ask the man behind the desk, but he was busy catering to a tough client, so Mack pulled the information up on her phone. Google said the Laundromat was only twenty-three minutes' walking distance from the apartment. With the way her body ached, Layani wanted to take a cab, but surprisingly there was not a single one passing by. She started to whip out her phone and call Akebo for a ride but decided not to when she realized that by the time he showed up, they could've been there and done washing already. Begrudgingly, she put her big girl panties on and endured the pain in her legs.

During the walk down the long city blocks, the women discussed their families back home. Mack had three sisters and two brothers, all of whom were younger than she was. They all depended on her to become rich and help move their family out of the ghetto. Layani had no one to talk about but Micah. Speaking of him made her miss him immensely. He was all she had, and she couldn't wait to be united with him again.

"I can't wait to meet Micah. He sounds like a pretty cool guy."

"He is the real deal, Mack. Me and that boy got out of the mud together. We've seen it all and done it all together. I don't know where I would be if I hadn't been placed in his foster home."

"One of these days, I'm going to find me a good one like Micah and settle down too," Mack admitted just as they approached the Sudz-o-matic Laundromat.

As Layani went to get some change from the coin machine, Mack walked the premises, looking for a free washing machine or two. She finally found two together in the corner near the back door that was open to let in a breeze. The place was jumping with patrons. There were kids running around playing a game of tag, a few older men at a table off to the side playing a game of dominoes while they waited, and a group of women looking up at the television hanging from the wall. *The Young and the Restless* was on, and they were all in. After giving Mack twenty-five dollars in change, she went to find a seat, but there were none, so she stood.

Once the clothes were in the washing machine, Layani forced Mack across the street to the purple-and-black boutique she had spotted through the window. Naturally, the last thing Mack wanted to do was window shop, but Layani wasn't taking no for an answer. Upon entrance, the women were greeted by a Dominican lady with orange hair.

"Welcome, ladies. I'm Salondra. Please let me know if you need help with anything."

"Okay, Mack, if I asked you to style me, what would you choose?" Layani looked around the store. Almost every piece in there was nice and affordable.

"Girl, I don't know. What did your fairy glam mother tell you your style was?" Mack shrugged while being funny.

"Let's not worry about my fairy glam mother. I like how you dress," Layani lied. Truthfully, Mack and Layani had two totally different dress codes. Mack was more of an edgy tomboy, while Layani preferred classy but sexy pieces.

"Well, what size do you wear?" Mack began thumbing through a rack of colorful leggings.

"I wear a six." Layani really wore a size four, but she had peeped Mack's size on some of the clothes in the bathroom.

"Cool. Sit right there. I'll be right back." Mack went about grabbing this and that.

Layani smiled, retrieved her cell phone, and called Micah while she waited.

"What's up, boo?" Micah yelled over the music in his background. He was hard at work in the studio as usual. Layani knew he always went there straight from work or before work.

"I miss you." She spoke into the receiver while imagining her man sitting in his favorite chair, playing with the keys. She loved watching him create masterpieces.

"I miss you more, baby. How is your day going?" Micah didn't really like to talk while he was in beast mode, but for Lay, he always made exceptions.

"It started out crazy as hell." She proceeded to tell him about everything she had done, including her morning run, which was two hours of torture, as usual.

"What's your budget?" Mack yelled from the back of the store. She was already carrying an armful of shit.

"Five hundred," Layani yelled back.

"Who was that?" Micah asked.

"My roommate, Mack." Layani wanted to tell Micah about her situation but didn't want to run the risk of being overheard.

"Let me guess, you ladies are out splurging with some advance money?" Micah laughed.

"Yeah, something like that."

"Well, have your fun now, but be mindful of how you spend. That shit will get away from you quick," Micah warned.

"Why don't you take a little something out of our account and treat yourself?"

"I'm not spending a dollar of your money." Micah shook his head as if Lay could see him. Although he had every right to stake a claim in a few of her dollars, his pride wouldn't allow him to. He was real man who wanted to work for everything he had. He thought it was weak for niggas to rely on their chicks for money.

"Baby, you deserve it," Layani protested.

"Girl, I'll have mine soon enough. Thanks for thinking of me, though."

"At least pay the bills up for a few months." Layani stared at Mack, whose arms were loaded with more clothing.

"I'm good, Lay. Now, get off the phone and finish shopping with your girl."

"Is that your way of getting me off the phone so you can work?" Layani giggled.

"Yeah, so call me later. I got to have this beat ready in two hours for Cash. Love you." Micah hung up the phone just as Mack walked up.

"I grabbed you some of everything, girl. You got dresses for the industry parties, casual wear for the studio, and a few flashy pieces in case somebody big come to town." Mack smiled, obviously proud of what she had selected.

"Thanks, boo. Let's go check out." Layani put the phone back into her pocket and stood.

"Aren't you going to try these on? I think size six may be too big for you."

"I don't have to because I won't be wearing them. You will." Layani smirked and walked toward the register.

"Wait, Lay." Mack stopped. "I can't take this stuff."

"Girl, you ain't got no choice, so come on."

"I don't like taking handouts," Mack admitted.

"Consider it a loan. Once your ass blows up, you can repay with me a little Versace and Chanel here and there." Layani laughed. It felt good to be a blessing to someone else. She knew firsthand what it was like to struggle, so it was no big deal to share.

"Thank you, sis." Mack wanted to cry, but her pride wouldn't allow it.

After shopping, the women walked back to the Laundromat so Mack could put her old clothes into the dryer. Next, they walked down two blocks to grab lunch at a local bistro called Nichols. The place was small but quaint and filled with people. The food was ordered at the counter and picked up by the grill.

As soon as they grabbed their food and found a seat outside on the patio, a small commotion broke out. People started screaming and shouting. Layani strained her neck to see what was going on. In her hood, screaming meant it was time to duck.

"Girl, is that who I think it is?" Mack started fixing her hair like her life depended on it. Layani squinted to see if she could recognize the tall man with adult acne and pickle nose. "Shit! The nigga is coming this way." Mack tried to calm herself, but on cue, her palms started sweating like crazy.

"Who is he?" Layani was clueless.

"Anthony Wright," Mack whispered as people followed behind the giant with their camera phones to record and take pictures.

"Who?" Layani asked with a frown. His name didn't ring a bell, nor did his face.

"He is the new starting forward for the New York Knicks," Mack mumbled.

That was when it all made sense. At the airport, Layani recalled seeing a newspaper article about the young ball player who had just renewed a seven-figure contract. No wonder bitches flocked to the nigga like magnets. Layani thought dude looked like the Predator with dirty dreads and a fucked-up face, but Mack was head over heels.

"What's up, ladies." Anthony approached the table with something in his hand.

"What's up?" Mack nodded, not missing a beat.

"My name is Anthony. I'm having a little celebration at the 40/40 Club. I would love to put you fine-ass ladies on the VIP list."

"What exactly are you celebrating, Anthony?" Layani asked like she hadn't just received the 411 seconds ago.

"Show up tonight and you'll find out." Anthony licked his crusty-ass lips. Layani wanted to gag.

"We'll be there as long as we get special treatment," Mack said, flirting.

"Your thick ass can get whatever you like." Anthony flirted back.

"Um-hm," Mack replied with her lips twisted to the side.

"For real, baby, just show up and I got you." He handed a gold envelope to Mack and watched her open it. Inside was a black invitation card with all the details to the party. "See, you already getting Black Cards and shit." It was a lame joke, but Mack played along.

"Hopefully, there is more where this comes from and the next Black Card got sixteen digits and an expiration date on it."

"Google me, baby, and you'll find out who the fuck I am," Anthony smugly replied as he walked away. He knew he was one ugly muthafucka, but he'd learned five years ago that money could make people look past his flaws. Like Jay said, there is no such thing as an ugly billionaire.

"See you tonight, boo." Mack winked and kicked Layani under the table.

Chapter Twenty-one

Mack folded her laundry, and the women walked back to the apartment building. Layani found a good spot on the side of a building with a colorful graffiti picture of a large halo and angel wings.

"Let's get some pics for the Gram."

"I'm good, fam, but I'll take yours." Mack dropped her bags and grabbed her friend's phone.

"Why don't you want to take pics? This background is everything." Layani posed for several pictures.

"Girl, I don't want my face in a picture with angel wings and a halo until I die." She handed Layani her phone. "I'm too superstitious for that."

Layani busted out laughing. "Oh, I am going to have a good time fucking with you, starting with this pole." On purpose, Layani split the pole, and Mack had a fit. She tried to trip Layani with her shoe, but Layani was too quick. She ran up the block and split another, waited for Mack to get closer, and split another. They ladies played like this all the way home.

Once inside their apartment, Layani and Mack went into their own separate corners. Layani set an alarm and dove into her bed like an Olympic swimmer. She slept for almost three hours.

As Layani and Mack got dressed for the night, they played music and sipped on a bottle of Cîroc.

"Girl, I can't believe our luck. We actually met a real millionaire today in the flesh." Mack flat-ironed her hair with the bathroom door open.

"Me either. I wonder who else will be at the party." Layani stood in the floor-to-ceiling hallway mirror, admiring her figure in a black Couture one-piece. Silently, she wondered if she was overdressed. Mack, on the other hand, was definitely underdressed in a vintage silver Gigi Hunter ensemble. Layani hadn't seen anyone wearing the nearly naked clothing line in forever, but Mack was working it. Tonight, it was apparent that she didn't come to play no games.

"Everyone who is anyone will be in the building tonight." Mack unplugged the flat irons and started touching up her makeup. "Money attracts money, and I can't wait to be in the midst of it all. I'm desperately trying to find me a husband."

"Desperate is an understatement. I can't believe you was flirting with that monster-face-ass nigga Anthony." Layani wanted to gag just thinking about it.

"Girl, bye! Niggas like Anthony don't come around every day. Fuck his face; I'm trying to secure my future. If rapping doesn't work out, that nigga will be my plan B, please believe me." Mack laughed, but she was dead-ass serious. Where she came from, it was rare to leave the hood. Now that she had the chance to change her environment and surround herself with people in different tax brackets, she was taking it and running all the way to the bank with that bitch.

"I hear you, but damn, girl, there got to be somebody else to have a baby with. That nigga sho' is uglyyyyy." Layani pretended she was doing a scene in the movie *The Color Purple.* "Your babies are gon' be ugly, bitch." She laughed.

"Ugly maybe, but they will be filthy fucking rich!" Taking her drink to the head, Mack didn't give one care about what Layani was saying. She was on a mission.

An hour and four pre-shots later, the girls were buzzing as they arrived at the club.

"Damn, look at this fucking line." Mack pulled the envelope from her purse and prayed like hell she wouldn't be embarrassed when she bypassed the line and gave it to the bouncer. "What if everybody got one of these?" she whispered to Layani, who was trying to walk in a straight line down the sidewalk. Her buzz was apparent, but she kept it cute and played it cool.

"Can I help you ladies?" The female bouncer looked like she was ready to give the girls a hard time. Every time someone with a name threw a party, hoes would show up out of the woodwork, trying anything to make their way inside. Most of the security men fell for fat asses and pretty smiles, but not Dot. She wasn't checking for none of these bitches.

"Yes, ma'am. I was told to give this to you." Mack smiled while handing over the invitation.

Dot inspected the card and knew it was official by the stamp embedded in the bottom corner. She handed it back to the girl, then asked for ID. Both girls proudly handed over their credentials. Dot put neon bands on their wrists and told them to have a good time.

Mack wanted to scream. She couldn't believe they got in. The inside of the club was on fire! The DJ had the entire dance floor packed with people doing the Wobble. Men in expensive suits chilled in various booths, as women in little dresses strutted across the floor like they were auditioning for *America's Next Top Model*. The scene was intimidating; however, neither Layani nor Mack broke a sweat.

"Damn, baby, can I buy your fine ass a drink?" Someone walked by and winked.

Layani didn't respond, but Mack said, "Hell yeah. Get her a Pink Pussy."

"A what?" Layani frowned.

"Don't worry. It tastes good." Mack gave her girl a thumbs up. The man nodded then headed to the bar.

"Girl, I don't need him buying me a drink. When he comes back, he's going to want to talk, and I got a man." Layani was beginning to think coming to this party was a bad idea.

"Bitch, do you know who that was?" Mack shook her head. For a Detroiter, Layani seemed too damn square.

"No, I don't know who he is. I don't care either."

"Gregory Patton. The number one NBA draft pick last year. The boy just signed a two-hundred-million-dollar contract with the Lakers. He has an endorsement deal with Nike, too!" Mack spoke while scoping the scene for her boo.

"Here you go, sweetheart." Gregory slipped behind Layani and handed her a pretty pink drink.

"Thank you," Layani said shyly.

"I'm G, and you are?" He extended a manicured hand with ice all around his wrist. The shit was damn near blinding.

"I'm Layani."

"Are you a model, Layani?" Greg whispered into her ear. "Because you are gorgeous."

"No, I'm a singer." Layani nervously sipped from the straw, thinking back once again to what her fairy glam mother had told her.

"Okay, cool. Maybe I can reach out to my connections in LA and get you signed." Greg thought Layani was just like every other female he met at the club, swearing to be a singer, model, or fashion designer. He always used his line about his connections to get into their panties and never called again unless the pussy was fire. Even then, he always strung them along until he was done with them and on to the next piece of ass.

"Aww, that's sweet of you, but I'm already signed to BMR." Layani smirked.

"Okay, that's what up." G was caught off guard and didn't know where to go from that point.

"Thanks for the drink. Maybe I'll catch you around." It felt good to bust his bubble. "Come on, girl, let's go find Anthony." Layani pushed Mack as far away from Gregory as she could.

After Mack had searched the club for nearly thirty minutes, the guest of honor finally walked through the front door. His entourage was in tow, and they all were dressed to the nines.

"Damn! I know there's such a thing as being fashionably late, but this nigga is four hours late," Layani thought aloud. The party started at nine, which was why she and Mack hadn't showed up until after midnight. Hell, the party was going to be over in a few hours. She couldn't believe Anthony paid all this money to miss his own damn party.

"Better late than never." Mack stood from the booth they had managed to snag, put on her best smile, and sauntered over to meet Anthony.

Layani wanted to tell her girl to tone it down, but she was nobody's mother. She watched as Mack whispered in his ear, then Anthony smiled. Whatever she was doing was working, so Layani sat back and kept quiet.

"Hey, thanks for coming." Anthony walked over to Layani. "Come on up to the VIP with me. You ladies are my special guests tonight."

Layani and Mack followed him, along with about ten other people, to the booth elevated off the floor. There were several expensive bottles of champagne chilling on ice and three waitresses standing nearby waiting to serve the crowd exclusively. Layani began to daydream about the day she would be able to throw an elaborate event such as this one.

"Soon, Lay . . . real soon," she mumbled to herself.

For a little over an hour, Layani sipped champagne and watched Mack run game on Anthony. Mack used every dance song to grind up on Anthony's dick. At one point, Layani even thought they could have been fucking. As she watched, several ball players had approached her to dance, but she politely declined. It might've been lame, but she eventually pulled out her cell phone and started texting Micah. She missed her boo and couldn't wait for him to visit so that she could grind on a dick like Mack.

Eventually, the I-love-you texts turned into sexual texts. Layani was deprived, and her vagina begged for some attention. Casually, she slipped away from the crowd to go to the bathroom. Once inside the stall, she placed her hand in between her legs and rubbed her clitoris for dear life. Layani had never done anything like this, but it felt so good. Within a minute, she had cum all over her hand and had to lean up against the bathroom door to catch her breath. As she sat there panting, the main bathroom door opened and Layani froze.

"Come on, bitch. Get in the stall before my wife come back."

A man's voice startled Layani, who peeked through the tiny crack to see what was going on. That's when she saw two black men and a white woman.

"No, no, you need to give me what you promised first." The woman held out her hand.

"Fine." The bigger of the men handed her a few bills and then removed something from his pocket and poured its content onto the top bill. Layani watched as the lady sniffed it.

"All right, cool. You have ten minutes." Heading over to the sink, the woman began to play with her hair while the men went into the bathroom stall beside her. Layani was in utter shock and confusion as she began putting two and two together. She felt as if she was going to have a heart attack when the men began making kissing sounds and unzipping their pants.

"Tell me how bad you want this," one man demanded.

"I want it bad, baby. Really bad," the other replied.

Immediately, Layani got sick to her stomach.

"Ohhh," he moaned, and then the soft strokes turned into hard pounds. Their sexual rendezvous was so hard it was shaking the wall connecting the stalls.

Layani moved away from the wall, but the motion caused her toilet to flush. Fearing they would kill her if they caught her, she unlocked her door and flew out of the bathroom like a bat out of hell. Thankfully, the men didn't stop fucking to see who she was, and the woman they paid to keep lookout was so high that she didn't care. With dry cum on her hand, Layani went back to the party and tried to stay out of view.

By four o'clock in morning, the after party had relocated to a penthouse suite at the Travertine Hotel Towers. Layani really wanted to go back to their apartment, but Mack begged her roommate to stay out for one more hour.

"Only one!" Layani warned as the small group entered the large living room of the suite.

"That's all I need. You're the best." Mack hugged her girl. "I owe you," she whispered.

"Layani, this is my boy Tiger. You can chill with him until Mack comes back. If you need us, we will be upstairs," Anthony said while whisking Mack away to the bedroom.

Layani wanted to protest being left alone with this stranger but she was too sleepy to put up a fuss.

"You got a pretty name, ma." Tiger was some tall, goofy-looking nigga with buck teeth. Mack had already told her his resume. The boy had bank, but Layani wasn't at all interested.

"Thanks. What's your government name?" Layani went over to the orange sofa with navy blue pillows and flopped down. Seconds later, she kicked off her heels, no longer trying to be cute. Her feet hurt.

"Terrence is what my mother named me," Tiger said before taking the seat beside her. Though he could have sat on the other sofa or at one of the chairs pulled up to the ten-person dining table, he chose to sit right next to Lay.

After a moment of awkward silence, Tiger reached into his pocket and removed a small tin box. "Do you party, baby?"

"Huh?" Layani frowned. Hadn't this fool just been at the party with her?

"You know . . . party?" He rubbed his nose and sniffed.

"No. Hell no." Layani knew what he meant when she saw the white substance inside the tin.

"Well, I do. So, excuse me for a second while I blast off." Tiger laughed.

"I thought all ball players got tested."

"We do, but the season just ended. I'll be cool by the time season practice starts up." Like it was no big deal, Tiger reached into his wallet and removed a fifty-dollar bill. He rolled it into a tight straw and sucked every morsel of the white stuff. Immediately, his eyes got watery and he sneezed. White shit and mucus dripped down his nose.

Layani excused herself and went into the bathroom. Once inside, she texted Mack and told her it was time to go. After no response, she called Mack's phone five times, but it went straight to voicemail.

Shortly after flushing the toilet and washing her hands, she opened up the door to see Tiger standing there. He no longer looked the same. His eyes were glazed and fixed on her like a beast fixed its eyes on its prey.

"Did you need to get in here?" Layani frowned. "Let me get out of your way." Layani tried to get past him, but he blocked her way.

"Where the fuck you think you're going?" Tiger looked down at Layani the way a lion would look at a lioness right before he penetrated her.

"Move, Tiger," Layani said with a little more bass in her voice.

"What the fuck you gon' do, bitch?" He unbuttoned his pants and released himself. His long dick was as limp as a wet noodle. Layani wanted to laugh, but she didn't want to piss him off.

"Look, Tiger, I ain't with this, okay? Just let me go." Layani was scared.

With one hand on his dick, Tiger wrapped the other around Layani's neck. He pushed her further into the bathroom and pinned her up against the wall. He weighed twice as much as she did. Though she tried to fight, Layani felt helpless. She wanted to scream but couldn't. Her oxygen supply was low. Tiger released his dick and began pulling at Layani's clothing with one of his hands still around her neck.

"Calm down. This will be over in a minute." With force, he lifted her dress and pulled at her panties so hard they ripped. As he tried to hold her leg up, she used everything she had to lift the other leg and kick the bastard in the balls. He released Layani's throat and dropped to the ground. She took her opportunity to run like a bat out of hell.

Tiger grabbed her foot, which caused Layani to hit the wall and fall. However, she wasn't down for long as she ran for the door like her life depended on it. Tiger didn't need any hallway video cameras catching him chasing her into the hallway with his pants down, nor did he need the bad press, so he decided to just let her go and hope like hell she didn't go to the police.

Chapter Twenty-two

Frantically, Layani ran down the hallway toward the elevator like an actress in someone's scary movie

"Come on. Come on." She pressed the elevator button over and over. Within a minute it arrived, and she hopped on. Only then did she exhale a sigh of relief. She didn't have on shoes, her outfit was torn, her panties were gone, and her hair was all over the place. Her makeup ran as she cried hysterically. She'd heard of the violence taking place every second in New York, but never did she think she would be one of the statistics.

"Are you okay?" A man's voice startled Layani, and she backed herself into the corner. The tears had her eyes blurry. She blinked rapidly to clear them.

"Layani, is that you?"

Layani couldn't catch the voice. With shaky hands, she wiped her face and got a clear vision of the other person on the elevator. "Dernard?"

"What in the hell happened to you?" He was completely disturbed by the sight before him.

"Someone just tried to rape me," she cried.

"What? Who?" Dernard reached into his pocket for his phone to call police.

"No, please don't call."

"Why not?" Dernard scratched his head.

"He's a ball player. I don't need a scandal like this coming out before my album. No matter how good I sound, I'll always be seen as a victim or the villain for getting him in trouble." Although Layani was obviously shaken, she was closed in her right mind. Dernard knew she had a point; therefore, he obliged her request.

"Ball player or not, this dude needs to pay for violating you." Pressing the button to the floor Layani had just come from, Dernard was steaming mad.

"He didn't rape me. He just tried to, but I'm okay now." Layani looked at Dernard and tried to smile. "Please don't go back up there. Can you just give me a ride home?"

"Sure, if that's what you want, but I'd like to show this nigga a thing or two."

"I'm sure." Layani nodded just as the elevator doors opened up to the lobby.

"My car is over there." Dernard removed his suit jacket and wrapped it around Layani to cover up the torn dress. When he realized her shoes were missing, he picked her up and carried her outside. Since Dernard had already called downstairs for his car, the valet had it waiting at the door. After putting Layani into her seat, he handed the man in the red coat a Benjamin and told him to keep his mouth closed before getting into the car and speeding away.

"Thank you for the ride." Layani wiped her face.

"No need to thank me. But are you sure you don't want to make a report? The station is about three miles from here." Dernard watched as the girl shook her head. "Can I ask how you even ended up here? The hotel is a long way from your apartment."

After getting her nerves together, Layani went on to explain the course of her day and how she ended up in the bathroom with Tiger. Dernard felt enraged and bad for his artist. She didn't deserve to be treated that way, and he hoped the unfortunate event wouldn't damage her permanently.

"Are you sure you're going to be okay? Do you think you might need to talk with someone like a therapist?" he asked cautiously.

"Yeah, I'm okay. I'm just glad you were in the right place at the right time," she admitted, having no idea that her boss was only at the hotel because he had just finished banging the back off one of his booty calls. "I'm from Detroit, where crazy shit happens daily, but New York is something different. I just feel so alone here."

"You're not alone. We're a team at Black Millionaires Records." Dernard patted the hand that was resting in her lap. There was a brief moment of silence before either of them spoke.

"I really appreciate the opportunity to fulfill my dreams, Dernard, but I think it's time for me to go home." Layani stared out of the window as they drove. In an instant, she'd made the decision to call it quits.

"I can't stop you from going, Layani, and I wouldn't dare try to, but I will say if you left right now, it would be the worst mistake of your life." Dernard sighed.

"I feel like I can't trust anybody now, especially not the roommate that left me hanging." Layani admitted she was feeling a way about her selfish so-called friend.

"You can trust me." Dernard's voice was low as he gently rubbed her hand. "Why don't you stay with me tonight at my house? Give it some thought, and we'll discuss it in the morning over breakfast after a good night's sleep. I don't think you need to be alone after all that has happened."

"Um." Layani hesitated, not knowing if this was a good idea.

"I don't bite. I'm not Tiger, and besides, my lady is at home anyway." Dernard smiled reassuringly.

"Okay." Lay finally nodded. "I think I'll take you up on your offer." Layani smiled back.

Nearly thirty minutes later, Dernard pulled the Aston Martin beyond the wrought iron gates and cut the engine before they got out. His home resembled a castle, just as Layani had imagined it would.

"Don't worry about clothes. Bianca has a whole bunch of shit with the tags still on it that you can have." Dernard slid his key into the door and twisted the lock.

"Where have you been?" A tall, thin white woman stood from her seat on the spiral staircase with her arms folded. Resting at her side was a bottle of Dom Perignon. "Who the fuck is this?" Her accent was thick. Maybe she was German, Layani thought.

"Bianca, this is Layani. She is one of my singers." Dernard introduced the ladies.

"And what the fuck is she doing here at nearly five o'clock in the morning, with her dress torn and bed head?" Bianca was on ten. "Don't tell me you fucked her, Dernard! Did you fuck this young bitch?"

"Baby, someone attacked her tonight at the Travertine Hotel Towers," Dernard explained in a low tone. "I told her she could stay here tonight so she won't be in her apartment all alone. She is from Detroit, so she has no one else to call."

He silently thanked God for Layani. Her incident had just saved his ass. If Bianca really knew why he was at the Travertine Hotel Towers, it would've been a very long night.

"Oh my God. Sweetheart, are you okay?" Bianca wrapped her arms around Layani and instantly dropped her attitude.

"I'm okay now, thank you." Layani nodded.

"Let me show you to one of the guest rooms, and I'll send Esmeralda up with some tea, okay?" Bianca practically fell over herself trying to please the poor girl after having put her foot in her mouth. "I'll get you some pajamas and personal items too."

"Thank you." Layani followed behind Bianca toward a room that was bigger than the studio apartment she and Micah had just upgraded from. The sleigh bed positioned in the middle of the floor was covered with thick white Egyptian linen. The mirrored bedroom furniture was sleek and dainty, and the fireplace beneath the television was cozy.

"Do you want us to report what happened to you tonight? Dernard has friends on the police force." Bianca took a seat on the bed.

"No, I told Dernard I don't want this scandal to break before I even have a chance to release my first album."

"I understand. The same thing happened to me when I was in Paris on my first modeling assignment abroad. I was attacked by a man who worked with the agency. The next day, I reported it, thinking that I was going to show him, and well, I guess they showed me."

"What happened?" Layani's eyes widened.

"They shipped my ass back to America so fast that you would never know I ever left home."

"When you got home, did you continue to model?"

"No, I hung up my catwalk and went to design school. I loved fashion too much to quit, but I knew being a model was no longer for me."

Standing from the bed when Esmerelda came into the room with the tea on a tray, Bianca excused herself to get Layani something to sleep in. When she returned a few minutes later, Layani was asleep on the bed. She left the items on the dresser and closed the door.

Chapter Twenty-three

As comfortable as Dernard, Bianca, and their house staff had made Layani feel, she was still on edge. All night, she tossed and turned. If she hadn't left her cell phone back at the hotel, she could've called Micah and told him about what happened. Although she would've probably regretted doing so, Layani knew it would've been a relief to lay her burden down on his shoulders. She always gave her problems to her boyfriend. Micah was strong and could handle anything. However, knowing him, he would've jumped on the first plane to New York and beat the brakes off Tiger's ass. Layani didn't want him to get into any trouble, so she decided to keep it a secret. For now, she sprawled out across the luxury bed and tried to close her eyes and go back to sleep.

An hour later, she was awakened, this time with a strong urge to pee. She tried to hold it and go back to sleep, but it was impossible.

"Shit!" she cursed. Bianca had given her pajamas and showed her to the guest room but failed to mention where the bathroom was. Cutting on the nightstand lamp, Layani peered around the room to see if she spotted a bathroom door. As luck would have it, there was only a closet. With the urge becoming stronger, she hopped off the bed and decided to go out into the hallway. It was almost eight in the morning. Maybe she could spot a servant starting their shift and ask for directions.

Silently, she trudged down the cold marble hallway, half asleep. Spotting a door at the end of hallway, she knew it had to be the bathroom.

"Yes!" she mumbled and sped up the pace. As soon as she turned the doorknob and cracked opened the door, she realized she had made a grave mistake.

"Fuck me, daddy!" Bianca screamed.

"Whose pussy is this, B?"

"It's all yours, daddy."

Layani's eyes widened at the sight of Dernard giving Bianca long strokes from the back. She wanted to turn and run, but curiosity kept her planted right there in the doorway. His penis was the biggest one she had ever seen. It was not only big in width, but length as well. Bianca's walls had to be deep to take it all. When he slid his dick inside of her, the shit completely disappeared.

"You like that, don't you?" Dernard asked Bianca, but he looked over his shoulder right at Layani. She nearly pissed on herself. She was busted.

"Baby, I love it," Bianca moaned with her head buried into the cushion of the couch.

Dernard had become even more aroused now that he had an audience. Therefore, he decided to put on a show. Stopping mid-stroke, he removed himself from Bianca's vagina and jammed his dick right into her ass. The pounding was so hard that it traveled from Bianca and sent a surge of electricity straight through Layani's body. Instantly, her nipples hardened, and her pajama bottoms were soaking wet with excitement. Dernard pumped harder and harder in Bianca while staring Layani down, and then it happened.

"Shit! I'm about to blow. Turn around and get this nut. Keep your eyes closed, though," Dernard instructed, still looking back at Layani.

"Yes, baby. Anything daddy wants," Bianca said with her eyes shut tight.

Forcefully, Dernard guided Bianca's head into his crotch and exploded all over her face. Layani had seen enough. Turning on the balls of her feet, she closed the door and left the room just as quietly as she had come.

"Got damn!" Layani exhaled after she was in the safety of the guestroom. Her nipples tingled, and her womanhood was once again on fire like it had been in the bathroom at the nightclub. She was panting and sweating like she was the one who had just been served. Her body yearned to be fucked like that right now. She couldn't wait for Micah to visit, but at the moment, she needed to get off again. With her back against the door, she slid two fingers down into her pants. The urge to pee was still present, but the need to come took precedence.

"Ohhh," she moaned softly.

BOOM. BOOM. The knocking on the door caused a little urine to squirt out.

"It's Bianca, sweetheart. Please come and join us for breakfast if you're up."

"Okay, give me a second," she replied after waiting a second. "Hey, where is the bathroom?" she hollered.

"Down the hall, third door on the left," Bianca said over her shoulder as she headed to the kitchen.

An hour later, Layani had showered, gotten dressed in her dress from the night before, and was ready to go. She followed the smell of bacon coming from the large chef's kitchen, where she was greeted by Bianca and Dernard. Both of them wore satisfied looks, and Layani knew why.

"Thank you, guys, for the hospitality. Can I use a phone to call for transportation back to the apartment?"

"Aren't you going to eat something? There is plenty of food." Bianca was dressed in a long silk nightgown that was see-through. Her nipples were erect, and her vagina was basically bare, with a skinny landing strip.

"Yeah, Layani, it would be nice for you to join us." Dernard smirked, which made Layani even more embarrassed. "Besides, we need to talk about your decision to stay or leave."

"I decided to stay. I'm not going to let Tiger block my blessing. He will get his in the end."

"I'm not going to lie. I am happy you decided to stay. Please grab something to eat before you go."

"No, I'm good, thank you. I just need to call a ride and I'll be out of your hair. Thank you so much for all you both did."

"Nonsense." Dernard frowned. "After what happened last night, I'm going to drive you back to your apartment and see to it that you are safe. I've already hired you and that fast-ass roommate of yours a security team. They start on Monday and will accompany you to all of your rehearsals and whatnot."

"Thank you, but I don't think that will be necessary. From now on, I just won't be attending any parties." Layani laughed lightly.

"You're my next star. I can't let anything happen to you." Dernard took a gulp of orange juice and stood from the table. He was wearing a pair of silk pajama pants and a black T-shirt. Layani could've sworn his dick was hard, but she wasn't trying to stare. "Let me throw on some pants and I'll be right back."

"I can call a cab or Uber, really. I'll be okay," Layani said to Dernard's back as he left the women in the kitchen.

"Bianca, you have a nice home." She tried to make small talk.

"Cut the shit, bitch!" Bianca looked at her with eyes of hate.

"Excuse me?" Layani was taken aback by the sudden change of attitude.

"Little bitches like you come sniffing around my man on a daily basis. Keep your hands off and we won't have any problems," Bianca warned.

"What the fuck are you talking about? Don't nobody want your man." Layani couldn't believe how this bitch had just flipped the script.

"Telling me you're not attracted to D is like telling me you weren't watching him fuck me in the study." Bianca's eyebrow raised.

Layani's mouth dropped. *Her eyes were closed. How could she have seen me?* she wondered.

"Come on, Layani. Let's get going," Dernard called from the hallway.

"You want to know how I knew, don't you?" Bianca laughed. "I could smell your cheap-ass perfume coming from the door."

Layani wanted to say something to defend herself, but she had been cold busted. Instead, she smiled and said, "You're mistaken, Bianca. I bet what you smelled was the perfume of that bitch he was fucking at the Travertine Hotel Towers last night." With that bomb dropped, she walked out of the kitchen, leaving Bianca red in the face. Low key, Layani felt bad because she had no idea what Dernard was really doing at the hotel and she knew

Bianca was going to let him have it when he got home, but she refused to be punked out.

The ride back to Manhattan was quiet, until Dernard broke the silence. "Layani, I just want to thank you for making the decision to stay here in New York to work on your career. It shows just how strong you are. Many women would have made a different choice."

"I've come too far to quit on account of some no-good ball player. Detroit girls are built Ford tough, in case you didn't know."

"That's my girl." He smiled. "You and I will make a lot of money together."

"Is that right?" Layani snickered.

"Hell yeah! You've got the voice, and I got the know-how. Together, we're unstoppable."

"You sound like Micah, my boyfriend." Layani didn't miss the sour look on Dernard's face.

"Look, baby, I'm going to keep it one hundred with you. You need to dump that nigga and get with a real one." There was no shame in his game, especially after he busted her looking at his dick. Dernard was ready to be all over Layani if she let him.

"Micah is a real one." Layani smacked her lips.

"Real recognize real, and that nigga ain't what you think he is." Dernard shook his head. "A real nigga would've never left you here alone in the jungle. You know why?" He looked over as she bit her lip.

"Why?" she asked.

"Because it's real niggas in the jungle like me, ready and willing to tear that ass up." His words were strong and direct. Layani was turned on but remained silent. "Let this seven-figure nigga show you what life in the fast lane is all about, ma." He dropped his hand into her lap and slowly slid it upward. "All you have to do is say yes."

Just before Dernard could scratch the surface of that kitty cat, Layani said no. Raising his arms in surrender, he retreated his hands to his side of the car. He didn't need a sexual assault charge today, so he backed off. Besides, he knew she was curious about what he had to offer, and eventually curiosity would get the best of her. It always did with women like her.

Chapter Twenty-four

The weekend had been crazy as hell, but thank goodness it was back to business. The following day proved to be another long one with workouts, two studio sessions, and a dance lesson. Layani was beat but thankful for the distraction. Her body rocked with pain, she had a headache, and she was starving. She still hadn't seen Mack but knew the girl was all right because Layani's purse and cell phone were sitting on the coffee table with a note written on an envelope.

> *Layani,*
> *I don't know why you left, girl. I was having a fucking ball. Anthony wants me to chill with him this week before he leaves to go out of town. Tiger told me you left your phone and shit. I guess you was in a hurry. He must like you because he gave me a few bands and told me to give it to you. Enjoy.*
> *xoxo*

Layani opened the envelope and saw a large rubber-banded wad of cash. She didn't even have the urge to count it. "Fuck Tiger and his hush money," she said aloud.

Just as she flopped down on the sofa and grabbed the phone to call Micah, a knock came at the door. Layani stood with a groan and went to check the peephole. Standing there was Dernard, looking as debonair as ever in a black Gucci shirt, white shorts, and black Gucci loafers. She stalled for a minute before letting him in.

"Nice place." He looked around as if he were just seeing it for the first time. Truth was, he had been there at least ten times before Layani took ownership. The last occupant was a seventeen-year-old by the name of Niyah. She was a singer from Washington, D.C. Her vocals were crazy, and her looks were bananas. Although the girl was young, Dernard couldn't keep his hands off of her. He put in work every chance she gave him, and she ended up pregnant as a result. Dernard begged her for an abortion, but Niyah wasn't hearing of it. She packed her bags and moved back home. The little boy would be here sometime soon, but his father couldn't care less. He'd already signed over his paternal rights, as well as a check for one million dollars. Niyah was hit with a gag order, and both parties were satisfied.

"Care for a water or something?" Layani casually brushed the loose strands of hair falling from her ponytail. She was nervous but tried to calm herself.

"Nah, I won't be staying long." Dernard took a seat.

"What brings you by?" Layani's heartbeat sped up in anticipation of what the reason behind the visit was.

"I sent you something and wanted to see your expression when it got here." Dernard crossed his legs and sat back.

Layani was puzzled, but then there was a knock at the door. Once again, she moseyed over to the peephole. This time, it was a deliveryman. She looked back at Dernard before unlocking the door.

"Are you Ms. Bell?"

"Yes, I am." Layani nodded.

The man extended a clipboard her way, and she signed. Then he wheeled the dolly into her living room and left several large boxes in the middle of the floor.

"What's all of this?" Layani asked aloud with excitement.

"There's more," the deliveryman replied before leaving to retrieve the other boxes.

"Don't open it until they all arrive." Dernard smirked.

Layani was eager yet nervous to see what was in all the boxes. Finally, after two trips, the last delivery was made.

"Go ahead, you can open them now." Dernard pulled a cigar from his pocket and lit it.

Cautiously, Layani used the tip of her nail to cut through the tape. Her eyes lit up with glee when she saw several tan shoe boxes with *Louboutin* written on the top.

"Oh my God!" she squealed before opening the next box filled with Alexander McQueen. Layani had died and gone to heaven. Every box contained designer shoes, handbags, and custom clothing pieces. Her favorite was a dress made of black crystals from Roberto Cavalli. The spaghetti-strap dress was ankle length with a train. The V cut in the front stopped just beneath her belly button.

"I want you to wear that when you receive your first Grammy nomination. I had it flown in especially for your big day." Dernard blew out smoke rings.

"I don't know what to say." Layani wiped a tear from her eye. She hated to cry in front of her boss, but this was truly overwhelming. Never in her whole life did she think having these types of things were in the cards for her. She thought the world had counted her out, yet here she stood, surrounded by things most people could only dream of having. Though she had spent a good amount of her advance money shopping for name brands, all of this stuff was real designer! Never in life did she imagine having a Roberto Cavalli gown flown in just for her, yet here she was.

"I don't deserve this. Not yet anyway. Let me work for it."

"Why don't you think you're worthy?" Dernard frowned. "Look at you." He stood from the sofa and walked behind her. "You're beautiful." He pushed her chin to face the wall mirror. "You deserve all of this and much more." His voice dropped an octave.

"Dernard, I come from nothing. I'm just an orphan from Detroit who's had to work for everything I have. I'm not used to people buying me things like this," Layani admitted. She wanted to take back her words because it sounded like she was dissing Micah, but she wasn't. Truth was, they had struggled together. Most of the time, he was the one who sacrificed and went without so she could have what she needed. Unfortunately, he always missed the mark with what she wanted.

"Maybe you just didn't have the right people in your life." Dernard leaned in and kissed Layani's neck. It was a daring move, but Dernard was known for throwing caution to the wind.

At first, Layani didn't move. She was completely caught off guard. She wasn't sure if she liked what he was doing. Again, Dernard kissed her neck and made small circles with his tongue. Layani's nipples hardened and vagina reacted just as it would've for Micah.

"I want to show you what life is like on the other side of the poverty line," Dernard whispered. "Let me do that."

"I got a man, though." Layani closed her eyes and tried hard to concentrate on Micah.

"What does your man have to me with me, ma? I got a woman." Dernard held the cigar with one hand and used the other to caress Layani's perky breasts. "I won't tell if you don't."

"I can't." She shook her head.

"You can't, or you won't?" Dernard raised a brow.

"Neither," Layani responded.

"Suit yourself." Dernard adjusted the collar on his shirt. "Females kill me. Y'all always talking about there not being any good men left, yet here I stand, and you're just going to let me walk out the door."

"I already got a 'good' man." Layani made air quotes with her fingers.

"Your dude is all right, but he could definitely be better." Dernard shook his head.

"What makes you an expert?" Layani folded her arms.

"If you were my lady, your life would be nothing but champagne wishes and caviar dreams. Yeah, the money your man negotiated for you was nice, but it was my bank account that covered it. My shit got so many zeros a nigga done lost count."

"Money ain't everything." Layani looked down at the floor.

"Think about what I can do for your career then. I can turn you into an overnight celebrity. Don't you realize that fucking with the boss is priceless?" Dernard turned and headed for the door. "Fuck with me, and I will see to it that you get the most studio time, the best tracks, and the best producers. Fuck with me, and I will make you a platinum-selling artist. With me, you will break barriers and solidify your name in the industry for decades."

"I'm sorry, I can't." Ashamed, Layani put her head down.

"Suit yourself, but just know the same way I give things, I can damn sure take them away. Have you ever wondered why you have a stylist, a trainer, and have recorded more shit than Mack?" Dernard didn't get too far past the door before Layani pulled his arm.

"I'm sorry. I didn't mean to make you mad."

"I'm not mad. I just don't like to waste time or money." Dernard used the statement as an opportunity to flex the platinum Rolex President on his wrist. "Layani, you're a good girl, and I can respect that, but in this game, being good only gets you so far. What you won't do, I know thousands who will do, just to be in my presence, let alone get a record deal."

"Okay, let's go into my bedroom so my roommate won't catch us," Layani replied with lust dripping from her tongue. It was something in his walk and the way he talked that had her open. Maybe it was the fact that she craved the sexual session that she had just watched him give Bianca, or maybe it was his platinum persuasion. Either way, Layani was ready to cross the point of no return.

Without another word, she led her boss toward the back of the apartment. She wanted to thank him for his generosity as well as satisfy the need she'd had since the club bathroom the night before.

Layani promised herself she would only let him dip in her lady pond just once. However, just like the women before her and the one before that one, Dernard had his way with Layani, and soon, she was begging for the dick!

Chapter Twenty-five

Days turned into weeks, and weeks into months. Before Layani could stop herself, she and Dernard were embroiled in a full-blown love affair by the end of the year. He used her for sex, and she used him for star status. In her eyes, fair exchange was no robbery. As promised, he expedited her career by giving her the best producers and songwriters on his squad. Her first single was already on the radio, and she had begun to book big shows in major cities. Everything was happening so fast that Layani could hardly keep up. People were beginning to know her name, and she was elated.

With back-to-back gigs and two-a-day rehearsals, this was the first free weekend Layani had had in a very long time. She was happy about it and sad at the same time. Micah was coming that day for his first visit, and Layani had been dreading the moment. In fact, for months she'd been pushing her visit with him back with stories about being booked and busy, until he finally put his foot down and said enough was enough.

Micah could tell something was off, but he couldn't quite place where the disconnect had come from. Unbeknownst to him, her feelings for him had definitely changed, and she hated herself for doing him wrong.

Although she was able to keep up the façade over the phone, she knew it would be nearly impossible to front in person. Micah knew her almost too well, inside and out. Silently, she wondered if Micah would be able to tell that another man had been inside her pussy. After Micah had booked his plane ticket two weeks ago, she told Dernard they had to chill so that her vagina could potentially shrink, but he wasn't having it. Despite her protest, he had fucked her every which way but loose every day since then, including that morning at the studio.

As nervous thoughts raced through Layani's head, the phone in her hand buzzed. She looked down to see Dernard's name on the caller ID, and her heart jumped. Quickly, she checked her surroundings before answering the phone.

"Hello."

"Your voice always manages to get my dick hard." Dernard caressed his manhood through the tan Armani slacks he was sporting.

"Is that so?" Layani smiled, completely forgetting about her nervousness.

"What are you doing right now?"

"I'm standing in front of the building, waiting for my boyfriend to pull up." Layani wanted him to know that she was expecting company so he wouldn't call or send any perverted messages for the next few days. The last thing she needed was a dick pic coming through in the presence of Micah.

"Baby girl, don't you know you're too old for a boy-friend?" Dernard looked down at the Italian loafers on his feet and then at the diamond-encrusted watch on his wrist. He didn't know much about Layani's *boy*friend, but he knew the nigga was definitely not on his level.

"Anyway, how long is this nigga staying?"

"He'll be here for the weekend," Layani replied with her head down. She was unaware of the yellow cab pulling up to the curb behind her.

"I guess that's not so bad. Are you lovebirds doing anything special?" Dernard pretended to be interested.

"Um." Layani paused. "I was going to take him to dinner at OPEY's tonight, and swing by the studio so he could see it. Then I'll probably take him sightseeing or something." She hadn't thought out the specifics, but she did plan to pack as much as she could in two days.

"Is he staying at a hotel?" Dernard asked.

"No. Why?"

"I just thought it would be uncomfortable to fuck your boyfriend in the apartment that my money is paying for. Not to mention fucking him on the bed we've already christened." Dernard was arrogant to say the least, but it was one of the things Layani liked about him. "I bet he won't make that pussy come like me."

"Dernard!" Layani gushed. Her insides were tingling, and her panties were getting moist. Just the thought of what he was saying had her about to erupt.

"Hey, baby." Micah wrapped his arms around Layani from the back, and she damn near had a heart attack.

"I've got to go. Bye!" She hung up on Dernard without another word and prayed like hell he didn't call her back. "Hey, you." She grabbed her chest. "You scared the shit out of me, boy."

"My bad, bae. Who was that?" Micah asked after kissing Layani on the lips.

"Nobody, just one of the producers," Layani lied.

"Damn, you've only been away for a year and you already acting like a diva, hanging up on people and shit," Micah teased.

"Shut up! Come on, let me show you around." Layani waved the doorman over to grab Micah's bag, and then they headed up to her apartment.

On the way up, Layani felt nothing but judgment coming from the doorman, who knew what was going on between her and Dernard. However, Layani couldn't care less as long as he kept quiet.

"Bae, this is some fancy shit." Micah broke the silence in the elevator.

"You haven't seen anything yet." As the elevator arrived on her floor, Layani pretended to be excited as she pulled Micah down the hall toward her place. Once she unlocked the door, Layani stepped aside and let him enter.

"Woo-wee!" Micah exclaimed. Without an invitation, he immediately walked around and began to check the place out. When he pictured Layani living in the Big Apple, he thought she would be staying in a tiny-ass box smaller than their studio apartment, but this was far from that. Truthfully, the plush dwelling put his mind at ease. He didn't want his most prized possession living in the ghetto, because she could've stayed home in the D for that.

"D-Money got you living good, and I wonder why."

"What? Why would you say that?" Layani snapped. Her guilt was weighing heavy on her heart. She needed to get her shit together.

"He knows he got a rock star on his hand, that's why." Micah went on with the conversation, totally oblivious to what Layani had just said. "This is just the beginning, baby. Plush apartments today, mansions tomorrow."

"Yup. This is just the beginning." Layani smiled, and Micah swooped her up into his arms. Immediately, her body got tense. "What's wrong?" He released the embrace.

"Nothing, baby. I'm just so happy to see you." She pressed her lips to his. "I really have been missing you."

"I missed you more." Micah planted three soft kisses on Layani's mouth, then her neck, and last her breasts. "Bae, I say we make the most out of our weekend and just stay here and make love from now until Sunday." Micah was practically unbuttoning his pants when Mack walked into the apartment.

"Don't let me interrupt." Holding up her finger as if she were in church, she tried to slide by. However, Layani used her entrance as a welcomed distraction.

"Mack, this is Micah. Micah, meet Mack."

"What up, doe." Micah extended his hand, but Mack took a hug.

"Come on, playboy. You know we are better than that. I feel like I've known you for years the way this bitch talks about you."

"Same here. It's nice to finally meet you in the flesh."

"What took your ass so long to come visit?" Mack wanted to know.

"I'm grinding, she's grinding. Our schedules conflicted for a little minute, but I'm here now, ya feel me?"

"I feel ya," Mack mimicked.

"So, how have things been going for you here in New York?"

"Shit, truthfully right now, I'm just making my own moves. The label got me on ice, but just like in B-more, I'll always find a way to skate." Mack didn't hide the fact that she was salty.

"Layani let me hear some of your stuff," he said, "and you sound good. I don't know why they ain't pushing the gas on you." Micah had had an ear for talent his whole life. From the first time he heard Mack rap, he knew she had the juice.

"It's all good. I know this is just a steppingstone. I will be where I need to be soon."

"Have you talked to Dernard about your career? Sometimes you have to make a little noise, Mack."

"Well, the CEO has been a little preoccupied lately, but you're right. I'll definitely holla at him soon." Cutting her eyes at Layani, she gave Micah a pound. "Look, I'm not going to hold you lovebirds. I just need to grab a few things, and then I'll be leaving you two alone for some privacy, but I'll be back on Sunday, Lay."

"Where are you going?" Layani wasn't looking forward to being alone with Micah for the next two days.

"Girl." She popped her lips. "Anthony is taking me home to meet his mother and his brothers." Mack started doing her version of the Milly Rock. "Bitch, I'm in there." Raising her hand high, she waited on Layani to slap her a five.

"Well, have fun and be safe." Layani pretended to pout. "I'll miss you."

"Ditto."

Chapter Twenty-six

As promised, Mack grabbed her things and left the apartment within thirty minutes. The minute the door closed, Micah removed his shirt and fumbled with the belt holding up his shorts.

"Bae, a nigga been fiending." With his dick about to burst from his shorts, Micah began kissing Layani's neck. She let him get a few kisses in before stopping him.

"Baby, let's wait until tonight so we can do it the right way. I don't want no wham, bam, thank you, ma'am."

"Do you know how long it's been? Even if we wait until tonight, it's still gonna be quick. Shit! You may as well let me get this first nut off now, and then tonight, we can put in some time." Again, he began kissing her body. "I'm talking foreplay, sixty-nines, the whole shebang, bae."

Reaching beneath Layani's dress, he removed her lace panties. After licking his finger, he began to rub her clit until her womanhood produced its own juices. In one motion, Micah bent Layani over the back of the sofa and slid his penis inside.

"Oh," she moaned, partially because it felt good, but mainly to keep up the façade of someone who hadn't been sexed by her man in forever. "Damn, daddy, your shit is so hard." She panted, but Micah said nothing as he stroked.

Instantly, her heart hit her feet as she wondered what thoughts were going on inside of his head.

"Baby, I'm about to come," she lied and screamed while making her vagina pulsate.

On cue, Micah climaxed with her. However, instead of coming inside of her, he pulled his dick out just in time to come on her butt.

"Is everything okay? Why are you so quiet?" she asked.

"I was just enjoying the moment, that's all." He winked and headed to the bathroom to clean up.

That night, over a lobster, crab, and crawfish pasta dinner at OPEY's the couple caught up on the happenings in each other's lives. Micah told her that he had been working hard on beats in his studio for a new artist who'd just come home from prison. Micah said the boy was about to blow up, and his debut album was featuring one of Micah's beats. He'd also produced a few songs for some local Detroit artists who were creating a new web series. However, he admitted that he was saving the best ones for Layani's album and couldn't wait for her to hear them.

Layani didn't have the heart to tell him that her label wasn't trying to hear any of his shit, so she slid right past that part. Instead, she told him about the crazy things she'd encountered during her stay in New York, of course without going into too much detail. She still had never mentioned the night Tiger tried to attack her and vowed that she never would.

Things were going great, until trouble showed up at their table wearing a custom Tom Ford ensemble and Prada loafers.

"Layani, imagine meeting you here." Dernard smiled wickedly. The tall, pencil-thin woman on his arm smiled to. She was no one special, just some arm candy for the night, but it still made Layani feel a way. She knew her lover was trying to get under her skin, and it was working like a charm.

"Dernard, what a surprise." Layani tried not to show her irritation. She could've kicked herself for even telling him where she and Micah were having dinner that night.

"What up, Dernard. I'm Micah." Micah stood to shake the man's hand. "I just wanted to thank you again for giving Layani this opportunity, and I appreciate you taking care of my lady in my absence." Though truthfully Micah could take Dernard or leave him, he recognized the power the mogul had. As an up-and-coming producer yearning to break into the music business, he always wanted to stay humble and professional.

"Brother, the pleasure has been all mines, believe that. Your girl is definitely a star!" Dernard spoke with sarcasm dripping from his lips. "Do you mind if I borrow her for just a second? I have some colleagues I would like her to meet. She'll be back before the butter on the crab gets cold."

"Handle your business, man." Micah sat down and proceeded on with his meal.

"Oh, I plan to." Dernard winked. "Enjoy your evening, Micah. Layani, we're in the back room."

Layani wanted to stay planted in her seat, but she didn't want to make things appear awkward, so she stood. "Baby, I'm sorry. I'll be right back." She excused herself from the table with a smile and followed behind the couple. Dernard and his arm candy headed to the back of the restaurant into a private dining area with frosted glass doors for privacy. Inside of the small room, there were several tables set with glasses, silverware, and plates, yet all of the chairs were empty.

"Where are these people I need to meet?"

"Have a seat," Dernard instructed with attitude. Without a fuss, Layani went to sit down in the chair, and he cleared his throat and pointed to the top of the table. "Sit up there."

Although Layani was confused, she did as requested after moving the dishes out of the way. Dernard grabbed a chair and positioned it right between her legs before taking a seat.

"Now open up."

"You want me to open my legs in here, like this, with her?" Layani looked from Dernard to his female escort. Though her and Dernard's sexual escapades had been known to get a little wild, they had never done anything with a third party.

"Don't mind her. Just do what I said." Dernard could barely keep his saliva contained in his mouth. Just the anticipation of what he was about to feast on had him hungry for her.

Knowing where this was about to go, Layani eyed Dernard seductively while lying back and parting her thighs like the red sea. He admired her light blue laced panties only briefly before diving in and pulling them down to expose her pink lady part. That beautiful sight was all it took before her magnetic force pulled him into her wet spot like a moth to a flame.

As Dernard sucked and licked, Layani shivered and moaned. Briefly, she closed her eyes. When she opened them again, she looked over to see Dernard's date sliding her hands around her own nipples, as she was getting aroused.

"Come over here and handle this." Dernard undid his pants and pulled the thick tool from beneath his CK boxers. On cue, his date placed her clutch down on the table, dropped to her knees, and began sucking his dick as if she were trying to figure out how many licks it took to get to center of a Tootsie Pop.

Layani was outraged and turned on all at once. She wanted to be mad at Dernard for putting her in this situation, but honestly, she liked it. Therefore, she allowed her mind to relax and let ecstasy take her away. Several minutes later, she came all over the table linen as Dernard came all over his date. Embarrassment made her want to hide her face in shame at what had just happened, but excitement made her want to do it again.

"Now go enjoy the rest of your night." Dernard used the table napkin to wipe his mouth.

Without a word, Layani slid off the table, adjusted her dress and panties, then headed back to her man.

Chapter Twenty-seven

The remainder of the weekend had gone extremely smoothly, despite Dernard and all his antics. After his pop-up at OPEY's, he tried to call Layani a few times, but she had temporarily blocked his number from coming through. Layani was so afraid Dernard was going to come by the apartment unannounced that she kept Micah out both Friday and Saturday all day. They took in some sights and even hit a few nightclubs. They also made love a few more times before the visit was over, and for a split second, things were back to normal. Though Layani craved the bad boy she'd come to like, she missed the comfort and safeness of the man she'd always loved. In fact, she was now sad to see him go.

"Just one more day," she begged with tears in her eyes.

"Bae, you are back to work in the morning, remember? You won't have time for me even if I stayed." Micah kissed her pouting lips and headed to the bedroom to get his belongings. He loved visiting with Layani, but truthfully, the visit made him eager to get back home. Being at the studio, meeting other producers, and hearing their work made Micah more motivated than ever. He knew he was already better than everyone Layani had introduced him to, but now he just had to grind and get his name out there. Micah knew he could do for himself what he'd done for Layani if he just stayed the course. His turn was coming. He could feel it.

"Come on, babe, your car is downstairs," Layani called out after getting the notification on her phone. She and Mack were sitting in the living room. Mack was on the phone with Anthony, discussing what they wanted to wear to an upcoming fashion show. They did corny shit like wearing matching clothes all the time. In fact, the gossip magazines had the couple in the "Bae Watch" category every week. Mack was gaining more celebrity for being Anthony's main thing than being a Black Millionaires artist.

"Lay, what the fuck is this?" Micah flew from the back of the apartment to the front. He was mugging the shit out of Layani. "Who the fuck do these belong to?" Holding up a pair of red boxers, Micah paced the floor. "You been up here fucking somebody else?"

Layani had seen this look before and knew that he was two seconds from losing it.

"Oops, my bad. I am so sorry." Mack dropped her cell phone, sprang from the couch, and snatched the underwear from Micah. "Me and Anthony got a little frisky last week while you were gone to rehearsal, girl. We may have ended up in your room on accident."

"Layani, don't fucking play with me. Are you fucking another nigga?" Micah had fire in his veins.

"Micah, bro, this is on me. My bad," Mack repeated.

"Bitch, you been fucking in my bed? Do y'all nasty asses do this every time I leave the fucking house?" Layani turned her attention toward Mack. She had to pretend to be just as pissed off as Micah. Otherwise, he was definitely not going to believe the lie.

"I'm so sorry, Lay. It was only once, and I swear it won't happen again." Mack looked remorseful as she took her cell phone and Dernard's boxers back into her room.

"Baby, I'm sorry about that." Layani walked up to Micah and hugged him. "That bitch is trippin'."

"Yeah, she definitely trippin', but all right, bae, let me get up out of here." Micah's temper had retreated. "You keep knocking 'em dead out here, and I'll be back soon." After pulling Layani in for a passionate kiss, he chucked her the deuces, grabbed his stuff, and left.

Once the coast was clear and Layani was sure Micah was on the elevator, she ran to her room and gave her girl the biggest hug.

"I owe you a bag."

"Bitch, you better just be glad my ass was here to lie for you, or you would've been in trouble . . . trouble." Mack mimicked the voice of Bernie Mack.

"Hell yeah, ain't no doubt about it. That nigga tried to play me." She couldn't believe that Dernard had pulled a female move on her. She always heard of bitches leaving underwear behind, not niggas.

"Girl, you need to cut Dernard scheming ass loose." Mack shook her head. Since her time in New York, she'd developed a bitter taste for him. Though she couldn't pin-point it, something about him seemed grimy.

"I can't leave him alone, girl. I'm hooked, Lay admitted.

"That nigga ain't nothing but trouble." Mack knew she had told Layani to secure her future, but who knew she would end up with the CEO of their label? Dernard was a womanizer, and everyone knew it. Layani was playing a dangerous game by shitting where she ate. If she wasn't careful, her house of cards would come tumbling down at any moment.

"You just don't like Dernard, do you?" Layani knew he could be an asshole sometimes, but he never acted that way toward her.

"Of course I like him, and I always will as long as he signs my checks. I just don't like him for you." Mack didn't want to see her friend end up hurt behind catching feelings for this fool.

"Dernard is no good, but leave it to you and I would've ended up with Tiger's rapist ass." That night back at the Travertine Hotel Suites was now a distant memory, so Layani was able to laugh it off.

"Leave it to me and you would end up with Micah. I love him, and he loves the hell out of your ass." From the times they'd talked on the phone and even the little bit she witnessed over the weekend, Mack knew Micah's heart was pure and his love was genuine.

"It's too late for lectures now. I'm already knee deep in this pile of shit." Layani knew Mack was speaking the truth, but when you're doing wrong, you never want to hear what's right.

For the remainder of the evening, the women continued to talk about life, love, and relationships until the wee hours of the morning. It was a conversation that Layani would cherish forever because it was one of the last real talks they would have.

Life eventually got in the way, and within a year, their friendship was put on pause. While Layani's music career took off like a rocket, with single after single going number one, Mack's never got off the ground. With Dernard putting all of his money and resources into Layani's freshman and sophomore albums, there was nothing left over for Mack. Eventually. she got tired of waiting for her moment and moved out of the apartment without a word to anyone. Layani came home one weekend after a press tour to find every trace of Mack gone, except for the pictures of themselves they'd framed a while ago.

Luckily, her relationship with Anthony was still on the up and up. Therefore, she was able to move in with him, and eventually they sent for her son to join them from Baltimore.

Sometime later, Layani was surprised to learned about Anthony popping the big question to her friend on The Shade Room. The news came almost two weeks after it happened at a private event with family and friends. Layani was hurt to say the least about not receiving an invite, but she was happy to see that Mack had said yes and was graciously transitioning from her role as a hardcore rapper to a doting basketball wife.

About eleven months after the engagement, she and Anthony welcomed a daughter named Mackenzie. Layani was elated for her happiness, but deep down inside, she felt so alone and somewhat abandoned by her one and only true friend. Now that Layani was famous, she had plenty of clingers and yes-men, but Mack was like a sister. She always kept it one hundred, even when Layani preferred her not to.

Wanting to fill the void he knew his girl was feeling, Micah offered to move to NY with the nest egg he'd saved. However, she always put off the conversation. She said she would be too busy to spend time with him, and he couldn't afford to quit work to go on the road with her. Therefore, they settled for visits every other month until even that became too few and far between.

Her world was lonely, but at least she had her music.

"Layani, girl, wake up. We have sound check after this, and then a meet and greet at five o'clock." Reah, the new road manager, informed Layani of their schedule as they pulled up to Power 106, a local radio station. She was headlining a show that night in Los Angeles at the Dolby Theatre.

"I'm tired. I just need to go to sleep." Lay yawned. They'd just flown in on the red eye from Wisconsin, where she'd performed late last night.

"Girl, you can sleep when you're dead." Reah pulled a Newport cigarette from behind her ear. She was a notorious chain smoker with a very raspy voice. "You're in the thick of things now. It's do or die, so come on, sweet pea, let's roll." The small woman snapped her fingers. Though she stood 4 feet 11 inches and weighed merely 123 pounds, she was a force to be reckoned with who didn't take shit from nobody, not even Layani.

"Can't we tell them I got sick or something?" Again, Layani yawned, barely able to keep her eyes open. After Layani's freshman album, *No Turning Back*, hit platinum on the Billboard charts a few months ago, Dernard had quickly thrown her on tour to capitalize on the momentum. In the past ten days, she had already done fourteen shows. Some of the major cities had even hosted two shows a night. Layani was happy with the direction that her career was heading, yet she wasn't prepared for everything that came along with being an overnight celebrity.

"Girl, being sick ain't nowhere on the itinerary, so suck it up, buttercup, and let's go." Rhea shook the tablet with the schedule in Layani's face.

"I'm really sleepy, Reah, I'm not even joking. So, tell me, do you see a fuckin' nap on the itinerary?" Layani was cranky. Her eyes were red, and bags hung beneath them.

"A nap? What's that? Welcome to tour life." Again, Reah laughed. Layani did not. "Come on and let's do this." Reah patted her client's knee while opening the door and stepping from the limo to light her cigarette.

After one more yawn, Layani slipped on a pair of oversized gold Cazal sunglasses to match her tan YSL pantsuit and then followed behind her road manager toward the large building.

Once inside the radio station, Layani couldn't help but smile. A group of dedicated fans lined the lobby with T-shirts, magazines, and posters.

"Ms. Bell, I love you!" someone screamed.

"I love you more." She blew kisses at various people, and the lobby erupted into screams. "Would you like me to sign this for you?" she asked a little girl holding a promotional picture she had taken for *Elle* magazine a few months ago. After the little girl nodded, Layani pulled out a tube of red lipstick and began putting it on. During the course of her superstardom, the fans had coined her "the lips" for the way her mouth was perfectly plumped and pouty. Therefore, instead of signing autographs with a pen, she simply pressed her lips on their merchandise, leaving behind a perfect kiss.

For twenty minutes, she met with dozens of fans and kissed over one hundred items before security whisked her away. Big Boy was ready in the studio to interview her.

"Here are your headphones. Just speak into that microphone when the light comes on," an assistant instructed and then counted down from five.

"Yo, yo, yo. It's your boy Big Boy coming to you live from Power 106. Guess who's kicking in my neighborhood today?" Big pointed at Layani to speak.

"What's up, L.A.? It's your girl, Layani Bell, just chilling in the cut with my favorite man on the West Coast, Big Boy." Layani smiled as if the radio listeners could see her.

"Speaking of your favorite man, I'm going to jump right in and ask you about the rumors that's been swirling about what's going on between you and D-Money. Are y'all an item?" Big Boy looked over to see her reaction.

"Boy, stop! Dernard is my boss. Where do people get their stories from?" Layani laughed it off the same way she did every time someone asked her questions about Dernard.

"Well, I ain't one to gossip, but there were a few risqué photos taken of you two last weekend at the VMA's. I mean, the split on your dress was mighty high, and where his hand rested on your back was mighty low." Big Boy chuckled.

"Honestly, we posed for a picture and it was blown way out of proportion. That's it, and that's all."

"Well, it's not every day that the CEO of a label shows up on the red carpet with his artist." Big Boy raised his hands in surrender. "I'm just saying I have never seen Weezy and Nicki take a picture like that," he pressed.

"No, you probably haven't seen them take a picture like that, but we've all seen videos of her giving him lap dances on stage." Layani smirked. She knew her rebuttal was bulletproof.

"Point taken, Ms. Bell." Big Boy backed up and moved on to the next set of questions, which were about her music, her childhood in Detroit, and some of the people she admired in the music industry.

**

After an hour of talking about the album, giving away free tickets, and speaking with callers, Layani was finally back in the car, headed to another meet and greet. "Reah, I'm tired. I can't do it," Layani whispered so the driver didn't overhear. "You know what I need."

"Hell no. Dernard would kill me if he ever found out." Reah shook her head. "I told you last time was the last time, Lay."

"Reah, I need it, and you know I do. Please don't make me beg." Layani removed her shades so Reah could see how bad she looked without her fix of speed, the potent amphetamine used to keep Layani alert and on her toes.

A few months ago, the middle-aged woman had introduced the drug to Layani as an attempt to help her keep up with such a demanding lifestyle. Layani was hesitant at first, thinking back to the advice she had been given at the start of her career; however, after back-to-back shows, countless hours in the studio and multiple daily interviews, Layani was desperate. It was supposed to be a one-time thing, but as with any drug, it had eventually become a habit, although Layani failed to see it as such.

"Come on, Reah. I will crash and burn tonight if I don't get it, and you know this."

"No." Reah stood firm on her decision.

"Didn't you say your grandson wanted that new iPhone for his birthday?" Reaching into her bag, Layani pulled out five hundred dollars. "This won't cover the whole phone, but this will at least cover most of it."

"Fine!" Snatching the money from Layani, Reah went into her pocket and slapped a little baggie into Layani's hand. "This is it! Next time, I won't be bought."

"Thank you! Thank you!" Layani was relieved to see her medicine.

As soon as the driver pulled up to the curb of the hotel, Layani asked him to step out for a second. He wasn't new to this type of thing with celebrities, so he played along. Once he was out, Layani licked her pinky finger and dipped it into the speed, then she rubbed it all across her gums. Because her body was used to the potent amphetamine, she had to repeat the steps five more times to get the feeling she desired.

"Um-hm." Satisfied, Layani folded the small pack and stuffed it into her bra. Seconds later, she put the shades back on and stepped from the limo, ready to conquer the world.

Chapter Twenty-eight

For the next few hours, Layani was on ten, and she felt amazing. Not only was she able to meet the fans in a hospitality suite at the hotel, take a few interviews with local reporters, and blow sound check out of the water, but she was also able to give an Oscar-worthy performance at the Dolby Theatre that night. In fact, at the close of her last song she received a standing ovation.

With tears in her eyes, Layani took a bow and left the stage. From behind the stage, she could hear the crowd chanting her name and begging for more. She was overcome with emotion and couldn't believe this was now her life.

"Now, that's what the fuck I'm talking about!" Dernard shouted when she entered the dressing room with makeup running from her eyes. "You killed that shit, Layani!"

"Oh my God. I didn't know you were coming." As she wiped tears from her eyes, he handed her a dozen red roses.

"You did that, baby. We have to go out and celebrate tonight." At that moment, Dernard was very proud of himself for signing Layani. She was his golden egg and didn't even know it.

"I appreciate the fuss, but really, I just want to head back to the hotel, take a bath, and fuck the shit out of you, baby." They were alone in the private room, so she felt comfortable to lean in for a kiss.

Just as they pressed their lips together, her phone started ringing from the bag on the couch. The ringtone indicated the caller was Micah. Layani let it go to voice-mail.

"Let's go then." Dernard licked his lips and grabbed at the python between his legs. It was an action he knew drove Layani crazy. "You leave first. Go take your shower, and I'll slide through there when the coast is clear." Now that Layani was gaining popularity, the pa-parazzi were always lurking in the shadows, so the need to play it safe was mandatory.

"Okay. I'll see you in a few." She kissed his lips and watched him walked out of the room.

Micah called her cell phone three more times, and each time, she let the calls go to voicemail. Lately, she wasn't in the mood to even talk to him anymore.

As Layani sat admiring her flowers, there was a knock at the door. After telling the visitor to come in, she watched Reah and a tall, light-skinned man enter. She recognized his face and immediately stood from her seat.

"Bishop! What are you doing here?"

"I was in town and heard you was performing, so you know I had to come check you out." Bishop was an established rapper from Canada, known for his R&B rap style. "What are you getting into tonight? I know this dope little spot around the corner that we could slide through if you're game."

"B, the only thing I'll be getting into tonight is my bed, but I do appreciate the offer."

"I respect that, but it will be a few industry folks there. I think sliding through would be a good look for you.

You can chop it up with your peers, make a few network connections, and then leave. I promise to have you introduced to everybody I think is important within an hour, no more than an hour and a half." Bishop pressed. "My girl Nadia will be there. You haven't heard this from me, but she is secretly scouting talent for an upcoming hip hop movie about artists from the nineties. She is trying to cast all current singers and rappers to portray the singers and rappers from that era. Me and her saw you playing Aaliyah."

"All right, an hour. Let me get dressed." Layani was sold.

Quickly, she called her team in to make her face up, curl her hair into loose spirals, and style her in a black Givenchy minidress with a gold belt and gold belt chains. The outfit was complemented by a pair of black leather, thigh-high boots with gold heel tips and a gold clutch purse. After giving herself the once-over, she met Bishop in the hallway.

Keith, her bodyguard, was posted on the wall. She told him that she didn't need an escort and to go back to the hotel. Since Layani wasn't high risk for danger, Keith had been ordered by Dernard to give her space whenever she asked. Without argument, he raised his hands in surrender and told her to be safe.

Together, Bishop and Layani headed the back way out of the theatre to his waiting black Suburban. Like a gentleman, Bishop held the door open for Layani to get inside. That's when they were ambushed by a group of photographers waiting at the entrance to snap pictures.

"Bishop, is Layani Bell the flavor of the week?" someone asked, referencing the new song Bishop had released with Two Chainz.

"I'm sorry about that." Stepping inside the SUV, Bishop closed the door.

"No worries. It's all good." Layani pulled out her phone and texted Dernard to tell him that she would be late. Micah called again, and again Layani ignored the call.

"Is that your man?" Bishop had peeped the picture on the caller ID.

"Yeah, something like that. It's complicated."

"I understand. My shit is complicated too." Bishop had been in and out of a five- year relationship with Kaya Sky, a reality television star. The couple was notorious for breaking up in the most dramatic fashion and then getting back together like everything was sweet just a month later.

For the ten-minute drive to Club Bliss, Bishop and Layani kicked it like old friends. She was surprised by how down to earth he was, and he was surprised by how easy to talk to she was. Though neither of them was checking for each other, that didn't stop the paparazzi from jumping to conclusions. By the time the SUV arrived at Bliss, Layani's phone was blowing up with notifications about her secret relationship with the Canadian rapper. The gossip articles were even accompanied by the photo of them getting into the SUV mere minutes ago. Layani showed Bishop the fake news, and he told her to do herself a favor and unsubscribe to those blogs. He advised that those sites were nothing but the devil and not to buy into the hype.

"Before you know it, you'll be pissed off and in your feelings." With a laugh, he exited the vehicle and held the door open for Layani. Of course, the paparazzi were waiting on them to make comments about the recent rumors of a relationship, but neither of them said a word as they flew through the crowd and headed to the door of Bliss.

A security guard was planted at the door, looking three sizes too big for his shirt. "Y'all enjoy yourselves." He nodded as they passed.

Inside of the purple-themed establishment, the vibe was very laid back and chill, as soft music from a live band played in the background. Almost every booth was filled with people doing hookah. Bishop pointed to a white girl with red dreads and headed over.

"Nadia and Cheese, this is Layani Bell. Ms. Bell, this is Nadia and her boyfriend."

Everyone shook hands and took a seat. A few minutes later, they were joined by Cee-Cee, C.B., Trucker, and Tammy Harris. At first, Layani felt out of place as the other celebrities rambled on about this and that, seemingly ignoring her. However, once McJay walked over and gently placed a soft hand on her shoulder and told her that she admired her work and was so happy to meet her, Layani began to feel as if she had a right to be at the table.

For almost two hours, the table of celebs talked about various things going on in the industry and in the world. They wanted to put their heads together to come up with what part they could play to make things better. Someone proposed the group do a big fundraiser for the underprivileged youth in Liberia, but another stated that they needed to help the kids in their own backyards before sending help to people across the globe. After the debate got a little loud, Nadia calmed things down by spilling the beans about her new movie. She admitted that she had invited all of them there specifically for the reason of picking them for certain roles. At that point, everyone was all ears and asked what characters they would be. Nadia told them she couldn't release the information yet but wanted to make sure they were all on board before she pitched the idea to Hillgate Media.

Everyone except C.B. was down. He had just signed a contract to do an international tour. However, he told her when she got her deal done in ink and had production dates and a location, to let him know and he would definitely try to work it in. Nadia thanked all of the artists for their time and promised to be in touch very soon.

Excited, Layani hugged Bishop and thanked him for the opportunity. She'd never thought of herself as an actress, yet the meeting was proof that she was on her way to conquer all lanes.

On her way out of the club, Layani stopped by the ladies' room. Luckily, there was no line, so she was able to go right into the stall. As soon as she pulled her panties down to pee, she saw an arm on the floor of her stall. "Hey. Someone is in here!" she hollered.

"Sorry, girl, my candy rolled over there. Can you give it to me when you come out?" a light voice replied. Wanting to be annoyed that anyone in their right mind would be searching for candy that fell on the bathroom floor, Layani smacked her lips and rolled her eyes. After flushing, she looked down and saw a green vial made to look like an emerald. Without thought, she picked it up and opened the door. Standing on the other side was a short, curvy woman with a clean-shaven head and a neck tattoo that said *Miami* in cursive. Layani couldn't remember her name, but she did remember the girl being on *American Star*, a talent search television show, and winning second place.

"Is this what you were looking for?" Handing the vial over, Layani headed to wash her hands.

"Yes, girl, thank you. This shit right here is the bomb. By the way, I'm Ava." After pouring a little of the substance onto the back of her hand, she sniffed, wiped her nose, and then screwed the vial onto her charm bracelet. It blended right in like a stone on a piece of jewelry. Layani was intrigued by the gadget and thought it would be a creative way to hold a secret stash of speed so she wouldn't have to keep asking Reah.

"Hey, where did you get that? I'm Lay." She didn't feel right giving the girl her real name while they discussed drug jewelry.

"I got this from the candyman." Standing in the mirror, Ava adjusted her dress. "He got the best candy on the West Coast. This shit is killing ecstasy. It will get you horny in minutes and have your pussy flowing like a real water fountain. My nigga love when I take trips to candyland, ya feel me?"

"Actually, I was talking about the bracelet," Layani admitted.

"Oh, shit, girl. I thought you was trying to get your super freak on." Ava laughed. "Here, you can have mine." Unhooking the bracelet from her wrist, she handed it to Layani.

"No, I can't take your stuff." Layani tried to hand it back.

"This is Los Angeles, girl, I'll have more by the end of the night. Consider the bracelet a gift from a new friend. If you don't want the candy, just pour it out." After giving a quick four-finger wave, Ava exited the bathroom.

Layani stared down at the bracelet and unscrewed the vial. She was about to pour it out when her mind told her that trying a little wouldn't kill her. Besides, she wanted to experience candyland with Dernard that night. Throwing caution to the wind, she emptied the vial onto the back of her hand and sniffed hard.

Ava was right. On the ride in the Uber back to her hotel, Layani was extremely horny. Her skin was hypersensitive, and her ears tingled with the smallest vibration. She couldn't wait to give Dernard everything she had, so she texted him: CUM GET THIS after getting off the elevator. When he didn't respond, she squatted down on the floor in the hallway, pulled her panties to the side, and texted him a picture of her moist vagina.

Once inside of her room, she removed all of her clothes and headed to the bedroom to get ready. Atop the bed was a white box wrapped in a red bow. Inside was a lace lingerie set. Her phone rang as she pondered over staying nude or putting on her gift. Excitedly, she looked at the phone and then frowned because it was Micah. Though she hoped nothing was wrong, she had to admit that his back-to-back phone calls were really beginning to irk her nerves.

After turning off the phone, she went back to deciding what to wear. However, there was no time to choose before hearing the knock at the door. Without even looking through the peephole, Layani swung it open, ready fuck and suck the soul out of her boo.

"Bitch!" a female yelled at the top of her voice before following it with a punch to Layani's face.

"What the fuck is wrong with you?" Layani hollered while holding her eye.

"I told you about messing with my man, but you didn't believe me. I guess it's time for me to show you." Bianca continued landing hits on Layani until she had no choice but to find her composure and return blows of her own.

WHAP! Layani caught Bianca in the nose before sending a blow to her stomach.

Bianca snatched the lamp from the table and tossed it at Layani's head. Luckily, she ducked and was able to tackle Bianca to the floor, where they rolled around like WWE wrestlers.

The cat fight lasted for all of ten minutes until Keith, Layani's bodyguard, heard the commotion inside and used his keycard to gain entry. He pulled Bianca off of Layani, but it was too late. The damage had been done. The superstar was now all scratched up and bruised. Bianca was black and blue too.

"Where the fuck you been?" Layani screamed in pure anger.

"I was in my room, using the bathroom. I'm sorry." Keith felt bad and knew his job was on the line. He made a show of detaining and dragging the white woman into the hallway by her hair.

"Call the fucking police." Layani was seething.

"Call them and I'll tell them all about you and D." Bianca hawked up a wad of spit and flung it toward Layani.

Dernard could hear the bickering from his room two doors down and opened the door to see what the problem was. He was just as shocked as Layani to see Bianca.

"What the fuck is going on?" Dernard asked Keith.

"This lady just attacked Ms. Bell," Keith replied.

"Take her into my room, please, while I see about Layani." Dernard sighed at the sight of Layani's battered face.

"That's right. Go check on your precious side bitch!" Bianca yelled.

Dernard ignored her and followed Layani back into her room. He couldn't believe the damage that had been done to her. It looked as if she'd been in the ring with an MMA fighter.

"I'm sorry, Lay." Dernard rubbed her shoulders.

"I don't think we should do this anymore," Layani cried. As much as she would hate to lose Dernard, she wasn't down for fighting over nobody. It just wasn't her style.

"Don't talk like that." Dernard tried to shush her.

"I'm for real. I can't be getting jumped over a dick that doesn't even belong to me. It was fun while it lasted, but it's over."

"Let's get married!" Dernard blurted out.

"What?"

"I don't want nobody but you. I'm ready to tell the world about our love. I'm tired of hiding the way I feel about you," Dernard declared.

"You love me?" Layani couldn't believe it. In all this time, he'd never ever uttered those words she longed to hear.

"I've been in love with you since I met you at the radio station back in Detroit." Dernard laid it on thick. "I'm done with these bitches, baby. I want you to be Mrs. D- Money. Will you marry me?"

It was as if time had stopped for them to bask in this moment. Never did Layani think she would end up with a man like Dernard. Never did she imagine living the life she saw on the television. This was her fairytale, or so it seemed.

The only catch was Micah.

"I'm sorry. I can't hurt Micah like that."

"Do you love Micah, or do you love me?" Dernard peered into her eyes. "Baby, if you tell me you don't love me, then I will leave you alone. I swear to God our relationship will only be about business. Do you love him or me?"

Layani loved them both, but she knew she could only have one. Micah had been good to her, but Dernard scratched an itch that she didn't even know she had. He lavished her with expensive gifts, he showed her new things, and he'd fulfilled his platinum promise to take her to the top. Removing Dernard from her life would be doing herself a huge disservice.

"Yes! I will marry you."

Chapter Twenty-nine

Like a gentleman, Dernard ran a warm bath and cleaned Layani up. He took his time washing her body and was especially careful wiping her face. The bath water must have taken a lot out of Layani, because she fell asleep in the tub. Dernard wanted to explore every inch of her nakedness, but instead, he put her to bed and went to fire Keith.

Keith already knew the deal, so he had already packed a bag and was gone before Dernard could deliver the news. When Dernard returned to his room, he found Bianca lying naked on his bed.

"Hey, get up and put some clothes on." He nudged her, and she rose with an attitude.

"What this fuck is—"

"Look, it's been fun, but I need you to grab your shit and get the fuck out."

"Dernard, are you serious?"

"Unfortunately, I am. You and I are done for good, Bianca." He coldly broke things off with her like the business mogul that he was.

For the better part of two hours, she screamed, cried, and tore up almost everything fragile in his room, but he didn't care. Once she'd tired herself out and dozed off, Dernard left the four thousand dollars he'd pulled from his pocket on the nightstand and then retreated to Layani's room.

Once inside, he removed his clothes and peeped into the bedroom to see if she had woken up. He silently hoped she was still down to have the hot, nasty sex she had promised him earlier, but she out like a light and snoring, so he didn't bother her. Instead, he crawled beneath the covers, cuddled up beside his soon-to-be wife, and fell asleep.

The next morning, Dernard woke Layani to tell her that he'd canceled her commercial flight to Las Vegas for the next show and replaced it with a private jet later that day so that she could sleep. She was so happy for the rest that she didn't get the chance to thank him before falling back asleep. When she awoke again, the room was empty, but there was breakfast waiting for her at the dining table. She wasn't really hungry, so she only grabbed a piece of turkey bacon and a slice of wheat toast.

Though her morning runs with Kandy K had ceased due to scheduling, Layani felt the need to go for a run. She needed to clear her mind after everything that had happened the night before. She couldn't believe she'd been attacked by Bianca, and she also couldn't believe she was about to marry a man she barely knew.

After dressing in a burgundy jogging ensemble and her gold Cazal sunglasses and lacing up her sneakers, Layani took to the streets. Her old security guard was gone and had been replaced by a thirty-something white man with massive muscles and a bald head.

"Hello, Ms. Bell. I'm Daren. I've been hired as your security guard." His accent sounded British. "Are we going for a run?" Daren looked down at her attire.

"I am going for a run, but you can stay here." Layani nodded and proceeded down the hallway to the elevator.

"Well, given the event that took place last night, D-Money requested that I accompany you everywhere until further notice." Daren pressed the elevator button, and they waited in silence.

Layani wanted to protest, but she didn't want to go back forth. Besides, she probably needed him in case Bianca was somewhere lurking.

Seconds later, they arrived in the lobby and began stretching. Just when Layani was about to exit the front door, someone called her name. Knowing the familiar voice all too well, she turned to see Micah. He was sitting on one of the seats in the waiting area.

"What are you doing here?" Layani was irritated.

"I took a few days off to come surprise you. I've been calling you nonstop, and you've been dodging me. What the fuck is up with that?" Micah's irritation matched hers.

"I've just been busy. I'm sorry." Immediately, her tone softened. She didn't want to piss him off and get into an altercation in front of the hotel staff.

"Busy with what? Or with who?" he barked. Having seen the story drop about her and Bishop had him beyond upset. On top of the initial picture of them getting into his SUV, another one surfaced with them all hugged up at a club that night. That coupled with the fact that she wasn't answering her phone really made his blood boil.

"Micah, are you serious?" Layani tried to touch his arm, but he snatched it away.

"Don't fucking touch me!"

"Is there a problem?" Daren stepped in front of Micah, who didn't reply with his words. Instead, he used his fists and landed a punch so hard Daren folded like a dollar bill. Though Micah was smaller than him, he was no punk and still nice with his hands.

Dazed and confused, Daren stumbled backward into wall, causing a shelf with brochures and booklets to fall.

In horror, Layani watched as blood squirted from her security guard's nose. "What did you do?" she screamed, catching the attention of the staff.

"Fuck him! You got one opportunity to tell the fucking truth. Are you fucking someone else?" Red was all Micah saw before grabbing Layani's wrist. "Are you fucking someone else?"

"Stop it! You're hurting me," she pleaded.

"So that's a yes then, right?" Letting her go, he punched the wall so hard it left a hole.

"Micah, I didn't say that," Layani cried. "Baby, come back," she called behind him as he walked out of the hotel. When he didn't respond, she followed him for nearly half a block, calling out his name. Finally, when he turned to face her, he had a tear running down both sides of his face.

She could tell he was beyond hurt, which made her continue to lie to his face like it would make everything she'd done behind his back better.

"Micah, I haven't cheated. I swear on my—" She never got the chance to finish her sentence before two police cars rolled up. With guns drawn, the officers instructed Micah to drop to his knees with his hands in the air and fingers intertwined.

Already knowing why the officers were there, Micah did as he was told. Someone at the hotel had called the police on him. Not wanting things to escalate further, he simply did as he was told.

Layani watched in silence as they placed Micah under arrest and placed him in the back of the squad car. "Micah, I'm sorry," Layani cried and tried to approach the car but was stopped by an officer.

"Ma'am, please step over here with me so I can take your statement."

"Micah, I'm sorry." She cried even harder when she noticed that he couldn't even look at her. She felt terrible for what had transpired because it was her fault, and her fault alone. "Please forgive me. Please," Layani whispered as the police car carrying the man who'd once meant so much to her pulled off.

As the scene wrapped, Dernard's limo pulled up, and he got out in panic mode as he searched the crowd for Layani. He spotted her with an officer, who was inspecting her face.

The officer asked, "Is this a result of his attack?"

"Of course it is," Dernard answered as he approached the pair.

"No, ma'am, he didn't touch me."

"What about the bruises on your wrist?"

"No," she lied.

"Officer, she is clearly a battered woman. She would say anything to protect that monster. She won't speak up, but I will. I care about her just that much." Dernard handed her a business card. "Please call me if you have any more questions."

"What?" Layani couldn't believe what she was hearing. "Micah did not hit me."

Though she continued to deny it, the officer looked skeptical. After taking down her information, the officer allowed her to leave with the promise of a call if they needed to follow up.

Once Layani and Dernard were in the back of his car, she began punching him in the arm. For the life of her, she couldn't believe Dernard was so shameless in his quest to pin a crime on Micah. His freedom was in jeopardy, and his reputation was on the line. Beating up a muscular security guard would gain him clout, but putting his hands on a woman was damning.

"Relax! That little nigga will be all right. Besides, what do you care anyway? You belong to me now, remember?"

Without another word about the situation, Dernard got on his phone and started making business calls, completely ignoring her. Layani didn't appreciate the comment, but she didn't feel like arguing, so she remained quiet.

When they pulled up to the hotel, Dernard told Layani to pack her things and be back downstairs in thirty minutes.

"Okay." Her tone was low.

Dernard didn't like her energy. "What's wrong? Do you still want to do this?"

"I do, but—"

"Well, if you do, then act like it. Put some a smile on your face and some pep in your step."

Layani forced a smile and headed up to her room. With thoughts of the day's events and the upcoming nuptials, her head was spinning. Though she was ready to live the life of her dreams with Dernard, she couldn't stop thinking about Micah. She wanted to help him but didn't know how. That's when she decided to stop by Reah's room.

After Layani knocked three times, the older woman opened the door, then ran back into her room. With a cigarette in one hand, she stood on a chair and used the notebook from the counter to fan the smoke detector with the other. Layani wanted to laugh, but she wasn't in the mood.

"Look, I need you to do me a huge favor, please."

"What's up?" Reah puffed.

"I'm about to leave with Dernard, but my friend Micah just got locked up. I don't know what the bail will be, but can I leave you my credit card to get him released?"

"What if he doesn't get bail set until tomorrow?" Reah knew sometimes things didn't happen as fast as we wished when it came to jail.

"Listen, if it takes until tomorrow, then stay here until tomorrow. I will cover for you with Dernard and the crew. Please, Reah, do this for me." The guilt over this entire thing was taking its toll on her stomach. She felt as if she were about to throw up.

"Lay, I have to make sure you're on point and on time to places on your schedule. I can't be in another state." Reah might've been a lot of things, but not about her business was definitely not one of them. However, she could see the pain in Layani's eyes, so she obliged.

"Fine, girl. Just leave me the card and his information. I will go down there and post his bail as soon as it's set, then I'll meet you in the next city. If anybody asks where I am, tell them I had a family emergency."

"Thank you, thank you." With a sigh of relief, Layani flew to her room to pack.

When Layani got downstairs, Dernard was standing outside the car, having a very intimate conversation with a woman whom Layani had never seen before. She was tall, thin, and sported a long purple lace front wig. She was the model type, just like Dernard liked them. His eyes were so focused on the woman's breasts that he didn't see Layani. However, the girl saw her and made a show of grabbing Dernard's hands and placing them on her bosom.

"Do you like what you see?" she asked flirtatiously, and Dernard licked his lips.

"What the fuck is going on?" Layani got up into Dernard's face.

"Baby, it's not what you think." Dernard was cold busted.

"How in the fuck are you going to ask me to marry you and hours later be all up in another bitch face? Fuck you, nigga!" Pushing past Dernard, Layani got into the car, and he followed suit.

"I told you it's not like that, now lower your got damn voice!" Dernard barked. "If anybody should be heated in this muthafucka, it should be me."

"You ain't got shit to be heated about." She bucked, and that's when Dernard tossed his phone into her lap. On the screen was her hugged up with Bishop and a long gossip article about their supposed date night.

"First of all, it wasn't like that. I ain't checking for Bishop."

"Fuck Bishop! I'm not worried about him. The shit that got me hot is the fact that you're taking media meetings behind my back. I know you met with Nadia about her little movie."

"And . . . so what?" Layani didn't see a problem.

"In what world is it okay to take meetings like that behind my back? How can you agree to some shit like that without consulting me?" Dernard was practically smoking he was so hot. "All the time and money I put into you, and you gon' let another motherfucker profit off the star status I gave you. How do you know I wasn't putting together movie deals for you and the rest of Black Millionaires on my own?"

Layani had never seen Dernard like this, and she felt bad. Though she didn't think what she did was wrong, she still apologized as if she did. "I'm sorry, Dernard. I didn't mean to upset you. I thought it was a good opportunity, that's all. I was going to tell you about it last night, but I never got the chance."

"Apology accepted. Just don't let it happen again. From now on, you have to let me decide the best moves for your career. I've been doing this for decades. Don't you trust me?" He peered lovingly into her eyes and planted a kiss on her forehead.

"Yes, I trust you." She nodded. Maybe it was his swag, or maybe Layani saw something like a father in Dernard. Whatever it was, this combination of affection was all it took to break down the walls of her world.

The remainder of the ride to the airport was silent, until the car stopped and Layani saw the private jet waiting for them on the landing strip. She couldn't contain her excitement.

"Baby is this for real?" She opened the door and ran toward the aircraft.

"Hell, yeah. This ain't no kid shit. This is how a grown man does things." Dernard laughed as he watched her grab champagne from one of the stewardesses.

"This is so dope, and I can't even take pictures." Instinctively, she touched her swollen face.

"Baby, now that you are about to be my wife, trust and believe there is plenty more where this comes from." Taking a seat on the cream leather recliner, Dernard removed his shoes and rubbed his feet across the mink floor rug. It was something he always did out of habit.

Layani excused herself to use the bathroom. That's where she unscrewed the emerald vial from her bracelet and poured the remaining contents onto the back of her hand. After sniffing the powder, she leaned back and let its effects kick in. Once her nipples began tingling and her vaginal walls pulsating, she exited the bathroom with lust oozing from her pores.

Only two minutes after takeoff, Layani introduced Dernard to candyland as he inducted her into the mile-high club.

Chapter Thirty

After landing safely in Las Vegas, Dernard sent Layani to shop while he prepared everything for their nuptials. He gave her his Black Card and told her to buy whatever her heart desired. Within two hours, she'd torn down Gucci, Louis Vuitton, Hermès, Chanel, and Prada. After coming out of the Tiffany & Co. store inside of Caesar's Palace, Layani pulled out her cell phone and dialed Mack.

"Hey, superstar." It was apparent by the tone in her voice that Mack was happy to hear from her girl.

"Guess what!" Layani beamed.

"Are you pregnant?" Mack held her breath.

"No, bitch! I'm getting married!"

"To Micah, I hope."

"Guess again." Layani laughed, but her friend did not.

"Did you meet someone new?" Mack knew it was wishful thinking.

"Stop playing, girl. You know it's Dernard. He proposed last night."

"Oh." Mack didn't try to hide her disappointment.

"Straight up, it's like that?" Layani walked down a way and took a seat on the leather chair in front of the Cartier store. She was told by the jeweler to come back in an hour to pick up the wedding band she had purchased earlier for her boo. It was simple in style yet equipped with three carats worth of flawless stones. She even personalized it with the words *Always & Forever.*

"I thought you would be happy for me, Mack."

"Layani, you know I don't like Dernard's ass for you."

"Are you jealous?" Layani boldly asked.

"Of what?" Mack was seething.

"Bitch, you know what! I heard you wasn't doing so well in the financial department. I also heard Anthony is a free agent this year and don't nobody want his ugly ass with them bad knees." Layani sucked her teeth.

"Bitch! First of all, who are you to be all in my business? Second of all, don't get it twisted! We still got money. Third of all, I'd prefer an ugly nigga with bad knees over a nigga with a team of bad bitches any day." Mack had no more words for her so-called friend. Without another word, she hung up the phone and deleted the number from her contacts.

Layani stared at the cell phone, dumbfounded. She wanted to call Mack back but decided some things were meant to be left alone. Someone once told her friends came and went. Although she was sad to see Mack go, she figured it was better to cut her losses now.

A few hours after picking up the ring, grabbing an outfit from Prada, and getting her nails done, Layani finally opened the door to her suite at the Bellagio. With all the time Dernard had, she almost expected to see flowers, balloons, and rose petals or something. Instead, sitting at the table was Dernard and another man in a suit. They were looking over documents, totally oblivious to her presence.

"Baby, I'm back." She removed her shoes, then went over to kiss her man. The taste of scotch was on his lips. "Who is this?"

"Layani, this is Jeffery Davenport, my attorney."

"Ms. Bell, it's a pleasure to meet you. Your music is amazing." Jeff smiled nervously.

Layani didn't get a good vibe from him, but she smiled and spoke anyway.

"I flew Jeff in with our prenuptial agreement," Dernard said casually.

"Pre-nup?" Layani was now on defense. "Don't you know by now I ain't no fucking gold-digger? Hell, I have my own money."

"Baby, calm down. I know you got your own money." Dernard gently rubbed Layani's arm. "Basically, this document is like a will, should something happen to me while we're married. It's certain things of mine that I want to go certain places. This document protects my wishes, that's all."

"Why isn't it just a will then?" Layani quizzed. "A pre-nup is what happens in the event of divorce." Layani wasn't as dumb as he thought she was. After all, she'd learned a thing or two from Micah.

"I need to read this." She pointed to the thick stack of paper.

Dernard eyed Jeff, who cleared his throat before speaking.

"Ms. Bell, you can read this if you like, but I can sum it up rather quickly if you let me." Jeff removed his rimless glasses. "It merely states that should you and Dernard divorce within five years, you each walk away with what you came with."

"What about my music? What about my name?" Layani asked, thinking about Tina Turner begging in court to keep the name she had worked for.

"Well, the music belongs to the Black Millionaires label already. As for your name, since it is your government name, it belongs to you." Jeffery placed a hand over the stack of paper and slid it toward Layani. "Fair and square, I promise."

Hesitantly, Layani looked between the men. Dernard could sense her reluctance, so he leaned in and kissed her lips softly.

"Baby, you are my world. You're my everything. I love you, and I can't wait to make you mine before the eyes of God. Please just sign the document so we can walk hand in hand into the sunset."

"I love you too, but I have to make sure this is right." Layani had learned from the last contract how shady Dernard could be.

"Don't you trust me?" Dernard peered into her eyes the way he always did when he needed to convince her of something. He knew that move got her every time.

"I do, but—"

"Baby." Dernard kissed her lips again.

"Fine." Layani sighed before grabbing the pen and signing on the dotted line.

With a huge grin, Dernard clapped his hands together. "I'm going to walk Jeff outside to his car. I'll be right back, and then we can head over to the 24-hour chapel."

"Chapel?" Up until now, Layani thought Dernard would at least try to plan something more elaborate, even on such short notice. After all, he was notorious for throwing last-minute mansion parties in almost every state that he visited.

"Yeah, babe, it was the one we passed on the way here. It had the big Elvis sign on the roof."

"Dernard, can't we do a little better than that?"

"Baby, you're getting caught on the wrong thing here. Who cares about the ceremony? It's all about the love we share and the rock" He grabbed her hand to remind her of what she'd be getting later. "Don't you worry. Everything is going to be perfect. Start getting ready. I'll be back after I walk Jeff out."

"All right, don't take long." Lay grabbed her dress and headed for the bedroom to hang it up.

Ten minutes after Dernard closed the door, Layani dashed across the hall to Rhea's room and knocked on the door. She'd called Layani while she was at the mall inside of Caesar's Palace and told her that she'd taken care of Micah's bail online and was able to catch an express flight to Las Vegas. By Layani's watch, Rhea should have just been checking into the room, and she was.

"Come in."

"Rhea, thank you for handling that thing for me. Are you sure the online payment posted?"

"Yeah, he should be out by tonight, if he ain't out already." She was standing by her window, taking a picture of the view.

"Cool! Hey, look, I need a little something, and I need it fast before Dernard comes back." Layani was desperate for another fix of speed since her nerves were on edge.

"I ain't got no more of that." Rhea shook her head. She could sense Layani was becoming dependent on the drug meant only to be a temporary fix for her exhaustion. It was small business in the world of narcotics. If Layani was going to have a habit, then it was time for Rhea to capitalize on it by putting her onto some major shit.

"What else do you have? I need something to take the edge off." Layani nervously looked back at the door as if Dernard would come busting through it at any minute.

"All I have on me is some powder. One of the boys in the band just asked me to hold it." Reah went into her bra and produced a bag of cocaine. Truth was, the drugs were hers. The minute she became Layani's tour manager, she began pumping the staff with the finest of her boyfriend's product. He was big dope boy from Saint Louis with connections in every state. Seeing an opportunity to make herself some big money, she began selling work to everybody on tour with a habit.

"Oh, hell no. I'm sniffing that shit." Layani frowned. "I can't be addicted to two things." Speed was bad enough.

"Well, suit yourself." Rhea shrugged and returned the baggie back into her bra.

"When can you get some more of my medicine?" Layani asked about the speed while tapping her foot impatiently.

"My connect can't re-up until a few weeks from now. I'm sorry, baby." She made a show of patting her breast. "But this shit right here will do it for ya."

"Shit!" Layani needed something, and she needed it now. The stressful situation called for a desperate measure. "Give it here."

"Are you sure, Lay?" Rhea appeared hesitant.

"One time won't hurt." It was a lie Layani told to make herself feel better about what she was doing.

With a sly smirk, Rhea, who knew exactly what she was doing, pulled a five-dollar bill from her pocket and rolled it up. "Use this. That way it won't come out."

"Like this?" Layani asked before taking a deep sniff of the potent powder.

Silently, Rhea watched as Layani dived into the deep end of a pond called "no turning back."

Chapter Thirty-one

Standing in the dressing room of the 24-hour wedding chapel, Layani eyed herself in the mirror. She looked gorgeous in the simple white Prada dress and veil. The smile on her face was there, but for some reason, she wasn't happy.

"Are you ready?" An Asian woman tapped on the door.

"Yes, I'm ready," she lied. Truthfully, she wanted to back out but didn't want to disappoint Dernard. He had been too good to her. Deep down, she felt like she owed him.

"Right this way." The woman led her into the cheaply made chapel with ratty red carpet and old church pews. When Layani envisioned getting married, she never had a place like this in mind.

"Meet me at the altar in your white dress. We ain't getting no younger, so we might as well do it," Dernard sang over the piano as Layani made her way toward him. He couldn't hold a candle to Jagged Edge, but his voice wasn't all that bad.

Thoughts of her parents flashed through her head. Would they be proud of her accomplishments? Would they be proud of the woman she'd become? Layani knew the answer to her questions was no; however, she was too far down the path of self-destruction to turn back. She knew what she was doing was completely wrong, but it felt so damn good, just like the cocaine floating though her bloodstream. Layani was on a high that no one or nothing could bring her down from, especially when Dernard pulled out a canary yellow ten-carat ring and placed it on her finger. Within minutes, both the bride and groom had exchanged vows, and then it was over. There was nothing special about the ceremony, not even the kiss at the end.

Layani felt cheated but didn't say a word. Instead, the couple went out for dinner at Tao with some of the record label staff, and then they hit the slots. No gifts, no big party, in fact not too many people out celebrating them had even bothered to say congratulations.

That night, Dernard was too drunk to even commemorate their first night as husband and wife. Layani told herself that the upside of shit being so bad now was that things could only go up from there.

The next morning, she grabbed her phone, went into the living room of the suite, and dialed ten digits she knew by heart very slowly. She didn't want to end things with Micah like this, but it was what it was. The deed was done, and she wanted to tell him before he read about it in the paper the next day.

"Thank you for bailing me out. Where are you?" He answered on the third ring. "I was just about to call you."

"Micah, we need to talk." Layani stared out of the oversized window from her hotel suite. The city was gloomy, and rain was pouring down on the window.

"Yeah, we do!" Micah exclaimed. "I don't know what the fuck is going on, but I don't like it. I think this space between us has allowed some bullshit to get in the mix, and that's my fault. I never should have let you go to New York alone. Last night, after I got out, I called and quit my job. I hate being away from you, and I know you need me now more than ever. Tell me where you are, and I'm coming." His bed felt cold without his woman. "I love you, girl. It's time to get married. I might not be able to afford the ring you want right now, but you better believe it's on the way."

Micah felt sure that his train was coming. He'd been diligently sending out his copyrighted beats to record companies, working on new stuff, and writing innovative songs. One day, he would have the life he always dreamed of, but today, all he wanted was to be next to his lady.

"Married?" Layani frowned. "Micah, it's too late."

"What the fuck you mean it's too late?" Micah was back on ten.

"Dernard and I eloped last night." She looked down at the boulder on her finger.

"Are you fucking serious?" Micah knew this had to be an April fools joke or something.

"Look, I just wanted you to hear it from me first." She sighed sorrowfully. "I wish you nothing but the best, but this is goodbye, Micah." After ending the call, Layani turned off her phone and wiped the tears from her eyes. Internally, she couldn't help but wonder if she had just made a huge mistake. She'd traded in Micah's love and loyalty for Dernard's platinum promises.

The churning in the pit of her stomach had her nauseated. She should've known then that a storm was coming her way. Karma was a bitch, and Layani was about to find out just how alive and well that bitch was.

Not long after they returned home from Vegas, news of Layani and Dernard tying the knot had social media in a frenzy. Most of the headlines read something like:

R&B PRINCESS MARRIES KING OF HIP HOP. People were calling their union the merger of the year. Immediately, they were booked for interviews and magazine spreads.

During the course of the year, Layani used the attention to plug her new work and book more sold out shows across the U.S. than ever. The hectic schedule was a mess, but with cocaine, Layani managed her shit like a professional.

Things went very well for a while, though lately it had been harder and harder to keep up the façade. Seemingly overnight, Lay had dropped a whopping thirty pounds, and people began to speculate, even her husband.

Cyn, Reah's assistant, popped her head into the dressing room. "Ms. Bell, there is someone out here claiming to be your aunt."

"I don't have any aunts." Layani had just taken a bump of cocaine from her charm bracelet and was beginning to feel the effects as she sat with her head back in the makeup chair. "Get rid of her."

"This woman is persistent, ma'am. She said she is your aunt Nova," Cyn nervously whispered. "She even brought a childhood picture of you and her as proof."

This information caused Layani to sit up in her seat and wipe her nose. Internally, her emotions were all over the place, but she didn't let it show.

"Let her in." Standing from the chair, Layani folded her arms and watched her so-called aunt come into the room with flowers and a Kool-Aid smile. "Nova, why are you here?"

"I heard you were coming home tonight, and I wanted to tell you in person how proud I am of you. Everybody in the family is, Layani." Nova set the flowers down on the coffee table in front of the sofa where Reah sat, going over paperwork.

"Family? Bitch, please. Y'all ain't family."

"Layani, I know you still have bitter feelings about the past, but I want to try to put that behind us and mend fences with you, baby. I love you, and I just want you to know that." Nova dabbed at the tears in her eyes.

"Alexis, hand me my purse," Layani instructed her makeup artist. Once the Hermès bag was in her hand, Layani reached inside and pulled out a few crumpled dollars. "Nice story, tears and all, Nova, but please understand that you shitted on me when I needed you the most. For that, I don't have nothing for you but the same raggedy fifteen dollars you had for me back then." After throwing the money at her estranged relative, Layani asked Reah to show her out and asked Alexis to throw the flowers out into the hallway trash can.

When she had the dressing room to herself, she un-screwed the charm from her bracelet and finished its content. Though she already had enough coke in her system to last for the next few hours, the stress of seeing Nova had her craving more. When Reah and Alexis returned to the room, Layani was high enough to be on Pluto. She was so high that she hadn't noticed the powder residue all over her nose.

"Lay, you won't believe this." Dernard burst into the dressing room to tell her that the Mayor of Detroit wanted to commemorate her first performance back home at Aretha Franklin Amphitheatre with a key to the city that night after the show.

"I don't need a key. I just want to perform and leave." To say she was apprehensive about being in her home-town was an understatement. She hadn't been back to Detroit since she left, and she knew there was a great pos-sibility she would run into Micah.

"What the fuck?" Dernard walked over to get a good look at his wife.

"Baby, what's the matter?" Layani tried not to slur.

"Are you fucking high?" Dernard couldn't believe of all the nights to be as high as a kite, she chose this one. Didn't she know her endorsements were in jeopardy?

"Yeah, I'm high. I'm high on life, baby." Layani laughed. Everyone else in the room was silent.

WHAP! Impulsively, Dernard backhanded Layani so hard she flew from the chair and hit the floor hard. He wanted to hit her again, but lucky for her, a knock on the door indicated that she had ten minutes to hit the stage.

"Y'all fix her fucking face and get her ready for show-time." Dernard didn't care one bit that he had just assaulted his wife in front of Reah and Alexis. They both were on his payroll and under a nondisclosure contract. No matter what they witnessed while working for him, they couldn't tell a soul. In fact, everyone on Dernard's payroll had nondisclosure agreements.

"Get the fuck up!" Wiping his brow, he tossed one last look down at Layani before exiting the room.

"Are you okay, girl?" Alexis flew to the ground to pick her friend up. Layani was bleeding from a busted lip, but it wasn't too bad.

"I'll be fine." Layani was too high to be embarrassed. She wiped her mouth and got off the floor like nothing had happened.

Thinking fast, Alexis painted Layani's lips with blood red lipstick to cover up the swelling. Rhea handed Layani her microphone and adjusted her ear buds.

"Rhea, let me get a little more before I go." Layani and Rhea both knew she didn't need anymore; however, for different reasons, greed interfered with both of their better judgments.

"Hurry up." Rhea went into her bra and retrieved the goods. Reaching into her back pocket, she grabbed a twenty and a five-dollar bill. After pouring a little white line onto the twenty, she rolled the five like a straw and handed it to Layani. There was a loud sniffing sound as Layani inhaled like she was trying to suck up the coke and the money too. With a cough, she wiped her nose and exited the room to take the stage.

The walk from the dressing room to the main stage was too much for Layani to handle. Several times, she had to stop, lean against the wall, and compose herself. Dizziness plagued the singer, and her bodily functions threatened to escape.

"Layani, what's wrong?" Rhea asked while following behind her. Instantly, she began to regret giving her that last hit.

"I can't hear you." Layani frowned. Rhea sounded far away, although Layani knew she was standing right there.

"I asked what's wrong," Rhea practically yelled.

"Nothing." Layani stood up and continued walking. "I'm okay." When she reached the stage, she could hear the crowd going crazy. They were screaming and chanting her name.

"Detroit's princess of R&B is here for one night only. Are y'all ready?" The host of the show spoke into the mic before the lights went off. Once again, the crowd went wild.

"What up doe, Detroit!" When the lights came back on, Layani was standing on stage. She was already sweating profusely and hadn't even sung one note.

Just as the beat dropped, Layani's voice cracked. The note she was supposed to hit came out super flat. "My bad, y'all. I have a cold. Can I start over? Is that all right?" she said, thinking fast. Of course, the fans obliged, and the beat started over.

Nervously, Dernard watched from the rear, along with Rhea and Alexis. They thought Layani was done for, but she pulled it together and began to sound impeccable, as always.

To the untrained eye, she was rocking the stage for nearly the entire ninety-minute performance. However, there were miscalculations in her steps a few times, and she was getting very winded. Layani felt terrible but somehow mustered up the strength to keep going. Just as she neared the last song, her body finally had enough. Midway through the chorus, she stopped singing and collapsed right there onto the floor.

Fans gasped as Layani dropped like a bag of potatoes. Still, it didn't stop them from recording the gruesome scene on their cell phones. Dernard raced to her side along with Rhea, Alexis, and few other staff members.

"Layani, stay with me. Help is on the way." With one hand, Dernard held Layani, and with the other, he dialed 911.

"I want to go home, D. I'm tired," Layani mumbled. With eyes rolled in the back of her head, she could see her parents floating in the rafters above her. They were calling her home, and she was ready to go. Closing her eyes, she inhaled then exhaled one last breath before everything faded to black.

Chapter Thirty-two

Sunlight crept into the window of Layani's hospital room, which caused her to stir. Wiping her sleep-encrusted eyes, she blinked rapidly, trying to figure out where she was. Her vision was blurry, and she was disoriented. She tried to speak, but her voice wasn't there. Immediately, she got scared and felt anxious, but then she heard a familiar voice, and her nerves calmed a little.

"Good morning, Sleeping Beauty." Mack was sitting in a chair beside the bed, surrounded by deflating balloons, gifts, and cards.

"Mack?" Her voice cracked and was low. "What happened?" Layani attempted to sit up, but her body felt weak.

"You almost died, that's what happened." Mack tried not to yell, but she was beyond pissed with Layani.

"Huh?" Layani tried to play innocent, but brief flashes of what had happened the night of her last performance were hitting her like a ton of bricks. "I thought that was a nightmare, but I guess it was real?"

"Bitch, what the fuck is wrong with you? Cocaine? Are you fucking serious?"

"Don't come for me. I've been going through a lot, Mack." Layani turned her head. She was ashamed of what she had been doing in the dark.

"Don't give me that shit!" Mack barked.

"Please stop yelling." Layani grabbed her temples.

"I'm sorry, but I'm upset. My friend nearly died. What do you expect?" Mack wiped the tears as they slipped down her face. She was so thankful that God had spared Layani's life. "I thought I had lost you for real. It's been a rough four weeks."

"Wait, I've been here for a month?" Layani was mortified.

"Yes, and the nurse told me this morning that though they were bringing you out of your medically induced coma, it will still be a few more days until you can leave."

"Where is Dernard?"

"Where you think he at?" Mack paused before looking at her friend sideways. "You know that nigga is somewhere laid up with the next bitch! He's only been here twice this whole time."

"Can you call him for me?" Layani believed her loving husband must've had a great explanation for his absence.

"Lay, he wanted them to pull the plug on you! The doctor actually had to explain to his trifling ass that you were in a medically induced coma, which is different than a normal one." Mack wanted to smack some sense into Layani but tried her best to remain calm.

"Call him, please," Layani asked again. This time, her eyes pleaded with her friend.

"Look at this." Instead of producing a cell phone, Mack reached into her bag and slammed a financial report down on the bedside table for Layani to see. "I had my lawyer do some digging, and your boy is broke, Lay. He wanted to let you die for the insurance money."

"Mack, I don't know what your lawyer thinks he found, but this is some bullshit. Dernard is a multimillionaire." Layani didn't bother reading the documents lying before her. Truthfully, she was offended by the accusation. "I thank you for being here, but your ass needs to go!"

"Suit yourself, Lay." Mack wasn't even surprised. "When you find out the truth, you know where to find me."

Layani watched in silence as her only friend stormed out of the room, yet she remained unphased. Within seconds of the dramatic exit, she was already over it and went on to dial Dernard from the phone in her room. After calling every number he owned twice, she started another round of calls. Once again, her search came up empty.

Just as Layani slammed the phone down in disgust, there was a knock at her door.

"Can I come in?" the recognizable stranger asked with a Colgate smile.

Layani tried to finger-comb her hair and sit up straight in bed.

"Micah—" Layani's voice got caught deep in the pit of her stomach. She'd been awful to him, yet here he stood in her hospital room, holding flowers, no doubt to check on her well-being. "I don't know what to say." She fumbled with her words after finally finding her voice.

"Don't worry. I didn't come here to talk or give out no lectures." Micah stepped closer to the bed and placed a hand on the bed rail. "I just wanted to lay eyes on you myself and make sure you're okay." He was holding a bouquet of pink carnations.

"They say I was in coma for four weeks." Layani purposely looked down toward the ground as she spoke. After all she'd done to him, there was no way she could look him in the eyes.

"Yeah, I heard on the radio, but it's a good thing you're okay now." Micah was now the one looking at the ground. "Well, I have to run, but like I said, I just wanted to check in on you first. Be easy, and I'll catch you later, all right?" He wanted to hug her, hold her, and kiss those lips he missed tremendously, but she was no longer his to hold and kiss. She belonged to the man he'd practically served her to on a silver platter, and for that, Micah would never forgive himself.

"Don't leave so soon. Tell me about your career." Layani didn't want him to leave, not yet anyway.

"Everything is everything. I'm maintaining." Micah shrugged while backing toward the door. Though he didn't say it, Layani knew he'd moved out of their house a long time ago and removed his name from every account they shared. She wasn't sure how he'd been getting by since quitting his job, but she knew he would manage just like he always did.

"See you around, Lay. Take care of yourself, all right?"

"What about my flowers?" Layani tried one last attempt to get him to stay. The truth was Layani knew nobody else was coming to see her, which was why she wanted to make Micah's visit last a little longer.

"Oh, damn. My bad. I completely forgot." Micah walked back over to her and gently laid the plastic-wrapped bouquet down on Layani's lap. For a brief moment, their eyes connected, until the sound of someone clearing their throat grabbed their attention.

"Ain't that cute." Dernard smirked from the doorway. "Just like old times, I see."

"It's not like that. Micah was just leaving," Layani blurted out before she knew it. She didn't mean to sound like Micah didn't matter, but Dernard made her nervous.

"Yes, I was." Micah cut Layani a look that would've killed her if it were a weapon.

"Don't leave on account of little old me." Dernard walked over to Layani and planted a sloppy, wet kiss on her lips. "Micah, pull up a chair and stay a while."

"I'm good. I got business to tend to anyway."

"That's right. I almost forgot you're the newest songwriter/ producer on my rival label. I hope that works out for you, man. I really do." Dernard was being sarcastic, but Micah paid him no mind as he chucked up the deuces and walked out of the room.

"Baby, where have you been? I've been calling you nonstop." Layani focused her attention on her man.

"I've been cleaning up the mess you left behind. Or do you even remember getting so high that you fainted on stage in front of forty thousand people?" Dernard looked her up and down. "Thank God it wasn't one of the bigger venues. What the fuck is your problem? Do you know how much money you've cost me?"

"Baby, it won't happen again." Layani felt bad. After all her husband had done for her career, she owed it to him to get her shit together.

"You damn right it won't happen again." Dernard gritted his teeth. "I'll take you out the game myself before I let you tarnish the brand I built."

"Baby, please calm down." She reached for his hand and noticed something missing from hers. "Dernard, have you seen my ring?"

"I took it off your finger the night you got here to ensure nobody would steal it." Reaching into the pocket of his jacket, he handed Layani a red box and watched her put the rock back where it belonged.

"It seems a little too big." Layani frowned.

"You just need to put back on a few pounds and it'll fit like it used to." Dernard shifted nervously. "Are you ready to get out of here?"

"Yeah. I need to get back to work, but the nurse told Mack that I wouldn't be discharged for a few more days." Layani spoke while eyeing her ring. Something was off about it, but she couldn't put her finger on it.

"Fuck the nurse, these doctors, and the hospital. Let's unhook this shit!" Dernard began unplugging things so fast that he almost ripped the IV from Layani's hand.

"Ouch!" she screamed. "I don't think this is a good idea."

"I need you back in the studio pronto!" Dernard removed his jacket and handed it to Layani just as her machines started to sound off. On cue, two nurses flew into her room.

"She needs to stay here for a few more days of observation."

"Lady, we're leaving now. You can either move or be moved." Dernard was on a mission.

"That's fine. You can take her, but first she'll need to sign a self-checkout form." The second nurse walked away and was back in less than a minute with an electronic tablet. Layani signed it, and with one swift motion, Dernard swooped her up into his arms and lifted her from the bed.

Still in her hospital gown, with only a jacket to cover her ass, Layani was carried out of the room and to the elevator, which had conveniently just arrived. Layani felt like Tina Turner being snatched from the hospital in such a hurry. She wasn't sure if that was a good or bad thing, but she didn't dare put up a fuss.

Chapter Thirty-three

Once back in New York, things went full steam ahead. As promised, Dernard had Lay back in the recording studio day in and day out. For nearly five weeks, she practically went without seeing daylight. Her new regime was a gift and a curse. On one hand, with her free time now being monopolized, she had no time to get high. On the other hand, with all this stress, the only thing she could think about was another hit.

"One more time, Lay." Supah Dupah, a funky fresh producer from Cali, spoke over the loudspeaker.

"I can't." Layani had just about sung her throat dry. In five weeks, she'd already completed fifteen songs. All of them were smashes, too. However, Dernard pushed her to make at least seven more as a backup plan. On top of that, the holidays were around the corner. Dernard had promised the world that Layani was making a Christmas album. She felt overworked and underpaid. Seemingly everyone around her was making money off her gift, but she hadn't seen a dime since saying "I do."

Dernard always paid for whatever she wanted, so she felt she really couldn't complain. Be that as it may, she liked her independence. The fact that she had no control over her funds anymore didn't sit well with her, so she decided that day's studio session was over. Now that she was thinking with a clear head, it was time to pay a visit to the bank.

"One more time and we should have it." Once again, Supah spoke into the speaker.

"We'll have to work on it tomorrow. I'm going home." Without another word, Layani blew out the candles she kept in the booth, grabbed her pea coat, and headed out.

While waiting for the elevator, she checked the time on her phone. There was still time to make it to the bank before they closed for the day.

As soon as the elevator doors opened, Layani felt herself grow irritated. Standing too close for comfort was her husband and some new piece of ass.

"Baby, I thought you had a session." Dernard tried to play it cool when he noticed his wife.

"Who the fuck is this?' Layani wasn't in the mood.

"Ms. Bell, I'm such a huge fan of yours. Can I have your autograph?" The wide-eyed, pimple-face girl went inside her crossbody purse for a pen.

"Who the fuck is this?" Layani completely ignored the young girl and asked the vital question to her husband.

"Her name is Dylan. She'll be joining our label temporarily as an intern," Dernard replied.

"Are you fucking this bitch?" Layani was in rare form today. No longer was she playing the meek and humble housewife.

"What?" Dernard stuttered.

"Five . . . four . . ." She began to count down his bullshit. She remembered the first time they were on this same elevator a few years prior. "Two . . . one." Layani was so mad, she had missed counting three.

"What is wrong with you?" Dernard tried to play it cool, but it was too late. In an instant, Layani completely lost it and went into ass-kicking mode. She whipped Dylan's ass something ugly, and then commenced to swinging on her husband. Once the doors to the elevator opened, she was apprehended by security.

Moments after being thrown from the building, her building, Layani was hit with camera flashes from the fucking paparazzi. Ever since her overdose in Detroit, those fuckers stayed outside of the studio. They were hoping to catch a bad picture of her, but not today. Like a diva, she smiled for the camera, pulled down her sunglasses, and sashayed to Akebo's waiting SUV like she hadn't just acted a fool on the elevator.

Wait until TMZ gets this info, Layani thought silently. All she needed was one more bad mark on her record, and she'd be well on her way to being coined the bad girl of R&B instead of hip hop's princess of R &B.

Layani didn't want to lose her fans or her endorsements, but she wasn't the one to be fucked with either. She knew Dernard had fucked that bitch, just like he had fucked her back in the day. The only difference between her and the others was the fact that she had a ring. For some reason, Layani thought that minor detail should make a difference, but it didn't. Dernard treated them all the same.

Nearly forty minutes later, the black SUV pulled up to First Bank and National Trust. It was the financial intuition Layani used at the recommendation of Veronica when she first came to the Big Apple. Walking up to the bank, she couldn't believe it. The building was dark and empty, a definite indication that it was closed. Her romp back at the studio must've eaten up her precious time.

"Might I suggest the ATM machine, Ms. Bell?" Akebo pointed to the machine near the door.

"I hadn't thought of that. Good looking out, Akebo." As Layani walked up to the ATM, she tried to convince herself that Dernard must've been sending her money direct deposit, instead of giving her paper checks for her royalties. However, her theory went out the window moments after sliding her card inside the machine. She punched in her PIN code, which was the year her parents died, and nothing happened. She always used the four-digit number for everything because it was a date she would never forget. Yet today, it wasn't working!

Quickly, she took a deep breath and tried the PIN again. This time, a message displayed on the screen, advising her to call the eight-hundred number being provided. Without hesitation, she grabbed her cell phone and dialed the phone number. After listening to the prompts and pressing the numbers she needed to get to her account, she was advised that it had been closed. The recording also said to speak with a live person, she would have to call back at eight a.m. Layani was more confused now than ever. She had a shit load of questions and knew only one man could provide the answer.

"Black Millionaires, this is Janet."

"Janet, put Dernard on the phone," Layani snapped after dialing the studio. Being pissed off was an under-statement! She was seeing red. How could her account be closed? Furthermore, where had the money gone that was in there?

"Who may I ask is calling?" Janet was only doing her job by screening the call, but Layani didn't see it that way.

"It's his fucking wife, bitch!" Instantly, she regretted her choice of words with the receptionist, who'd been nothing but nice to her, but it was too late to retract them.

"Ms. Bell, Dernard left shortly after you. I think he—" Her words were cut off by the abrupt ending of the call.

Layani dialed her husband's cell, which went straight to voicemail, and then she dialed the house number. Apparently, he was ignoring her, but it was all good. She knew she would catch his ass sooner or later. For now, she decided to calm herself down and have Akebo take her home, the same one Dernard owned where she'd stayed the night of Tiger's assault on her.

With her eyes closed and her head back on the seat, Layani tried to recite some bullshit phrase she'd picked up during her online rehab coaching sessions. The chant was working right up to the minute Akebo pulled his SUV into the driveway. Once Layani's eyes opened, things again went from zero to sixty.

"What the fuck are you doing with my stuff?" She practically sprang from the moving vehicle like an action hero.

SCREECH! Akebo had to slam on the brakes just to keep from running his client over.

"Why do you have that?" Layani watched as an unfamiliar man carried out one of her platinum album plaques.

"No English," the black man said and kept it moving to the waiting truck. Layani knew he was full of shit but decided to approach the next man walking her way as an attempt to get someone to answer her.

"Sir, why are you taking my possessions?" Her eyes pleaded with the young white man. He was wearing a black muscle shirt with gold letter that said VIPER RECOVERY.

"Are you Mrs. Perry?" He looked down at his clipboard.

"Yes, I am," Layani said while eyeing two more men rolling a rack of her expensive clothes past her. "Is this bastard putting me out because I beat his bitch down in the elevator?" Layani was flabbergasted.

"Huh?" The man raised a brow before shaking his head. "I don't know about any of that. I am here on behalf of my boss, Viper. It appears your husband made a few bad bets, and this is the end result." After producing a business card and handing it over, he could tell Layani was still in the dark. "Your husband has a gambling problem. He's two million in the hole, and his extensions have all run out. Viper said it's time to collect, so that's what we're doing."

"Are you serious?" Layani rubbed her neck. She could feel the tension growing.

"Yes, ma'am. Everything he owns belongs to Viper, including this house." He paused, giving his words time to sink in.

"The house?" She frowned. "Viper owns my house, too?" It felt as though the world was crashing down on her.

"Look, you seem like a nice lady, so I'll give you a few days before you got to be out." The man patted her shoulder. His gesture wasn't much, but Layani was relieved that at least she had somewhere to sleep that night.

"Thank you, sir." She was sincere, but her gratitude was premature. Minutes after letting her keep her home, the man blatantly reached out and snatched the diamond necklace Layani was rocking right off her neck. With no remorse, he brushed past her and told his boys it was time to go.

"Viper said get the wedding ring too!" one of the men called out.

Quickly, Layani balled up her fist. They were not about to take her most prized possession.

"We already have the ring," the white man replied after checking the itemized list on his clipboard.

Layani uncurled her fist and looked down at the ring on her finger. That's when she noticed the band was starting to change colors. "Son of a bitch!" She knew it looked funny when Dernard gave it back to her at the hospital. The motherfucker had the audacity to give her a fake. "Damn," she mumbled while pulling it off and tossing it to the ground.

Layani felt deflated as she stood there watching those robbers pull off with truckloads of her belongings in broad daylight. "This can't be happening." She spoke aloud to herself while entering the empty house. She needed a hit of something now more than ever, yet she remained chill. Pulling her cell phone out, she dialed Dernard once more. Surprisingly, this time he answered.

"Layani, you've really fucked up this time!" he hollered. "You're looking at a massive lawsuit and possibly jail time for assaulting that girl on the elevator."

"Right now, I'm looking at an empty-ass house, and my necklace just got snatched." Although both of Dernard's scenarios were real and she should've been worried, Layani had bigger fish to fry at the moment.

"What are you talking about?" Obviously, he didn't know what in the hell was going on.

"Does the name Viper ring a bell?" As Layani spoke, the sound of her voice echoed off the bare walls.

"Fuck!"

"Dernard, they took everything!" she screamed. "These niggas even swiped the got damn appliances."

"I'll be there shortly. Until then, lock the door!"
Click!

Chapter Thirty-four

Anxiously, Layani paced the living room floor for nearly two hours while waiting on Dernard, who had no intention of ever showing up. It was eerie being in such a large place by herself. As an attempt to calm her nerves, Layani went over to kitchen counter where her purse sat and grabbed the paperwork Mack had given her at the hospital. Line for line, she read the truth about her no-good husband. The prenuptial agreement Dernard and his lawyer had convinced Layani to sign was an actual document giving Dernard all the rights to her name, music, and her money. The document advised Layani that she was worth nearly three million dollars, and it all belonged to Dernard. Furthermore, Layani had also signed away her right to any future paydays. His conniving ass had conned her into working for free.

"That bastard!" Layani spat.

Dernard was nothing but a fronting-ass nigga. His business had been in trouble long before Layani even came on board. However, he'd found his saving grace the day they met in Detroit. He knew her angelic voice and golden looks would catapult her to the top of the music industry's ladder. In turn, she would take his label's name with her.

Unbeknownst to Layani, she was the reason Dernard was even getting respect these days. Everyone knew he was a clown but gave him props for launching the career of such a superstar. Layani was the reason Black Millionaires was still receiving funding from other bigwigs and endorsements from major brands.

Layani held star power, and she didn't even know it. She was worth millions, yet here she stood, in an empty house with not even a dollar in the bank. This thought alone brought tears to her eyes. It was a low blow to her spirit that she couldn't handle. She had survived cancer and the death of her parents, but this was the final straw that would break the camel's back.

Quickly, she grabbed her phone and stood to her feet. There was only one way out of this situation, and that way was upstairs. On the way up, she sent Mack a text: **Friend, I'm drowning here. Save me before I do something stupid!**

The message was sent with the hope that Mack would read it and call her before she reached the door to the en suite bathroom connected to the bedroom that she once shared with Dernard. However, the call never came. Maybe Mack was unavailable, or maybe she was done playing Captain Save-a-ho. It didn't matter the reason, because Layani had already made it to the vanity cabinet where she kept her personal items.

Inside a box of tampons, she kept a nice stash of cocaine. She hid it there because it was the last place Dernard would ever look.

After removing the contents from the box, she glanced over at her phone to see if it would light up with her friend's name on the caller ID, but it didn't. Slowly, she went about the routine of pouring the white substance into five lines on the granite bathroom counter. This was a lot of cocaine, but she needed something to really take the edge off. She wanted to be numb.

"I'll worry about the consequences tomorrow," Layani mumbled before putting the pre-rolled dollar bill she'd hid with the coke up to her nose. Like a pro, she went from line to line until all of the cocaine was ingested. Instantly, her nose began to burn then bleed.

"This is that good shit!" She smiled before deciding to fill her Jacuzzi tub with warm water. "Might as well take one last bath before I get put out." This time, Layani chuckled. The potent powder was really getting to her.

Piece by piece, she removed her clothing. Next, she turned on the FM/XM radio wired throughout the walls. She flipped through the stations until she came across WJLB. That was her favorite hip hop station from back home. As the music played, she bobbed her head and stepped into the warm bath water.

The beat sounded familiar, but the words didn't. Nonetheless, Layani was vibing. She felt good . . . maybe too good.

"This is your girl Chaka, hanging here in the studio with none other than my main man, Micah, the hottest new producer on Hood Boy Records. He's responsible for that new French joint. He did the new Cane and Drip collaboration, as well as that hot new joint we all just had the pleasure of listening to by Detroit's own Big Jon."

Layani wanted to sit up in the tub, but the high she was experiencing wouldn't allow it.

"So, Micah, you hit the scene seemingly yesterday and set it on fire. How does it feel to be making all this noise?" Chaka asked.

"It feels surreal." Micah chuckled. "Seems like yesterday I was making beats at home. Now I'm flying from city to city, making hits with some of the greats."

"They say success brings jealousy. Have you lost a few friends yet?"

"My circle is so small I hold conversations with myself. In other words, there ain't no friends to lose," Micah replied.

"I completely understand!" Chaka chimed in. "Well, are there at least any special ladies in your life?"

"I'm taken, if that's what you're asking." Micah paused.

"Come on, man. What's her name? The people want to know."

"My lady is the incredible J Marie." He sounded happy.

Layani wasn't sure how she felt about that but continued listening, nonetheless.

"For those of you who don't know, J Marie is the fashionista/socialite who's best friends with Kim." Chaka dropped knowledge on her listeners. "Now, word on the street is you used to be engaged to Detroit native Layani Bell—well, should I say Layani Perry now."

"Is that the word on the street?" Micah played it off.

Layani felt hurt that he wouldn't claim her, much like she hadn't claimed him not too long ago.

"Well, you did help launch her career, right? Can you give us that much?" Chaka pressed.

"I did work with her back in the day before she became a superstar and all." Micah laughed lightly.

"What was she like?"

"What do you mean?" Micah was growing irritated.

"Well, home girl is off the chain now. Word on the street is that Ms. Bell has a cocaine habit, and after that nasty little incident on the elevator earlier today, I don't know about where her career is headed now." Chaka smacked her lips.

"What elevator incident?" Micah asked.

"Didn't you hear about her kicking some intern's ass at Trap House Studios today? The elevator surveillance was leaked by someone in the security department. It's all over TMZ." Chaka was proud of herself for being the first to drop dime about the situation live on air.

Layani didn't want to hear any more about how fucked up her life was, so she slipped farther into the tub. She wanted the water to cover her ears. She knew it wouldn't change what was being said about her, but somehow, not hearing it did make her feel better.

Where did I go wrong? Her mind raced back to when her career took off. In the beginning, all she wanted to do was sing. Never in her wildest dreams did she imagine her story would end with words like *broke* and *addicted*.

Who have I become? Whoever it was, Layani didn't like it. She closed her eyes and prayed for a new start. Oh, how she wished she could go back to that studio apartment with Micah. Oh, how she wished she had never signed that deal to sing for the devil, nor fallen for his platinum persuasion. More than anything, Layani wished she had never snorted that first line of cocaine, taken that first speed hit, or ventured into candyland. Now it was too late.

Or was it?

Buzzz. Buzzz. The vibration of her phone atop the toilet caught her attention. Mack was calling to save her! She blinked rapidly and tried to lift herself from the tub, but it was useless. Suddenly, her chest began to hurt, and it was hard for her to breathe. Her body felt like dead weight, and she was instantly lightheaded. As the water rose rapidly, Layani willed herself to elevate her head before it reached her mouth and nose. When that didn't work, she tried to use her toes to turn the water off.

In her haste to numb the pain, she must've snorted entirely too much cocaine to function. Add in the stress

of hearing Micah talk about his new life on the radio, and
Layani thought she was having a heart attack. Her limbs
were failing her, and her breaths were more strained now
than ever. Her heart was hurting uncontrollably. She
willed herself to get up one final time, but all she did was
make a big splash in the water.

"Help," she whispered through strained breaths, but
it was useless. She was all alone. She knew this was it,
and there was no one to blame but herself. Maybe it was
better if she died.

*There is life after death, right? The afterlife has to be
better than this anyway*, she thought. Closing her eyes,
she took one last breath and let the water overcome her.
Her brain wanted to fight, but her body just went with the
flow. Up and down, her body jerked as her lungs filled
with water, and within minutes, Layani was gone.

In the days following her death, friends and fans from
all over the world would come to mourn the young icon.
Just like the others who had died before her, they would
say she was gone too soon. However, Layani was now
at peace. She'd taken one final bow, and the curtain on
her life had finally closed. In such a very short time,
she came, she saw, and she conquered. Her story may
not have been the fairytale she hoped for, but her name
would be forever etched in stone. Layani was finally
famous.

The End